*The Adventures
of Good
Comrade Schweik*

**** *The Adventures*
********** *of Good*
** *Comrade Schweik*

HELMUT PUTZ

Translated from the German and abridged by
Susan Gillespie and Rochus E. Bassauer

FREDERICK UNGAR PUBLISHING CO. • *New York*

Translated from the German
Die Abenteuer des braven Kommunisten Schwejk
By arrangement with the original publishers
Bechtle Verlag, Munich

CONTENTS

Part I

THE MADMEN
AND THE WISE MAN

MINOR HAPPENINGS—
MAJOR
CONSEQUENCES

✳ ✳ ✳ "Frau Lehmann," demanded the little round man of indefinable age, as he seated himself at the table in his combination kitchen-and-living room in a suburb of Dresden, on a February morning, anno Domini 1956, "where is today's newspaper? First thing in the morning, you're supposed to put my newspaper on the table."

"Downstairs in the mailbox," replied Frau Lehmann in her nasal Saxon accent. A dyed-in-the-wool Dresdener, she was the man's housekeeper, a beneficiary of accident insurance who was forced to earn a little extra on the side. "You'll have to fetch it yourself this morning. I'm sick. I've picked up something or other."

"What?" asked the little man, pressing Frau Lehmann.

"The usual flu, I suppose. I've had the same thing every year since I can remember. I'm fed up with it."

"Don't say that!" retorted the fat little man, in tones of gracious rebuke. (It should be said at the outset that he was a world-famous figure.) "Other people would gladly be in your shoes."

"How do you mean?"

"Old Herr Lersch, for example—a reactionary, I admit, but an intelligent, honest man. He told me as much. And he's a punctilious, dependable person in all conscience. For thirty years now he's also been plagued by flu—in the fall, in his case. Last October, on a Monday I think, I remember his saying the time had come round again. In the morning his bones already felt like lead, and by the evening he could barely drag himself to his usual apéritif, sacrificing the last ounce of strength which only a good cause—mark my words, Frau Lehmann—can summon up. But like a true friend he didn't betray his condition to the other gentlemen, lest their imagination run away with them and they become infected on the strength of it. Normally he doesn't leave the regulars' table until three-thirty or a quarter to four —this time it was only half past two, he was so done in. On Tuesday, Wednesday, and Thursday he lay in bed, couldn't get up, and a friend visited him . . ."

"One from the regulars' table?" asked Frau Lehmann, interrupting the renowned verbiage of her illustrious employer.

The great man wrinkled his brow. "No. The regulars were already down with the flu. Don't interrupt me, Frau Lehmann. How often do I have to tell you that? With your predecessor, the dear-departed Frau Müller, may she rest in peace, I was not accustomed to it."

Nothing was more agitating to Frau Lehmann, who understandably had secret matrimonial designs on her protégé, than the latter's frequent references to Frau Müller, whose spirit stubbornly seemed to haunt the apartment and refused to be banished to those regions where, in the opinion of Frau Lehmann, a good Christian, it indubitably belonged: bowels of Inferno.

"Do preserve me from your Frau Müller," she said sharply, clattering pots and pans over the gas oven. "It's not your place to plague me with her. Nowadays things are different. A housekeeper today is a valuable treasure, to be tended and pampered, not annoyed—and don't you forget it. All of Dresden, Leipzig, Rostock—you name it—is crying out for housekeepers. Even Moscow, so I've heard. And in West Germany, or America, housekeepers are so unique they're brought breakfast in bed by their employers. What d'you imagine you'd do if I left you, Herr . . ."

At this dangerous moment the little rotund man asserted his mastery of the situation. Cutting his housekeeper short, he simply asked with a certain undertone, "How do you know that, Frau Lehmann?"

"What?"

"About conditions in the West. Do you listen to enemy broadcasts?"

"No!" cried Frau Lehmann. "I beg your forgiveness, dear Master. Forget what I said. I wouldn't be disloyal to you either, never. So then Herr Lersch was visited by a friend . . . and what comes next?"

The famous, rotund little man was doubly satisfied —first, because of his lightning success over Frau Lehmann, and second, because at last he could return to that intelligent reactionary, Lersch, who was so enamored of streptococci.

"So Herr Lersch," he said, "told his troubles to the friend—that he'd been afflicted by this sickness for thirty years. And the friend knocked three times on the nearest piece of wood and answered, 'Touch wood—not I! In thirty years I haven't had flu once. I've never been sick at all.' Herr Lersch was somehow alarmed for his friend and interposed, 'But listen now, that can't be healthy either.'"

A clock struck seven. The great man let it strike, then he continued, "So you see, Frau Lehmann, *that's* the way things are. *That's* the way you must think of your flu. Then in the long run you'll even get attached to it. Queerer things happen. You need only open the newspaper and read about some fellow who's had his diamond wedding anniversary. What does he have to say? That he has gotten more attached to his wife than a bug to a jam jar. Where's my breakfast?"

For the second time Frau Lehmann forgot to weigh her words, for she said: "The coffee water hasn't boiled yet. Here we go again, that's Socialist gas-pressure for you!"

The great man coughed, got up from the table, and with a look which said clearly that he hadn't heard anything, announced that in the meantime he would fetch the newspaper.

Frau Lehmann set the breakfast dishes on the table, then bread, margarine, and ersatz honey.

"In March we're supposed to be getting two hundred grams of Hungarian bacon per person, they told me yesterday in the fish market," she said, as her employer returned with the newspaper. "Or one hundred grams of salami. But it isn't definite yet. Depends where the Hungarians want to do their exporting."

The little round man said nothing. He sat down, opened the newspaper, and tried to immerse himself in the day's news. This maneuver, however, was doomed to be thwarted, for Frau Lehmann, just like a woman, had not the slightest intention of giving him any respite.

"That's assuming we get anything at all," she added tartly. "Assuming the West doesn't buy up all the bacon and salami and help line the pockets of the Socialist camp. Then maybe we'll get peppers—second choice, of course . . ."

The master cleared his throat, rustled his newspaper, but there was no holding Frau Lehmann.

"That's the way it went with the Polish geese last Christmas," she droned on. "The West Germans gobbled them up, and we got an extra five pounds of Polish potatoes per head for the holidays! Remember?"

This direct question the great man had to answer, willy-nilly.

"Even the West Germans *eat*, they do not gobble, Frau Lehmann," he said dryly.

"Don't push your West Germans down my throat!"

Frau Lehmann, for whom the West Germans were a sore point, now started to shout:

"And when did they send us the last package, may I ask? Christmas. And what was in it? *Canned* American goose! Well and good, that saved Christmas for us. But Christmas is long over and done with. What do the West Germans imagine we live on in the meantime? What do they think I can serve up in the months between? Don't thrust your West Germans at me!"

Frau Lehmann regarded the little round man, whose age was indefinable, challengingly.

He attempted to meet her gaze. The odor of ersatz honey rose in his nostrils.

"Now, at long last, I would like to read my newspaper," he said, lowering his eyes. Once again his head disappeared behind his paper, *Neues Deutschland.**

Frau Lehmann poured boiling-hot coffee into his cup. Except for the slosh of the coffee, there were five seconds of uninterrupted silence in the kitchen. Because the unfolded newspaper shielded him from her, Frau Lehmann could see only the nether regions of her lord and master.

"Nice knees you have," she said with sudden tenderness, as once again her purpose in life—against all odds, to secure a husband—rose before her mind's eye. "Almost like a young lad's."

"In Moscow," noted the other from behind his newspaper, "they have something else."

"Such as?"

"The 20th Party Congress."

"Well, I must say! Here I am telling you about your nice knees, and you react with this sort of thing. As if there were any connection!"

"They seem to be having a fine old time out there," continued the great man unswervingly. "Nikita Sergeyevich Khrushchev, our newly beloved father in Moscow, said—wait a minute—he spoke for five hours and said . . ."

As he read, his right hand reached out from behind the newspaper, grasped his coffee cup and lifted it to his mouth. He fancied a sip and started to take one. The cup met his lips, he tilted it. A second later, strange, inarticulate sounds burst forth—snorts, a yelp, then a clattering of china. The first word that rocketed upward was a dreadful oath.

---

* *Neues Deutschland* is the official party organ of the German Democratic Republic.

"Holyjosephhellanddamnation!" he shouted, neglecting that world-wide fame of his which should have restrained him. "Frau Lehmann! Your goddamned coffee! My mouth! My fingers!"

Clapping his scalded fingers over his mouth, he jumped up, and with his free hand, flung down the newspaper.

To hell with it, with you and everything else! Goddamn Nikita Khrushchev, your goddamned Congress in Moscow!

Little things lead to big ones . . .

"To hell with your breakfast, Frau Lehmann! Where's my overcoat?"

With these words the victim of scalding coffee bolted from the room.

The suburban train in which the little round man rode to work resembled on that day a mobile institute for deaf mutes. Not a human sound was to be heard; even the smokers suppressed their morning coughing fits. When the train had left the station and the great clatter of wheels had died down to a monotonous rhythm, an almost graveyard silence followed.

"Seat free here?" the great man out of politeness asked in the very first compartment. Inside sat three people: an elderly married couple and a man with a red necktie, about thirty or thirty-five years old.

Silence.

Go to hell, Comrades, thought the little fat man, and took a seat.

The married man blinked at him through thick spectacles. He was, unhappily, a far-sighted person to whom the Planning Office had for years assigned spectacles to alleviate shortsightedness. His wife knitted. One of her knitting needles was steel, the other plastic. The plastic needle actually belonged to a sister-in-law in Zwickau, a good soul, who was always glad to lend out such things when she was asked. The steel needle was an heirloom, handed down from a grandmother.

The man in the red necktie seemed to be sleeping. He was leaning with closed eyes against a corner-seat by the window.

It was a cold day in February, but the cars were not heated. The passengers hid their noses meekly in turned-up collars. Only a drunken man, returning from a wedding-party, which had not broken up until dawn, asked the conductor what was wrong with the damned heater. The conductor, prepared for such eventualities, pressed into his hand a leaflet from the Ministry of Transportation, from which the passenger might conclude that the victory of Socialism demanded such sacrifices.

The train shivered. It had resumed its journey.

"This morning, Comrades, I burned my fingers," said the little round man, who found the silence in the compartment oppressive.

Something stirred by the window. The man in the red necktie hadn't been asleep after all.

"You did what?" he asked, sitting up.

"Burned my fingers. Did a fine job of it, too."

The married couple exchanged horrified glances. The knitting needles stopped twitching.

"Well, in that case," came the voice from the window seat, "what had you said?"

"What do you mean, said?"

"You've just informed us that you got your fingers burned?"

"Right, Comrade."

"Then you must have said something."

The married couple exchanged not a word, but rose simultaneously as if by command and silently left the compartment.

"So what *did* you say?" asked the man with the red necktie, resuming the conversation. "If you got your fingers burned, then it follows you must have said something."

"No. I spilled hot coffee, Comrade. Just a sip—but that was enough, I assure you. Holy Maria! It was still boiling! Have you ever had that happen?"

The other grabbed suddenly at his necktie and shouted in a fury, "Are you trying to make an ass of me, Comrade?"

Unpleasantly taken aback by his outburst, the little round man said, "How could you think that? You're a perfect stranger to me. A perfect stranger is not someone you can, if you'll pardon the expression, make an ass of. Why, it's not possible! If you were my father or mother, let's say, then I could, excuse me again, make an ass of you. That would be quite different. But not a perfect stranger!"

The perfect stranger didn't know what to say. He relapsed into silence and leaned back into his corner.

Now he's insulted, the little fat man thought to himself. And I don't know why. I didn't mean to insult him.

"My housekeeper," he said, measuring his words carefully, in order to give the gentleman in the red necktie a better impression of himself, "told me this morning that we're supposed to get salami or bacon next month. From Hungary. Do you think we shall?"

"Do you mean to say you don't think so?"

"But of course!"

"Very well then, why do you keep talking so suspiciously?"

"I talk suspiciously? There must be some misunderstanding, there's no reason whatsoever why I should talk suspiciously, Comrade."

The other was silent. For some time he looked out the window with obvious disapproval.

"Walter Ulbricht," he at last declared, "recently said that in five years we will not only catch up with, but even surpass the West."

"In *how* many years, Comrade?"

"In five."

"That means by 1961?"

"Yes."

"I don't believe that, I must say."

"You don't believe it?" shouted the man in the red necktie, jumping up.

"No. I believe it will happen two, maybe three years sooner."

The man in the necktie came to the conclusion that he would have to play for higher stakes if he were to win any points over his fellow passengers. For this reason he blurted out suddenly, "And what do you say to Stalin?"

"To Stalin?" The little round man in his seat by the door strained his eyes into the distance, all the way to the mausoleum on Red Square in Moscow, and pronounced in solemn tones, "Saintly Joseph Stalin! There is no one else to touch you—for me, there never will be anyone else to touch you! Are you satisfied with that?" he asked the man by the window when he had returned from his reverie. The latter, with a happy look, replied, "Yes, entirely. I am satisfied." His eyes glowed with predatory joy. He tucked back his red necktie into his jacket. It was a typical gesture of satisfaction, which one often observes in men of excitable disposition.

"So you pronounce yourself a Stalinist?" he said, smiling, to the little fat man.

"Of course!"

"And intend to remain so?"

"Until my dying day."

"I am satisfied," he said again. "What's your name?"

"Schweik. Why do you ask?"

"Spell it!"

The little round man spelled out his name. He demonstrated, in doing so, that one of his character traits was compliance.

"First name?" asked the other.

"Joseph. Why do you ask?" Schweik inquired, now thoroughly mystified by his questioner.

The train was approaching a station. The whistle blew.

"Joseph Schweik," repeated the other thoughtfully. He had a feeling he had heard the name before, but for the moment it escaped him where. "Good. Take a good look at this," he said, "then you'll see what it's all about. We'll get rid of . . . get . . . rid of your difficulty."

Good-natured Schweik was actually only mildly surprised to learn from the identity card that had been handed to him that he had fallen into the hands of a secret policeman named Sand. He was unable, much as he now tried, to account for this turn of events. But then many others in the same situation had found themselves equally baffled.

"The rest will be clear to you, Schweik," pronounced Secret Policeman Sand.

"Perfectly."

"You will come with me?"

"In my opinion you're making a great mistake—but I'll go with you anyway, because I have to. I know the form."

"You know the form?"

"It won't be the first time I've been to jail," said Schweik, looking calmly at his captor. "I knew many jails inside-out—long before you came into the world, young man."

These words of Schweik, which bore testimony to an exemplary inner composure, annoyed Comrade Sand, who would have been happier if his victim, as was usually the case, had broken out in tears or trembled.

"I am going to bring you before Comrade Olbert, Schweik," he said sharply. "He'll make short-shrift of your arrogance, I assure you."

"There must be another misunderstanding here," answered Schweik as the train halted; in his case there was no question of arrogance. Arrogance deserved to be punished and was a characteristic of people with capitalist views—not people in the Socialist camp, who had long since been free of all arrogance.

Sand gave Schweik another piercing look, but on Schweik's face, which was the picture of innocence, all the secret policeman's glances shattered.

The train came to a halt. Sand ordered Schweik to descend. They could reach the SSD* more conveniently by streetcar from this station. The two men walked

* SSD = State Security Police.

down the platform, in sight of all. The elderly woman with the knitting, who had taken a seat with her husband in the next compartment, began to cry. In answer to a sympathetic onlooker, she said she was crying because she had just been reminded of the coming anniversary of Lenin's birth.

"Of his death!" she corrected herself aghast, as she saw her husband suddenly turn pale.

SCHWEIK'S ACQUAINTANCE WITH DR. OLBERT

✳ ✳ ✳ Joseph Schweik sat in a quiet little single cell and wrote a letter to his housekeeper:

Dear Frau Lehmann,

It is not easy for me to tell you what has happened to me. If it looked this morning before breakfast in our kitchen as if things might catch up with you, dear Frau Lehmann, not with me, the tide has turned in the meantime. I myself have been overtaken by fate, even though the reasons for it remain entirely incomprehensible, which would not have been the case with you. I am writing to allay your fears—perhaps that I have been lured away by some frivolous female. Those days are past. I am aware of your stubborn doubts of this fact, for which reason I must remind you that I am also aware of the many erotic traps you have set for me. You know I have always been as cold as a block of ice, and that's exactly how I am toward every other female, too.

Save the newspapers for me until I return. If the caretaker asks when I am going to help him clean out the cellar, tell him maybe not this week, but the one after. You will gather from these lines that I am innocent. The matter will soon be cleared up. There is only *one* person in the whole world who doubts this, and that is a certain Herr Sand, a young, inexperienced man—by profession a secret police-man—who arrested me. For these reasons it would be en-tirely foolhardy of you, dear Frau Lehmann, to consider deserting me now as fast as you can, to save your own skin, because at the moment it may seem to you that I'm an enemy of the State. Appearances are indeed deceptive!!

Many prison greetings,
your

Joseph Schweik

P.S. Frau Lehmann, from the papers it's only the sports section you need to . . . .

Outside in the corridor, footsteps approached. Schweik's pen ceased moving. His letter (whose original misspellings it hardly seems necessary to reproduce here, since Schweik's image would be neither helped nor hindered by them) did not quite reach completion. The footsteps halted in front of Schweik's cell door. Keys rattled, the lock grated, the door was pushed open, and a uniformed individual over six feet tall called sharply, "Schweik!"

"Here!"

"Follow me immediately!"

Schweik, who saw the hour of his rehabilitation at hand, did not have to be summoned twice.

In the corridor he strode so firmly along that the guard could scarcely keep up with him and said, "What are you running that way for? Don't run in front of me!"

"Why not?" answered Schweik, without slacken-ing his pace. "I know my way around here. I've been here often enough. Have no fear I'll get lost."

Impressed, the guard fell silent. He too, exactly like

Secret Policeman Sand, was used to quite different behavior from his charges. But he had the kind of soft heart which is known to dwell in certain giants, and, rather than being irritated by Schweik, he instinctively respected him. And so, when Schweik had led him with a sure step along four corridors and down three flights of stairs, he said without a trace of his original sharpness, "You impress me, Herr Schweik."

"You're not the first one," Schweik assured him. "There have already been quite a few before you."

Two corners later they had reached their goal, and Schweik halted in front of a door on which hung a sign with the inscription "Wet Paint."

"So, here we are," he said.

"You really have found it, Herr Schweik," said the guard in tones of praise, "like a homing pigeon. Not only the wing, but even the right door. If only all enemies of the State could be as helpful. That's what we need, then people like me would have an easier time of it."

The guard looked down with concern.

"Not everyone has my memory," Schweik said to him. "I only have to be told once that enemies of the State whose names begin with the letter S are taken care of behind this door, and I know it for good. Up there is where B's go. Right?"

The guard's respect for his prisoner knew no bounds, and he was even about to open the door for Schweik, as if he were a bishop, but the latter prevented him by remarking, "Never mind. I'd rather take care of that myself, so that no paint gets on my suit. I don't want the day to be crowned with something really unpleasant like that."

With such bearing, such equanimity, Joseph

Schweik stepped over the threshold of the room for enemies of the State whose names began with the letter S.

This room was the realm of the academically trained police official Dr. Olbert, who was thin as a rail and eaten up with ambition. Not his own ambition, but, what was still worse, that of his wife. Frau Olbert kept her husband's ears ringing with the word "career." Many hours of overtime had already borne fruit in several eye inflammations. Just at present, he was suffering again from such an inflammation. Until recently he had been in the provinces, for the greater blessing of the population in the prefecture of Zeulenroda, whence he had also brought his dialect with him to Dresden. It was one of his habits to explain continually that one should not underestimate him, to which he always added a "Let that be a warning."

With smarting eyes he looked toward Schweik, who presented his compliments.

"Good morning. But I'm sure you spend too much time working. Your eyes will be sure to pay you back some day."

"Do we know each other?" asked Dr. Olbert, surprised.

"It wouldn't surprise me," Schweik sighed, looking around for a chair. "But we haven't met each other here before. You must be new here."

"How do you know about my eyes?"

"The trouble is quite obvious. They're all swollen already," said Schweik with a professional air.

He could discover only one other chair; however, it was covered with a pile of documents.

Schweik removed these documents, laid them with a

friendly "Permit me" on Dr. Olbert's desk, and eased himself contentedly into the chair. He crossed his legs comfortably.

At this moment, if not earlier, Dr. Olbert realized that—if he were not to go to the dogs—he could no longer let the initiative be taken away from him.

"If you think you can continue that way here, you're mistaken. I warn you. Your name is Schweik?" he said testily.

"Joseph Schweik, Your Honor."

"Do you know you have a famous namesake? Or, let's say, an infamous one. So you can be glad you're not that Schweik, but another one."

And Schweik actually did seem to be glad of it, for he lowered his eyes, while a little smile played around his mouth. But even this smile was too much for the dreaded Dr. Olbert, and he shouted, "Stop grinning! There's no grinning here! Who do you think you are!"

Applying himself to the actual cross-examination he had in mind, he asked severely, "Where were you born?"

"In Prague, Your Honor."

"In Prague?" Olbert's voice suddenly sounded uncertain. "How so, in Prague?"

At this clever question, Schweik shrugged his shoulders.

"Because I was born in Prague, Your Honor."

"Then how did you end up here in Germany?"

"Because in 1945 they threw me out of Prague," Schweik said cheerfully. "That was customary in those days."

Olbert's hopes rose again. He heaved a sigh of relief.

"So you're a German after all," he said.

"No, Czech, Your Honor."

The blood suddenly shot into Dr. Olbert's head, increasing the smarting of his eyelids, as Schweik continued candidly, "They kicked me out of Prague because I collaborated with the Germans during the war, so they said. I had made good deals with the Germans, they said, because from time to time I had sold them a mongrel that they took for a thoroughbred. My bad luck was that after the *Putsch* not one of the German officers on whom I'd unloaded the mongrels was to be found, so no one could testify against me. That's where my defense broke down, as the lawyers say, Your Honor. But don't worry; in the meantime I've learned a few things, you can be sure of that."

"Unloaded mongrels!" groaned Dr. Olbert, involuntarily echoing Schweik's expression.

A storm was raging in Olbert. The information about the profession that Schweik had practiced in Prague left not a ray of hope. There were not two Schweiks, but one—and only one. To be precise, *that* Schweik who had won world-wide fame in literature, on the stage, in radio, film, and television. An unfortunate fame, in the opinion of many—among whom was Dr. Olbert.

"So you are that Schweik, after all"—a muffled cry escaped Dr. Olbert—"that blemish on the history of the Czechs.

"You'll be sorry about that," he interrupted himself, and, realizing he must pull himself together, suddenly struck the table with his fist. "Very sorry!"

He grew silent again, immersed in thought. Finally he rasped out distracted, "I would never have thought you were still alive."

"I can no longer die," said Joseph Schweik, born in Prague, age indefinable. "I am immortal, that's what the experts say who've already read about me and understand such things. I myself don't know why, any more than you do."

As he spoke, Schweik's voice sounded neither enthusiastic, nor imposing, nor triumphant. It sounded exactly the same as ever.

"You are *what?*" Olbert asked him angrily.

"Immortal."

"We'll see about that!"

With these words, in which one could discern a declaration of war by World Communism against Joseph Schweik, Dr. Olbert's first cross-examination came to an end. He had Schweik led away, because first and foremost he wanted his shock and agitation to die down. It was imperative that at the next cross-examination he should be ice-cool and superior and make what is known in the vernacular as short shrift of his famous adversary.

"Schweik," began Dr. Olbert in a serious tone two hours later, opening a file which, as was only natural, was still very thin. "Here I have your file, beginning with today. Don't underestimate me, I warn you. You are now in Germany. And you are dealing with Communism. That's an entirely different breed of cat from the old Austrian-Czech humbug, in the days when you led all of Prague—I mean the entire former dual monarchy —around by the nose. Here the wind blows from quite another quarter, as you'll find out soon enough. So I warn you again. I am a man who strikes while the iron is hot. I have acted accordingly wherever I've served."

"Where *do* you come from, Your Honor, if I may

ask?" interrupted Schweik with a note of genuine interest. But Dr. Olbert ungraciously ignored the question and continued, "Schweik, you explained this morning to Secret Policeman Sand that you do not wish to renounce Stalinism—not even on your dying day, you went so far as to say. Or do you perhaps wish to deny that now?"

"*Deny* it!" retorted Schweik incredulously, "I'd have to be a crass idiot to do that. We're all enthusiastic Stalinists—have been so for a long time. Or perhaps you're trying to suggest that you haven't been one yet and would like to become one now, for the first time?"

Apparently Dr. Olbert, in spite of the intelligence vouched for by his title, didn't know what to reply to this, for once again he merely said, "Don't underestimate me, Schweik, I warn you."

"You're mistaken there, Your Honor," remarked Schweik soothingly. "In fact I think a great deal of you. And because I do, I'd like very much to learn more about you—make inquiries, if that's a better way of putting it. You ignored my question as to your background . . ."

"Schweik!"

"Let me finish, Your Honor. My point is, that were I to know where you came from, I could then tell you whether I've ever been in the area, or at least traveled through it. Do you follow me?"

"Schweik, I warn you again. You very seriously underestimate me."

"No I don't . . ."

"You do indeed underestimate me!"

"Certainly not!"

"Yes you do!"

And so on, five times over.

It was a perfect example of a vicious circle, from

which for the moment Dr. Olbert seemed unable to escape. At last he shouted, "God Almighty, to hell with
you! I'll get the better of you yet! In Zeulenroda I got
the better of everyone!"

"You come from Zeulenroooda!" Schweik said
with a cry of deliverance, stretching the "o" like a rubber
band. "Why didn't you say so right away and stop
beating about the bush. In my mind's eye I'd already hit
upon Weilenbach. That's a little town near Sonnenberg.
I don't know exactly how I came up with that; it just
suggested itself to me. So you come from Zeulenroda.
Unfortunately I haven't been there as yet. But I know
from a bowling buddy, that he has to pay alimony
there . . ."

"Goddamn it! By all the . . ."

"But otherwise, when he's not thinking about his alimony, he's a very jolly, original fellow, I can tell you,
Your Honor. Always ready for a joke, even though
they're always bugging him about not being a member
of the SED.* Last month he went into a lingerie shop. A
young salesman, a novice still trying to win his spurs,
dashed up to him and asked him what he wanted. 'Underpants,' he said. 'For you?' asked the salesman. 'Not for
the King of England!' said my bowling buddy—a man
with a golden sense of humor, you'll be quick to
note . . ."

"Schwei . . ."

"You haven't quite let me finish. 'Very well,' the
salesman asked, 'have you anything particular in mind?'
'All I have in mind is a pair of lilac-colored underpants,'
said my friend. 'Lilac-colored?' asked the salesman. 'Yes,

* SED = German Socialist Unity Party, the name of the Communist party in East Germany.

that's right, lilac-colored,' said my friend. 'There's no such thing as lilac-colored underpants,' said the salesman. 'Let me speak to the manager,' said my friend. The salesman ran and told the manager—and what did he say? 'Ask the man if he's queer.' 'I'd prefer to leave that to you, Sir,' answered the salesman, 'even though I'm trying to make headway here.' At that the boss himself went over to my friend and informed him officially from the management that there is no such thing as lilac-colored underpants, not in the whole world—not even in the West, where they have everything. My friend merely smiled. And then he said, 'Haven't you ever seen white lilacs?' "

In Schweik's candid, mildly gleaming eye, which hadn't for an instant evaded Olbert's reptilian glare, appeared an expression of encouragement, as if to say, "Very well, now it's your turn, now you can say what you think of my bowling buddy."

But not another word escaped Olbert's lips. Dr. Olbert suddenly came to the conclusion that there was something basically rotten about this cross-examination, that somehow he must have started off on the wrong foot—*how*, heaven alone knew. In any case the matter was beyond rescue; that seemed plain enough, for today anyway. These thoughts raced through Dr. Olbert's head and decided him to break off the hearing, go to the eye specialist, and that night in bed try to fathom out where and how it was that he had slipped.

"We will continue tomorrow," he said abruptly to Schweik, and had him led away.

On the way back to the cell, Schweik confided to the gargantuan guard who accompanied him that the new examining official—Dr. Olbert—was, in his, Schweik's opinion, an unfortunate person: moody, full of inner neuroses, inconsistent. In a word, difficult.

"That's right," agreed the guard only too readily. "And what a lot of trouble he's always causing us! Comes from the provinces, the little beggar, and wants to teach us, here in Dresden, how to handle prisoners. Did I handle you properly, Comrade Schweik, not too strict and not too easy—or didn't I?"

"Nothing to worry about, Herr . . . what did you say your name was?"

"Burger, Richard Burger."

". . . Herr Burger. I'll be glad to recommend you. But actually there was something else I wanted to mention about Dr. Olbert. He doesn't come to the point. It seems as if he has something entirely different on his mind than the things you end up discussing with him. That's typical of moody people, I can tell you. Have you noticed that about him?"

That wasn't the half of what he'd noticed about that fellow, answered the guard; for example, the clown would drink milk when he was thirsty.

You really couldn't get anywhere at all with a man like that, replied Schweik; even cannibals would have no regard for such a person.

Burger, who was an old boozer, and always tipsy by noon—which also explained his companionable conversation with Schweik—now suddenly felt a pang of deep brotherly sympathy for this new prisoner. He therefore looked cautiously up and down the corridor, and when he saw that the coast was clear abruptly bent down to Schweik, who barely came up to his shoulder, and said softly:

"Watch yourself with that bastard, Schweik! When he told me to bring you up he said: 'That good-for-nothing will get ten years for sure. I'll arrange that in no time.' So you'd better see to it that he pulls in his horns."

"We're already on the right track, Herr Burger."

Inside his cell, Schweik noticed that his letter to Frau Lehmann had disappeared.

That night he slept reasonably well, better anyway, than Dr. Olbert. When the latter told his wife about his first fiasco with the prisoner Schweik, she said that he absolutely must make good this setback; he owed it to his career; a police official who wanted to get ahead couldn't afford any blunders, not even if the fellow was innocent; he must convict everyone—and especially political suspects.

Frau Olbert was a completely uneducated individual, the daughter of a Party activist, but pretty and sensual, and, besides, twelve years younger than her husband, who was her slave.

"The name Schweik doesn't mean a thing to you, my dear," sighed Dr. Olbert. "You know your way around in bed all right, but not on the battlefields of literary glory."

Did he think it would be better the other way round? asked Frau Olbert with the self-confidence of sex appeal.

It wasn't that.

"So there you have it, dear. Then just don't worry me about your Schwaik, or Schweek, or whatever his name is. What's the trouble with him?"

"Plenty of people have already broken their teeth on him."

"Why, all the more incentive for you to finish him off," said Frau Olbert, switching off the light over the marriage bed. "That will be a real step forward. That's exactly the kind of prisoner that's worth while. Good night."

It was silent in the dark bedroom, until after a while again, saying, "No. Not tonight. First finish off that Schweek, or whatever his name is."

Dr. Olbert continued to toss and turn on his pillow, unable to fall asleep. And when his eyes finally did close, it was no refreshing rest he enjoyed; instead he was pursued by a troublesome dream.

A little man appeared to him, looking very woebegone, but wearing a king's crown on his head. Before Dr. Olbert could pull himself together, the little man said in a tearful voice, "Think of me, old boy." Whereupon in his dream Dr. Olbert sank to his knees and stammered, "I was just obeying orders. I can claim subjection to authority, Your Majesty."

"That's not what I meant," said the little fellow with the king's crown.

"I offer you my service as a police official, Your Majesty."

"I don't need any. I no longer need any service at all. But think of me, old boy."

"Who are you, Your Majesty?"

"Pyrrhus."

In the morning Dr. Olbert felt complete exhaustion in all his limbs. He looked unwell, so unwell in fact that, when he asked his worried spouse whether she had paid the rent this month, she absent-mindedly asked him in reply how much pension she would get as a widow, if she were to be in that position, by chance.

Embittered, Dr. Olbert left for the office. His bitterness turned against Schweik, who was the cause of everything. His eyes hurt. He ordered the guard on duty —a certain Kauschke, who was interested in only one thing in the world, namely fishing—to fetch Schweik. Kauschke hated political prisoners like the plague, because at those times when he was not fishing he was forced to occupy himself with them.

"Where's our Herr Burger today?" Schweik asked him, since he had no intention of going their mutual way silently. "Still asleep? I like to sleep myself, when I can. How about you?"

"Shut up!"

"Or perhaps he missed the streetcar and will be coming on the next one. Where does he live?" Schweik continued undaunted.

"I told you to shut up!"

Schweik was silent, but could only hold out until they got down to the third floor, where he continued, "Overcast weather today. It would be nicer if it were nicer out."

"I'm telling you for the last time to keep your damned mouth shut, holy crucifix!"

"Pardon me, but you are murdering the language. The way you said it, the holy crucifix is supposed to hold its tongue. But I assume you meant me—right?"

Herr Kauschke rolled his eyes and gnashed his teeth, but Schweik continued in his chatty way, "Overcast weather has its advantages, too, of course. Then the pike bite."

He naturally had no idea what a lucky vein he had struck with this comment, for now Kauschke could hold out only five steps farther, before asking Schweik, "Do you fish?"

"Not exactly," answered Schweik, happy that he had at last managed to strike up a conversation with this cold fish. "But the father of a girl I had some forty years ago used to do so. He forbade her to have anything to do with me, the old eccentric. The mother had died, so the girl could thank God that on overcast days the coast was clear in their apartment, because her father went out after pike. We took advantage of every overcast day and were never disappointed. Since that time I know that fishermen are very reliable people."

"As far as I'm concerned they're the only real people," said Kauschke, giving expression to his deepest conviction.

"There's also a fisher who lives upstairs from me," said Schweik, holding on to this favorable topic with all his might.

"Maybe I know him. Where does he fish?"

"Actually nowhere. He is only *named* Fisher."

Anyone else would probably have thrown Schweik down the stairs upon hearing this, but Kauschke was such an impassioned angler that he only said, "If you think you can make a joke of that, Herr Schweik, then you're mistaken. The name Fisher means that at least some distant ancestor of his was a fisherman. That's how such names originated, in the old days. People were named for whatever they did most or most often, or for all I know with the most enjoyment, or for what they did best."

Kauschke stood still and asked Schweik if he could imagine that, whereupon Schweik replied that he could imagine it to a certain degree; however, there were some names where a decent person would have to call a halt to his imaginings. In the heat of battle Kauschke denied this, and when Schweik defended his standpoint he challenged him categorically, "Give an example!" Whereupon Schweik gave him one: "Privy!"

Meanwhile Dr. Olbert, sitting behind his desk, had already looked at his watch three times and asked himself what could be holding up that damned Kauschke with Schweik, who was long since due for a dose of de-Stalinization. With a fourth glance at his wrist watch, he got up, to see himself whether everything was in order.

He discovered the two men on the stairs, where they were leaning on the banister and continuing their conversation with animated gestures. As Dr. Olbert approached, he could make out only an incomprehensible fragment to the effect that the name Hunter was so common because of the ceaseless hunt for lice and vermin in former times.

The bellow with which Dr. Olbert interrupted their discussion would have swept the courtyards of three German barracks.

Back in his office with Schweik, he resumed the hearing with the following words: "I'm adding to the charges against you. You undermine the morale of the guards, you demoralize them."

"What's happened to my chair this morning?" rejoined Schweik with concern.

The chair, invisible to Schweik, stood in the next room. Dr. Olbert had removed it with his very own hands, because in his reflections of the previous night he had realized that the chair must have been one of the mistakes in the first hearing.

"You will remain standing, Schweik!"

Schweik bent forward and placed his hands on his knees with a martyred look.

"I should like to bring to your attention, Your Honor, that ever since World War I, I have had rheumatic knees. I stood around on the stairway with Kauschke for so long that now my knees are making themselves felt. You should have come sooner, out there, then that could have been avoided. I was just wondering whether we shouldn't take a seat, when you surprised us. Did you see how startled the guard was? He was so overcome that his mouth kept opening and closing, but not a word came out—like one of the carps he's probably yanked from the water, from which no doubt he caught the habit. Did you notice that, Your Honor?"

But Dr. Olbert, who had made an iron vow not to be distracted by anything this time, said sharply and loudly, "You wish to deny that Stalin committed crimes?"

"Holy Moses!" cried Schweik. "Now you've startled me too, Your Honor. I beg of you, don't say such a thing. If it's just once, I can overlook it. And above all—not so loud! Otherwise they'll hear you in the corridor, or through the wall, and you've had it."

"Stand up straight, Schweik!" shouted Dr. Olbert no less loudly, and Schweik, in order to pacify his interrogator, obeyed immediately. "Do you or do you not deny that Stalin committed crimes?"

"For heaven's sake, Your Honor, stop shouting that way! You make me afraid for your neck. Apparently it will put you at ease if I don't deny it. Very well then, I don't deny it—if that will pacify you."

"Whaat? All of a sudden you no longer deny it?"

Olbert was now roaring so deafeningly that Schweik,

remarking that the opposite seemed more likely to calm him down, quickly added, "All right, I deny it."

And in fact Dr. Olbert did stop bellowing. With restored composure he wrote something in Schweik's file and commented, "So much for item one."

He continued to write for a while and then, once again fastening his inflamed eyes on Schweik, said, "In addition, you have failed to denounce an enemy of the State."

"I, not denounce an enemy of the State? Why, I don't even know an enemy of the State."

"You know one very well."

"Who, may I ask?"

"Your housekeeper."

As he removed Schweik's letter to Frau Lehmann from a drawer of his desk, Dr. Olbert's smile was at once triumphant and derisive. He started reading in a loud voice:

". . . If it looked this morning before breakfast in our kitchen as if things might catch up with you, dear Frau Lehmann, not with me, the tide has turned in the meantime . . ., etc. . . ."

He ceased, let the letter fall, and barked out, "What about 'catch up with you,' Schweik? Out with it! What's been going on with your housekeeper?"

Dr. Olbert expected that Schweik would struggle and writhe under the impact of this surprise attack, that he would lose control of the situation, but that was an error of judgment, for Schweik said with delight, "Well, what do you think of that! So that's where my letter ended up. I looked for it everywhere and was afraid it was lost. So I can finish it now, after all. You've undoubtedly noticed, Your Honor, that at the end there are a couple of words missing. Herr Burger, who by the way is a very likeable person, Your Honor, and one you should hang on to, interrupted me."

"What did she do, your housekeeper, that's what I'm asking you!" screamed Olbert, his face flushed.

"My housekeeper?" Schweik smiled indulgently. "She does plenty of things, all very foolish. Has your eye fastened on anything in particular, Your Honor?"

The catchword "eye" reminded Schweik of something else, and he continued, "By the way, how are your eyes, Your Honor? They look even more swollen than yesterday. I bet they're painful."

"Schweik," said Dr. Olbert in a surprisingly soft voice, after a period in which silence had reigned over the two men, "Schweik, I warn you, I'm telling you for the last time. You are no longer in Old Austria. The whole world knows what it means to have dealings with Communism. It's no accident that millions tremble before us. We do not hesitate to wade in the blood of our enemies. So do not underestimate me, Schweik. Believe me, I am giving you good advice . . . And now you will tell me what's going on with your housekeeper!" he suddenly screamed out once again.

"With Frau Lehmann?"

"Who else do you think—goddammit! D'you have ten housekeepers?"

"She poured scalding water into my coffee cup, Your Honor. She's a fool, and has designs on me. You should meet her, Your Honor."

"I *have* met her!"

"You have?" asked Schweik, surprised. "Has she kept house for you too? She told me that before that accident with her hip she had worked in a factory."

He knew People's Enemy Lehmann, Dr. Olbert said slowly, giving his words extra emphasis, because he had her arrested, naturally on the basis of "this letter here . . ."

Noticing that Schweik for the first time showed signs of bewilderment, he continued in the same tone, "She's locked up not far from you, Schweik. She howls like a lap dog, or more precisely like a *bitch*."

"You shouldn't have done that," Schweik replied seriously. "She'll be a pain in the neck for all of you."

"For us?" asked Dr. Olbert, smiling sarcastically. "Why for *us*?"

"You won't be the least bit happy about Frau Lehmann's hearings. She has an old bladder complaint which, to put it bluntly, inevitably comes into its own when she's excited. That's why I think the hearings will get on your nerves—even more than on Frau Lehmann's. Your carpets will suffer from it."

At this piece of news Dr. Olbert had a strong conviction that enough had been said for the moment; that once again he had had all he could take; that he could no longer stand the sight of the prisoner's moon-shaped face; that he needed a break.

"Kauschke!" he called out to the guard who stood outside the door, "Take him away!"

Once outside, Kauschke was afraid Dr. Olbert might be sneaking after them, and spoke not a word to Schweik. When Schweik asked him whether he, as a fisherman, knew how high was the water content of the human body, he ignored the question.

Not until they had reached the cell door did he abruptly open his mouth again, to retort, "You won't get me into hot water again, I guarantee you that."

Dr. Olbert rang for a secretary, in order to dictate his intermediary report for typing. Along came the elderly Fräulein Wagner, an old crocodile of a secretary, hard-boiled and with a heart of stone. She had already served ten years with the Dresden SSD and every day witnessed unheard-of things without a twinge of emotion. She was a hopeless old maid, and for this simple reason every man who was sentenced to ten years' hard labor or penal confinement, whatever his crime might be, did her heart good.

Dr. Olbert began dictating: "Prisoner Joseph Schweik . . ."

"Which Schweik?" asked Fräulein Wagner, her key-tapping coming to a halt. "The one from Prague?"

Dr. Olbert answered in the affirmative.

"Good God!" cried the secretary.

This exclamation showed that even Comrade Wagner could still be caught off balance.

Dr. Olbert asked what was the matter with her, and Comrade Wagner replied that he could only ask such a thing because he hadn't been transferred to Dresden until recently.

"What is that supposed to mean, Comrade Wagner?"

"That means that otherwise this Schweik would mean something to you too, Comrade Olbert. We've been frequented by him before."

"Here too?" exclaimed Dr. Olbert. "I thought it was only earlier, in Prague, that they had him by the collar."

It is easy to see that this conversation between Dr. Olbert and Comrade Wagner would have dangerous repercussions for the prisoner Schweik; repercussions with which Schweik was soon to be acquainted—at his next hearing with Dr. Olbert.

This time Dr. Olbert was absolutely sure of victory, and people who are totally presumptuous tend toward the dangerous vice of irony; that is common knowledge.

"Now let's see what we have here for you," said Dr. Olbert, ushering in Schweik's Waterloo with bland irony. "This'll be a pleasant surprise for you!"

He had before him a file, or more precisely a mountain of files. This monstrosity was so thick that Dr. Olbert could scarcely see Schweik over the top of it. On the cover was written in black India ink, partly in capital and partly in small letters:

SCHWEIK, Josef

Dr. Olbert stroked the cover again and again with loving hands, and said with exaggerated irony, "It took two men to carry this file to me. One in front and one behind, as if it were a little buried chest full of Maria-Theresa thalers. What do you say to that?"

Schweik's eyes were fastened on the Indian-ink letters on the cover. "You could have sent that giant Burger. He could have done it alone," he said half-distractedly.

Stay calm, don't get irritated! thought Dr. Olbert to himself and then continued speaking, measuring his words with heavy irony: "I thought you were a person to be trusted, Schweik. But I must have been mistaken; for a trustworthy person would have told me right away that I didn't need to start a new file for you, because there has been one on hand for some time now. And what a file! I have permitted myself, assuming you wouldn't object, Herr Schweik, to nose around a bit in this file, as certain people would say. But I had to break

off again, because I never could have taken so much at
one sitting. The number of black marks is extraordinary,
Herr Schweik. I've never seen such a collection as the
one you've been working on for forty years. Tell me,
how does it feel to have so many black marks on your
record?"

Schweik said nothing, and Dr. Olbert, sure of
victory, interpreted this as remorse—which filled him
with satisfaction.

It was only natural that the expression "black
marks" was one of Olbert's favorites, and it was therefore
just as natural that he wanted to hold on to it awhile
longer.

"A normal human being, Schweik, would collapse
under the weight of so many black marks. Do you remember the male nurse who strangled his paralytic
rich old aunt and was supposed to be executed last
Friday, although his superiors testified at the trial that he
was the best male nurse in Dresden? What happened to
him? He collapsed under the burden of his black marks
and hanged himself Thursday night. And he had only
tripped up once. . . . But you, Schweik, you've been
tripping up ever since you were weaned. And mostly on
political things. You clashed with the Emperor Franz
Josef, with the monarchy; after 1918 you blabbed all
over the Czechoslovakian republic that the treatment of
the Sudeten Germans would lead to no good; naturally
at the time of the Protectorate you *yourself* played with
the SS. But besides that you also collaborated with the
Germans, which is why you were expelled from your
native country in 1945. And no sooner did you arrive
here, than it started all over again. For example, in 1946
you were denounced—but that was just part of it—

because after a radio celebration week on the occasion of Stalin's birthday you said there was no sense in over-doing it: where the Emperor himself would have gone on foot, even Stalin couldn't drive in a six-horse coach. And now, when the time for these kinds of opinion is ripe, what do you say now? Naturally just the opposite. With so many black marks . . ."

Dr. Olbert broke off abruptly, his feeling of satis-faction suddenly expired.

"Are you even listening to me, Schweik?" he began again after a short pause. "You're not listening to me at all. I warn you, you underestimate me."

Indeed, for some time now Schweik's thoughts had been in a quite different place.

"I've been debating the whole time, Your Honor," he answered, his hand on his chin, his index finger on the tip of his nose, "what we should do about my name on that file cover there. Impossible to correct it, that's easy to see. The whole name will have to be rewritten on a new piece of cardboard and pasted up over the old one. I can't imagine why I never noticed that until today."

"What?"

Dr. Olbert really croaked out this simple short "What?"—which proves how completely he had been disconcerted.

"That my name is written incorrectly," Schweik replied.

"Your name is incorrect?" asked Olbert, looking at the file. "What do you mean?"

"It is unquestionably incorrect, Your Honor. If an innkeeper wants to give me credit under that name, then no one—least of all myself—could care less. But a file like this is a very different matter." Schweik raised his voice meaningfully. "It's an official *document*."

"What's wrong with your name, Schweik? The 'i'? Do you write it with a 'y'?"

"Nope."

"With 'ck'?"

"Wrong again. You're on the wrong track, Your Honor. The 'Josef,' that's what's at fault. It's spelled on this file with an 'f' on the end, and my name is spelled with 'ph.' "

Dr. Olbert had an overwhelming urge to say all kinds of things in reply, and at the same time—in one great explosion, so to speak. But as it happened, as is always the case in such circumstances, he said nothing at all.

Meanwhile Schweik launched forth again, with much vigor; "Paper and pencil we've got, so it might be possible to get to work on the matter right away. But what about glue? Not every desk drawer has glue."

There was scarcely a circumstance which could have thrown a more distinct light on Dr. Olbert's sudden confusion and lethargy than the fact that he actually pulled open all the drawers and scrambled everything in them together in the search for glue.

In vain.

Dr. Olbert produced everything imaginable—twine, colored pencils, eye ointment, a tonic for conjugal vitality, two maps of Dresden before the bombings, stamps, a list of office numbers in the building from the time when it had been occupied by the Bureau of Finance— he came up with everything but glue.

After this fiasco Dr. Olbert needed a cognac—a good stiff one. Not one from Bautzen or Karl-Marx-

Stadt, but one from Rudesheim,* one he could only drink unobserved. In the right-hand pigeon-hole of his desk was one such bottle. It had been confiscated from an enemy of the State who had received packages from a married sister in West Germany.

"We will continue after lunch," he said abruptly to Schweik. Then glue would be on hand.

By the door, Schweik turned once more to Dr. Olbert and said politely, "Enjoy your meal, Your Honor."

But he should have said, "Good health," for the meal with which Dr. Olbert refreshed himself, as soon as he was alone, consisted exclusively of half a dozen cognacs.

"I don't know," began Dr. Olbert at the next hearing with Schweik, which was already the fifth or sixth, "whether I've mentioned that you shouldn't underestimate me. I warn you!"

He had just heard it for the first time, Schweik replied frankly.

Dr. Olbert glanced at his watch and said, "We have until three, Schweik. Then I have to go to the oculist. Before that I shall make short shrift of you."

Schweik asked him if his lunch hadn't agreed with him, since he seemed so excited, or what else it was that had upset him.

And as Schweik saw that Dr. Olbert was about to flare up again, he asked him quickly not to get excited, to stay calm, since otherwise he, Olbert, might get on to the subject of Stalin again and accuse the latter of crimes, which could get him into very hot water with any other witness than himself, Schweik.

* That is, one from West, *not* East, Germany.

"Hold your tongue!" shouted Olbert. "I see clearly that you are aiming for Paragraph 51. You want to be declared feeble-minded. But absolutely nobody can be so feeble-minded as you're trying to make yourself out to be here."

Then he wanted to begin once more, methodically, at the beginning. He opened his file and said, "You're a yardmaster at the Dresden freightyard?"

Schweik replied in the affirmative. He wanted to add that he was a yardmaster only out of necessity, since he had been restrained, due to the lack of demand for dog-traders. But Dr. Olbert cut him short by declaring categorically that, from now on, his questions were to be answered only with a "yes" or "no."

Meanwhile he was leafing through Schweik's file, stopped, glanced at random at one of the pages, struck it with the palm of his hand and said, "Here . . . nineteen hundred and forty-eight . . . accused of sabotage . . . three freight cars of machines from Zwickau, supposed to go to Belgrade, you put them on a train to Dortmund . . . to West Germany . . . Adenauer's government . . ."

Olbert's voice increased in volume with every word he barked out.

"Adenauer's government!" he repeated, yelling. "It's enough to drive one mad!"

"No."

"What do you mean 'no'?—that that's not enough to drive one mad?"

"No," was all Schweik answered again, although it was plain to see he had plenty of other things on the tip of his tongue.

"But it *is* enough to drive one mad!" Olbert's hand

slapped down on the file. "Three freight cars to Dortmund! Is such a thing possible?"

"Yes."

"What do you mean 'yes'?"

"Yes."

"Goddammitall! Yes. No, no, yes—what's that supposed to mean? Answer my questions, or I'll . . ."

Whatever threat Dr. Olbert had up his sleeve was
not given an airing, for Schweik, who loved nothing in
the world more than letting himself go and speaking
freely and unconstrainedly, broke in with relief, "Now
you're being more reasonable, more accommodating,
Your Honor. That's sensible of you. I've met some colleagues of yours who weren't so sensible as you. 'Yes'
means that I did send three freight cars to Dortmund, and
'no' means that it wasn't to Adenauer's government."

"Why not?"

"Because at that time Adenauer didn't govern in
West Germany. He didn't take over until 1949."

Flabbergasted, Dr. Olbert realized that Schweik was
absolutely right, and because Schweik was absolutely
right, Dr. Olbert offered to box his ears as they had
never been boxed in Schweik's life before.

But Schweik was not intimidated; he simply realized
the more clearly how vital it was to continue his explanation and clear himself. So he said: "And as for
sending the three freight cars to Dortmund, I can explain
that too. It was a matter of the quota. We yardmasters
had just gotten a new brigade leader at the freight yard,
who called on us right away to agree voluntarily to a
higher quota. The obligation up until that day was
80 freight cars per yardmaster, and now we had
agreed to 110 cars a day. It just so happened that I was

the first one to be on duty with the new quota. Until closing time, everything went off smoothly. I shunted 107
cars—so that it was a real joy to see, Your Honor. You
can't imagine what it was like, at your dry desk job,
with pen and ink. But then it was suddenly closing
time, and nothing could be done, not on your life, Your
Honor. I needed 3 more cars for the quota. There
were enough cars around, for instance a whole dozen
with machines for Yugoslavia. But for shunting, as
everybody knows, you need not only freight cars standing around, but also trains with which to couple them.
Unfortunately it turned out that on that day there
weren't any more trains going to Yugoslavia; there was
only one going to West Germany . . . Do you see what
I'm leading up to, Your Honor?"

Schweik's question would have left many a man
besides Dr. Olbert speechless; and the latter's mouth
merely hung open, so that Schweik was forced to accept the lack of response from Olbert and continued: "I
didn't want to be like the others and say to myself on
the very first day, 'Go to hell with your quotas, Comrades.' So I ran to the new brigade leader and asked
him, 'What should I do?' 'Do whatever you want!' he
roared at me. 'But fill that quota! I've already reported
our decision to the Planning Commission for Socialist
Railway Yards of the GDR.' What could I do, Your
Honor? I took the three cars I needed—that was three
with machines for Belgrade—and coupled them to the
train for Dortmund. The quota was filled."

"There's just one thing I don't understand," said
Dr. Olbert at last. "Why you weren't shot there and
then, why they didn't shoot you on the spot."

Schweik smiled forgivingly.

"On the contrary," he said, "I was even publicly praised. At first it didn't look as if I would be, you're right about that, Your Honor. Four Comrades from the SSD came and got me. The prosecution demanded ten years for sabotage, twelve years is what they gave me, and I served fourteen. But only fourteen *days,* Your Honor. Then they released me with much pomp and ceremony. And why? Because fourteen days later the Yugoslavs deserted Russia and Stalin, and they thanked me for not having sent the machines to those traitors to the Socialist cause. Such luck can only be had in a country like ours, I give you my word on that, Your Honor. In a capitalist country you can't have such luck, but our citizens know that by now, they don't have to have it drummed into them any longer . . . One more thing, Your Honor," Schweik exclaimed hastily, as he saw that Dr. Olbert was about to say something. "You don't have to bother yourself about those machines for Dortmund either. In fact, the people in Dortmund sent them back right away, without prompting. 'For heaven's sake!' was written with chalk on one of the returned machines. That was all they permitted themselves in Dortmund."

"Schweik," Dr. Olbert said in a muffled voice, "I see that one cannot engage in any kind of conversation with you, or in anything at all. Now I shall have to make short shrift of you . . ."

"That won't be possible, Your Honor. I'm afraid we won't have time."

Schweik actually said "we."

"Why not?" asked Olbert, automatically glancing at his watch.

A second later he sprang up.

"Goddammit! Already three! I have to go. The doctor won't see me if I arrive a minute late. Those rascals get their salary whether they do anything or not."

In Cologne or Munich or Karlsruhe that wouldn't happen, rejoined Schweik. There the doctors slaved and lived in misery, because the government didn't take care of them.

"I hope you'll feel better!" he wished Dr. Olbert sincerely, as the two men parted once more.

In Dr. Olbert's case it turned out that a stay in the clinic was suddenly necessary, if he were not to go blind. During the examination the doctor also incidentally discovered a considerable hormone imbalance.

"That too . . . Schweik is responsible for that too," Dr. Olbert muttered between clenched teeth.

Olbert returned for just an hour to his office, to take care of the most pressing matters. He passed Schweik's file on to the State Prosecutor's office with the following memorandum:

The prisoner Joseph Schweik admits the political offense of which he is accused. What he could not be induced to admit is a political offense by his housekeeper.

Olbert.

OLD ACQUAINTANCE

✳ ✳ ✳ Thus, before the day was over, Schweik's file found its way to the Dresden State Prosecutor's office; Department I/1a—Political Offenses. Four State attorneys tried simultaneously to pass it on to each other, until it finally ended on the desk of the most good-natured of the four: a certain aged Herr Zollner.

Did I say "good-natured"?

That was a mistake. State's Attorney Zollner was in fact anything but good-natured. He was a classic example of a wolf in sheep's clothing; he only looked good-natured. His voice, his drinker's nose, his gestures, his paunch—everything about him made a "good-natured" impression. And then, too, he was accustomed to repeat expressions like ". . . I'm sorry to say," ". . . I can't help you," ". . . If you'll excuse me," which also helped conceal his claws. But if there was ever a case of a man's appearance being deceptive, this was it. In reality, Karl Zollner was a bastard to end all bastards, a real fire-eater of a State attorney.

Herr Zollner and the Dresden State Prosecution

were, in many people's eyes, one and the same thing. Some even held that Zollner was older than the Dresden State Prosecution itself, since for as long as they could remember, Karl Zollner had been prosecuting them for political offenses. Four different regimes had made no difference. While the State Prosecutor's office had changed its name, its divisions, its aims—Karl Zollner had remained faithful and unaltered. An ideal State attorney!

His family life was limited to parakeets, which made his apartment small, in return for which he bestowed upon them human virtues. He found them more intelligent, more affectionate, less deceitful, and better behaved than that two-legged mammal, Homo sapiens.

In other words, Karl Zollner was an old bachelor. But that by no means indicates that he was a man of more than average intelligence. On the contrary, in his younger years, looking for a wife, he had chased after the weaker sex with unsurpassed zeal. Six engagements had been the fruit of his labors—but that was all. In the end, not one of his fiancées had married him, in spite of that deepest wellspring of female concern, the problem of how to be provided for.

The reason was simple: Herr Zollner had halitosis like an old father confessor in a confessional.

Now such a thing may be suffered in a confession box, where one is prepared for penance anyway, but not in bed, which raises entirely different expectations.

To people who have halitosis, even their best friend doesn't mention it, out of exaggerated tact—that is common knowledge. As a result, the victims themselves remain ignorant all their lives of the cause of their communication problems. Some of them grow bitter, some become melancholy. A continual "Why?" bores into them; they can't help hating people, and their hearts swell with a great love for dogs, cats, or parakeets. And why? Because no one tells these unfortunates they should see a dentist or a stomach specialist.

Herr Zollner was the prototype of the old bad-breath sufferer. To tell the truth, he served as a model for my description of these outcasts. In conclusion, I can only say that every one of us should pray daily on his hands and knees that he may not fall into the hands of a State attorney with bad breath.

And now, Karl Zollner, of all people, ended up with Schweik's file!

It was not the first time the two had met; this was, so to speak, a matter of course for Schweik's file.

It follows that there was no need for Karl Zollner to study the whole file before calling Schweik in. He knew him—and that, as they say, only too well! He merely had to read over the uppermost pages, which Dr. Olbert had filled out with Schweik's most recent political offense.

State Attorney Zollner read, shook his head slightly, smoked a cigar, a Sebastopol, which had to be relit after every puff, and finally concluded by announcing in a good-natured tone:

"This time I've had enough. This time I'll make an end of him. I swear by the life of Nikita."

Nikita was the name of Zollner's feathered favorite of the moment.

And Zollner immediately ordered Schweik to be brought before him.

When they were ready to begin, Zollner repeated good-humoredly, for good measure:

"This time I've had enough. This time I'll make an end of you, Schweik, I swear by the life of Nikita."

"Nikita?" Schweik's good, honest, full-moon face composed itself in wrinkles of grief. "Then that means that in the meantime Joseph has died or flown away? I remember you still swore by him last time. My condolences, Sir."

"You can spare yourself these tricks, Schweik. I can no longer allow myself to be moved to clemency. You may have gotten by with such tricks in Prague in the old days, but not any more, not in Communist Dresden today. If nobody has told you that before, then now at long last you must take it to heart. The old days in Prague are over and done with, if you'll excuse me. So I'm sorry to say that it's all over with you. We've known each other eleven years now, but I tell you again, this is positively the end, I'm sorry to say. Again and again you've gotten in my way and made work for me. Altogether it must be fifty or sixty years I've tried to pin on you. Not to mention one death sentence. But the Devil knows how time after time you somehow managed to weasel your way out again. Either your stupidity was taken seriously, or the political situation changed, or things even went so far, in your younger days when thank God I didn't have anything to do with you, that a world war conveniently came along and you managed to get sent to the front, to prove yourself. In the Second World War it was the same story. Even then, after some shady dealings, you succeeded in escaping to the Russian front—as a German soldier. How you managed that, Heaven only knows. And you were promptly supposed to be executed again. But lo and behold! as a doomed man in that Russian winter, when the execution squad had to spend your last night with you in the only house far and wide, you succeeded once more in getting them all on your side, so that they shot into the air, although they were members of the SS! Which was interpreted as divine judgment like a broken noose in the Middle Ages, because the bullets had missed you by mistake, they said. Some divine judgment!"

Herr Zollner was so upset over this divine judgment that he suddenly and very ill-humoredly began to pound the desk with his fist, screaming:

"But this is the end of such divine judgments!"

His furious glare pierced Schweik to the core, and since he couldn't see any signs of success with Schweik, who was smiling happily at the recollection of those ill-aimed bullets, he continued even more sharply than before:

"Under the Monarchy until 1918 I exterminated republicans, and afterwards, under the Republic, monarchists. Before 1933 the extremists, left and right, didn't have a chance with me, least of all the Nazis. After 1933 the anti-Nazis trembled before me, especially the Communists. I cleaned out Communists and, after 1945, anti-Communists. I'm telling you all this so that you'll see I leave no loopholes—I can't help you. And I also suggest that you wipe that smile off your face—understand!"

Schweik's thoughts returned to the present, and he endeavored to maintain a serious expression, while Zollner added:

"Yesterday I finished off anti-Stalinists, and today I finish off Stalinists, I'm sorry to say. You know very well why you are here, Schweik . . . you're grinning again! Why!"

At last!

At last the key word had been spoken, the one Schweik had been longing to hear ever since his forced departure from the suburban train; and that was also the reason why he was smiling anew.

"Because I *don't* know it, Sir."

"What don't you know?"

"Why I'm here."

And Schweik's expression of perfect innocence was so convincing that Zollner, who was about to say something biting, only sighed and said:

"With a face as stupid as yours, I could almost believe you."

"I really haven't the faintest idea, Sir. I swear to you by your Nikita."

"And why haven't you said so before?"

"Because with Dr. Olbert the conversation always led in an entirely different direction," Schweik replied, also with a sigh. "I don't know why. But please don't think I mean to say anything against that gentleman— not at all! He was a very well-educated man with good manners. Biting his fingernails or spitting on the floor is completely foreign to him. And in his politics he's even more reliable than you are, Sir. Only communication, as I say, just broke down between us, when we two spoke to one another. With you, it's different, Sir. But you have to take into consideration, after all, that you and I have already had considerable practice together. Dr. Olbert hasn't had that yet."

Whether consciously or unconsciously, Schweik had put a certain emphasis on the word "yet" which could not bode well. State Attorney Zollner unhesitatingly interpreted it as provocation and decided to put an immediate end to his senseless discussion of whether

Schweik's political aberration had been intentional or unintentional.

He rose, strode up to within an inch of Schweik's nose, looked him in the eye and said:

"Ignorance of the law is no excuse. That is an old rule of jurisprudence, as old as the law itself, I'm sorry to say, Schweik, if you'll excuse me. So what do you expect to gain? Besides, you still owe us so many years from earlier offenses that it couldn't possibly be unjust. I shall ask for the usual twenty-five years, and this time you won't weasel your way out, either. We have your admission of guilt. That's it, then! I can't help you, Schweik, I shall have to make an end of you, I'm sorry to say."

"By all the saints in Heaven!" shouted Schweik, who had already shrunk back several steps away from Zollner.

"Don't bandy the saints at me, Schweik. The saints have served their time. Perhaps someday things will change once more, then maybe the saints will even impress me again. When that happens, we'll grant you amnesty as well too, Schweik. So stop making such a fuss about your twenty-five years, like an infant!"

"But I didn't mean the twenty-five years."

"Then what do you mean?"

"Your smell!"

"My *what?*" exploded Zollner.

And Schweik, whose absolute frankness was also one of his distinguishing characteristics, repeated:

"Your smell, Sir. I mean from the mouth."

Karl Zollner stood like a pillar of salt, while Schweik continued:

"You've never come this close to me before, otherwise I could have told you that much sooner. It's absolutely unbearable. Why don't you go to a doctor or a dentist? Don't you have a good one? Or don't you trust doctors? If you like, I can recommend you a nature-healer I know of, who practices privately, and doesn't ask too much either—he even gives diluted hydrochloric acid to clear up difficult cases. That's guaranteed. Shall I give you his address?"

Zollner stared absently into space. So *that's* it! *That's* why they ran away from me, avoided me, why they never wanted me at the regulars' table, for a game of cards, or in the bowling club. So *that* was it!

The scales dropped from Zollner's eyes.

Why didn't anybody ever tell me, so that I could do something about it?

But this Schweik, he's told me! The first decent, honest person in my whole life . . .

And I was going to show my gratitude by giving him twenty-five years . . .

Zollner's miraculous metamorphosis, which went down in the history of the Dresden State Prosecutor's office, had begun.

"Herr Schweik," he said, when he finally found his voice again, "I thank you from the bottom of my heart . . ."

Tears began to rise in his eyes, he swallowed, shook Schweik's hand again and again, and continued, "I won't make a long story of it. You wouldn't understand, anyway, what's happened so suddenly. At this moment you see before you a different Karl Zollner than in all the long years full of misunderstandings between us. The old Karl Zollner no longer exists. We can't stop the proceedings against you now, things have gone too far for

that. But don't you worry about a thing. I'll have you
cleared. And as for this Herr Olbert and his methods—
Stalinist police methods, I'd call them—I'll find time to
take care of him too."

Herr Zollner, in his confusion, rose to the heights
of exaltation and crowed, "You'll be rehabilitated once
and for all, Herr Schweik. You'll be paid damages for
your arrest."

But Schweik, a convinced adherent of the philosophy that a bird in the hand is worth two in the bush,
only said, "Perhaps you could put me in a communal
cell until my trial?"

Touched to the heart by so much modesty, Zollner
granted Schweik the immediate fulfillment of his wish,
merely requesting him to confine himself to neutral
topics in his cell conversations before the trial—no
political ones, heaven's sake. "It's on account of the
microphones, Herr Schweik."

Schweik answered that that was nothing new to
him, and that he was not afraid of those microphones—
on the contrary, they could only help his cause.

And he would no longer have to look to his own
defense, State Attorney Zollner informed him next; what
on his account remained to be done, that was now something which was someone else's responsibility—a certain
Karl Zollner.

"And you know him, Herr Schweik—am I right?"

Joseph Schweik was the kind of man who is always
ready to go along with a joke, so he asked, "What did
you say his name was?"

"Zollner."

"Zollner? Isn't that the well-known Dresden lawyer?"

State Attorney Zollner smiled a bit self-consciously.

"And you say he is going to take over my defense?" Schweik added. "But I haven't the money for a star lawyer like that."

"There won't be any charge, Herr Schweik."

"Such generosity!" Schweik exclaimed emphatically.

They parted friends.

When Zollner was alone, he thought back over the events of the past hour. Now he could give free rein to his tears. He arose, went to the door, and locked himself in. A bungled life passed before his eyes.

State Attorney Zollner, who could no longer count the death sentences he had procured for his victims, most of them honest democrats, wept with self-pity.

*T*WO NEW *ACQUAINTANCES*

❋❋❋ Pleasant   days   dawned   for Schweik.

State Attorney Zollner did everything in his power to make his friend's sojurn a bed of roses. He presented him with a cell, which Schweik still raves about.

It was a so-called de luxe cell, of which the State Prosecutor's Office had half a dozen at its disposal. Its advantages: a flush toilet, mattresses, freedom from bedbugs, a squeakless lock. In addition, the windows could be opened by the prisoners themselves, and the bars were painted in bright, friendly colors. These cells were usually occupied by foreigners from the West, who had been mistaken for spies. Nonforeigners kept in them were regarded not as full-fledged traitors, but rather as harmless strays who could still be taught to tread the path of virtue.

Into one of these little paradises, these—to use the appropriate literary expression—"gilded cages," Schweik was admitted.

As he was being transferred, he pointed out to the

guard who accompanied him that there was one advantage in changing your living quarters in prison—you didn't need answers.

The guard was a medium-sized man whose main philosophy in life was that change is the essence of political regimes. He answered that he had nine children at home, and you had to take that into consideration.

Then it wouldn't surprise him, Schweik continued, to hear that the movers were losing money, because so many people who had formerly changed their residence in the outside world now confined their moving to prison.

If you have nine children you have to nourish them, the guard philosophized. That was the foremost duty of a father.

Schweik, latching on to the nine children, said, "With nine children I wouldn't like to be in a removal man's shoes nowadays, you can be sure of that."

"*I'm* the one who has nine children," the guard now insisted.

"You do!—have they given you much trouble? Or is your wife one of those women who are so sensitive that, no sooner do you write her a love letter, than she's expecting?"

"Feeding them is my chief headache," replied the guard in a troubled tone, not joining in Schweik's laughter. "But what am I to do, Herr Schweik? It's my duty as a father to feed them. Thirty years ago I entered the professional world as a supervisory official for the Dresden State Prosecutor's Office. How could I have then anticipated what fate had in store for me, in the shape of nine children? With nine children you're tied to your profession once and for all—do you see what I mean, Herr Schweik?"

"Nine children," Schweik said understandingly, "are a problem that can only be solved if they are illegitimate, assuming of course they are brought into the world by women who are married, that's the main thing."

The guard sensed Schweik's sympathy. He assumed he was trying to switch the subject to less dangerous ground. So he replied that naturally he always kept his eyes open for witnesses, when he was discussing things you could only mention to preferential prisoners—their horizons were so much broader.

"Where do you live?" Schweik asked after this confession from the guard.

"Leipziger Strasse 14. Second floor left."

"Are your floors still in good shape or d'you have dry rot?"

If the guard needed further proof that Schweik really understood him, this question would have removed the last shadow of a doubt.

At home, besides dry rot, nine children, and a wife who was very sensitive, the guard also had a father-in-law, a widower who shared his home and was a devotee of spiritualism, because it enabled him to communicate with his deceased wife. Summarizing all this, the guard said to Schweik that no one could blame him, in a situation like that, for having wished many a time that he could trade places with one of his prisoners.

"Do many prisoners pass through your hands?" was Schweik's next question.

The guard gave Schweik a searching look, as if to ask whether his question was in earnest.

"For heaven's sake!" he said reproachfully. "You

must know that, Comrade Schweik! Take today, for example. You're the eighth one I've had to transfer. Each one has cost me an hour. And I've had corns for years."

"Well, congratulations!" exclaimed Schweik. "Me too! You don't have to say another word."

"What do you do about them, Comrade Schweik?"

Schweik answered that it was the duty of his housekeeper to do something about them. But even her homely remedies, some of which went back to the Germanic migrations, had only disappointed him, time and again.

Since the topic "corns" is inexhaustible (although there is no sense talking about them, for a real case of corns can't be helped), Schweik gave a shrug of resignation and asked, "What were the other seven prisoners like?"

"All political," replied the guard, whom the mutual fate of being cursed with corns had made Schweik's complete confidant. "First a deviationist, then a revisionist, then a sectarian, then two ordinary counterrevolutionaries, then a Trotskyite, and, last of all, another deviationist. And after you, Comrade Schweik, I have to fetch another one who is accused of each of the seven deadly sins: Revisionism, Deviationism, Objectivism, Practicism, Reformism, Trotskyism, and Sectarianism."

Schweik could only break out in the same exclamation as before, "Congratulations!"

Schweik's new home received him as the day was drawing to a close. The rays of a sufficiently bright light bulb were reflected on two enormous bald heads, whose beams first attracted Schweik's glance as he crossed the threshold.

"How do you do, Gentlemen," said Schweik.

"That's what I like, when you can tell right away that someone's brainy, and don't have to rely on a long conversation to do so. That saves time. How are you feeling, Gentlemen? You don't look too bad."

"Well, well," he continued after a brief but satisfying look around, "this looks pretty bearable—almost like a health resort. Does the toilet flush when you pull the handle?"

Schweik answered his own question by successfully operating the toilet, which inspired his praise.

"Just like the Ritz. Only there it costs money."

The testing of the mattress, by several rapid downthrusts of the hand, ended also with Schweik smacking his lips in satisfaction.

Finally, Schweik stood in front of the cell window, gazed out into the dark winter evening and said, "Now the only thing left is for you to tell me that our dwelling faces south, Gentlemen."

He waited in silence for an answer—the first he had really waited for since entering the cell.

One of Schweik's bald-headed cellmates was called Long, the other Altdorfer. Long replied, "I'm sorry, but we haven't verified that. We are occupied with other matters."

And Schweik, who grasped the situation in a flash, exclaimed, "Aha! I see. You're even more brainy than I thought. Even in prison you're only interested in things of the mind."

It was true. Long and Altdorfer were two very learned men, yet such simpletons in workaday matters that in their mental world such things as prison microphones did not even exist.

"I assume," said Herr Altdorfer, now addressing

Schweik for the first time, "that you too have been involved in a mental conflict with Communism. I imagine
that goes without saying."

In Schweik's mind a brief struggle took place. On
the one hand he felt flattered; on the other, he thought
of the microphones. The microphones won, and Schweik
replied, "No, you're mistaken there. I am a stranger to
all conflicts with Communism, whether mental or physical. For my part, Gentlemen, there's nothing I enjoy
more than being on good terms with Communism; that
is really the most enjoyable thing in the world, believe
me."

"Then why are you here?"

"I wish I knew!" sighed Schweik. "I'm innocent, in
any case."

Altdorfer and Long were silent. They immersed
themselves in reflection and came to the conclusion that
Schweik didn't yet trust them. But intellectuals as they
were, they were also tolerant, and could even understand Schweik's reaction.

"We must first establish a relationship of mutual
trust," said Herr Long before falling asleep.

Herr Long was a well-known Dresden philologist,
who had become involved in a particularly tragic way
in a mental conflict with Communism. At night, in his
dreams, he muttered disconnected words of a strange
nature—for example: Justice-encouragement-law-minis-
try, streetcar-tramway-conductor, producer's-manufac-
turer-widow, advertising-publicity-article, motivation-
inducement-research. And many more like these.

After each of these words, Herr Long laughed
sarcastically in his sleep. He wakened Schweik, who

asked him first thing the next morning what these expressions meant.

"That is connected with my tragic arrest," Long replied with an air of secrecy.

Schweik could no longer restrain his curiosity and asked to be put in the picture. But Long hesitated and said that while Schweik could have complete confidence in him and in Herr Altdorfer, who was to guarantee that they, on the other hand, could count on him? In fact, a relationship of mutual trust had not as yet been established between them.

Schweik met this need promptly, by confessing that he already had had clap four times—three times while wearing the national uniform, as a soldier.

"Good," said Herr Long in a schoolmasterly tone, "that's more like it. That establishes unqualified mutual trust. Are you a psychologist?"

"To some extent, yes," said Schweik.

Long sat down at the table. Schweik followed his example, as did Herr Altdorfer, whereupon Long began to recount the story of his arrest.

"The tragedy of my arrest is a tragedy of my profession. I am a philologist—a passionate philologist, in fact. For that reason I cannot depart from certain basic tenets of my profession. As a philologist I had to speak out at last, although for a long enough time, nevertheless, I refrained from doing so. I'm a nonpolitical person, and basically I don't care one way or the other about Communism. Workuta, Katyn, Torjau—none of that interests me. That doesn't enter my field. But what does enter my field is this: Communism terms the countries in its control 'People's democracies.' And that is philologically unbearable. I was forced to take an opposing stand, although I knew that the expression 'People's democracy' had long since become a hallowed phrase of Communist terminology. But what does it mean? Democracy is derived from the Greek and means, literally, people's (*demo*) rule (*cracy*). So 'People's democracy' is a senseless redundancy and means nothing less than 'people's people's -cracy,' or 'people's people's rule.'

"Well, I opened my students' eyes to this. I forbade them to use the phrase 'People's democracy,' either orally or in writing. A few unteachable ones, among them the son of Dresden's Lord Mayor, who also attended my school, refused to listen to me. For that, I naturally accorded them unsatisfactory reports."

Long sighed.

"I shouldn't have done it, I sometimes think in a moment of weakness. But then I pull myself together again and think: it was my duty as a philologist. Am I right, Herr Schweik?"

Long's tragic fate, the fate of a true martyr to his profession, naturally inspired Schweik to relate similar cases from his circle of acquaintances. Nonpolitical cases, that is.

"That goes without saying, Herr Long. You remind me of a policeman I knew in Prague, long before the war, a traffic policeman named Upletal or Apletul or Uplatel or Eplutal—no, I'm confusing him with someone called something different, Peisl, I think. In any case he was a 'traffic cop.' He was a tough son-of-a-gun who failed the admissions test three times, so after the fourth time he was all the more devoted to his job. Cases like that tend to become pathological, Gentlemen. For instance, I could tell you about another policeman named

Sturm, one I met more recently here in Dresden. The poor devil fell prey to Watt-Waste. You know Watt-Waste, that symbolic figure invented by Comrade Leuschner himself, so that we all save electricity, because that way, thanks to our savings' tactics, if we don't use any, the West will suffocate in its own electricity and we'll catch up with it. Gentlemen, that is strategy. Officer Sturm couldn't think that far ahead, I admit, but that didn't prevent him from asking himself, as a mere policeman and Party member, how he could declare war on Watt-Waste. What did he finally come up with? He was a local celebrity after he announced one day that Comrade Leuschner could be proud of him, because in his night patrols he had decided to leave his regular flashlight at home and make his rounds with an old kerosene lantern his wife had found in the attic. To this day, he still wonders why after that he was assigned solely to daytime duty.

"So much for Sturm. Now back to the other one— Preisl, his name was, if I'm not mistaken. One day in Prague he happened to be walking home from work at half-past six, when an old car came careening down through a vineyard, with its driver shouting out the window, 'Get out of the way! My brakes have failed!' The traffic cop was just opposite a one-way street, a one-way street going the other way, understand, Gentlemen, and the car headed straight for it. In a single bound, the officer reached the middle of the road and screamed 'Stop! You can't go in here!' Whereupon the driver again shouted, 'Out of the way! My brakes have failed!' He must have been a superior sort of person, otherwise I imagine he'd have screamed, 'My goddamn brakes won't work!' Anyhow, superior sort of person or not, the officer only had eyes and ears for his duty and went on shouting, 'Halt! I can't let you in here! This is a one-way . . .' That's as far as he got; next thing he knew, he was lying flat on his back and a moment later he gave up the ghost. His last words, as the car shot out the other end of the street, were, 'I couldn't let him in here.' "

"So far as things of the spirit are concerned," commented Herr Long, who couldn't keep silent another minute, "your policemen are pretty irrelevant."

Long's glance wandered from Schweik to Altdorfer, who nodded in agreement, and Long said to Schweik, "Herr Altdorfer is also of my opinion."

"I know what you mean all right, Gentlemen," said Schweik. "You mean the spirit of the Western world or of Christianity—I've heard that mentioned a couple of times already."

Herr Long got to his feet and strode up and down meditatively in front of the table several times before saying, "You mean the absolute spirit. Only that rises above Communism. Every conflict with Communism must be spiritual in nature, or it is meaningless."

For a moment, Schweik's answer might have given rise to the fear that he would say something political; but his train of thought proved to be strictly military. "So you do mean the spirit I thought you meant, after all—although I don't think quite so highly of it as you do, Gentlemen," said he. "The spirit I do think a lot of is the alcoholic kind. Whatever you feel on that score, Gentlemen, and even if you tell me a hundred times that that joke is as old as the hills—the more alcoholic the spirits, the more the fighting spirit. Have you ever been at the front, Herr Long? And you, Herr Altdorfer? You both shake your heads—I guess not. Because otherwise you would have known which side wins, according to a law of nature, when two companies join battle, and one of them is full of alcoholic spirits, and the other full of the spirit of the Western world. Have you ever asked yourselves why the Roman legionaries clobbered the Germanic tribes whenever they felt like it? Because they were up to their ears in wine, and the German mead was like water by comparison. Or why the Hungarians got as far as Lechfeld? Because of the Tokay wine. Have you ever gotten in a fight in a bar? Sober and inspired by the spirit of Christianity, you approach this task with a heavy heart. Usually you give in entirely. But with twenty Slivovitz under your belt, you should see how easily you can stand up even to ten enraged woodchoppers. And as for giving in—not a sign of it!"

Long and Altdorfer sighed. Then Long, who appeared to be the speaker for both of them, said, "We do not associate with woodchoppers, Herr Schweik."

"You've taken the words right out of my mouth, Herr Long," added Herr Altdorfer in an undertone.

"Then try it some time with scissors-grinders," Schweik advised the two of them. "I recommend them highly."

Schweik's third suggestion nominated the unfortunately near-extinct profession of goatherds.

Again Altdorfer and Long exchanged looks, until Herr Altdorfer, who must have been extremely agitated —otherwise he would scarcely have been so talkative all of a sudden—arrived at a new realization, which he formulated by commenting, "I don't think there's any sense in this."

This suited Herr Altdorfer; he was an inveterate

pessimist. And what is the phrase pessimists always prefer above all others? The phrase "There isn't any sense in . . ."

On the other hand, Herr Altdorfer also exemplified the self-taught type of man. Things that fell into the laps of others, he had had to fight for. After elementary school—the only school he had attended—he had decided to devote himself exclusively to private studies. Now, as a rule, such people study everything. Herr Altdorfer developed into a universal genius, who had a word to say about atomic physics as well as all matters relating to world politics, cancer research, philosophy, or the fruit harvest in southern Tyrol. Small wonder that, especially in public schools which needed a speaker for a topic such as "The Influence of the Monsoon on the Sociology of the Papuans," to name only one example, this saying had grown up. "But then, what is Herr Altdorfer there for!"

One cannot blame experts in atomic physics, world politics, philosophy, and cancer research for being pessimistic. So in Herr Altdorfer's case, one thing reinforced the other—his personality and his education. The story of his mental conflict with Communism was also unusual, nor was it any less tragic than Herr Long's.

In his private publishing company, Herr Altdorfer had brought out a pamphlet in which he developed the thesis that the Communist State, like every other state before it, must inevitably decline, unless it grasped the vital necessity of revolutionizing education by doing away with all universities, and thus forcing aspiring students to teach themselves; for only autodidacticism cultivated true scholarly thinking.

Altdorfer's arrest had furnished another splendid

vindication of his pessimistic convictions. He distributed this pamphlet at Dresden's main railroad station. Beforehand, however, he had said to his wife: "I go to my martyrdom. From the distribution of the first pamphlet until my arrest, not an hour's time will elapse."

There elapsed exactly twelve minutes.

With this gentleman Schweik now became involved in a conversation about the intelligence of the common people.

Herr Long happened to be enthroned on the toilet, otherwise probably he—and not Altdorfer—would have carried on this conversation with Schweik. He made haste to escape the fate of being condemned to silence.

"The common people are simple-minded," said Herr Altdorfer, after Schweik, who had heard the story of Altdorfer's arrest, remarked that none of the common people would ever publish such a pamphlet. "That requires intelligence and education, Herr Schweik."

"The common people really are simple-minded," Schweik agreed with conviction. "Take for example the janitor where I live. He imagines that for a pack of cigarettes I'll help him heave coal."

He begged Schweik to concern himself with the pamphlet, Herr Altdorfer replied with dignity, and not to change the subject to coal-heaving. Besides which, he said, Schweik's example was ill-chosen, for it introduced the problem of the relativity of things. It would have been much more simple-minded of that janitor if he had offered Schweik fifty packs.

Schweik answered Altdorfer's grave words by pointing out that he, Schweik, hadn't wanted to change the subject to coal-heaving; on the contrary, all he had tried to do was to point up the relative dumbness of the janitor and thus of the common people. That there was a great difference between publishing a pamphlet and shoveling coal he could see well enough himself.

"Very well then, let us stick to the subject of publishing pamphlets," Herr Altdorfer reiterated. "Such things can never be expected from the man-in-the-street. What does he have on his mind? He eats, he drinks, he reproduces—but what he totally lacks is an eye for the true meaning of things. He isn't the least bit interested in them. That has always been so."

"You're absolutely right," Schweik agreed. "An eye for the true meanings of things has always been something that only the most brainy and educated people have had, not the common people. The Jesuits, the professors, they've always been proving things in learned books. For instance, they proved five hundred years ago that there were witches, and that the best way of dealing with them was to burn them at the stake. And of course they proved also that the sun revolved around the earth. The common herd couldn't positively have noticed anything of the kind. And today? Today the professors prove to us that the earth is a sphere. But actually it's pear-shaped, that's the latest novelty. My janitor had a good laugh about that! Go ahead and laugh, idiot, I thought to myself, so far as you're concerned the earth is as flat as a pancake."

Altdorfer's hope that his opinions could make an impression on Schweik remained unshaken. He said: "The causality of matter, the law of cause and effect, also applied to the existent philosophies, the revaluation of all values, of which Nietzsche was the first to speak— what man-in-the-street is interested in all that? Not a soul—you'll have to agree with me there, Herr Schweik."

"Certainly not my janitor; you're right about that."
Under Altdorfer's piercing glare, Schweik shifted the
blame to someone who was not present, and Herr Altdorfer, whose nerves were beginning to be unpleasantly
affected by this janitor, cried indignantly, "Leave your
janitor out of it, once and for all, Herr Schweik! Let's
stick to the business of publishing a pamphlet. I can assure you that that requires intelligence and education."

"And this here," said Schweik, rubbing his thumb
and forefinger together.

"Money?" Herr Altdorfer gave a contemptuous
wave of the hand. "Money comes only third or fourth
in the order of things."

He waved his hand again. It was easy to see, even
if he didn't contradict this assertion, that Schweik privately rejected Altdorfer's standpoint.

Altdorfer looked Schweik in the eye and said, "You
don't seem convinced?"

"The most important thing is dough," replied
Schweik with unusual obstinacy, rubbing his thumb and
forefinger together again. "You can't shoot without
powder."

Herr Altdorfer felt insulted and addressed himself
to the rear corner, which Herr Long still occupied.
"That's precisely the attitude of the proletariat—just
money, money, money! Can't you grasp what I'm trying to say?" he rejoined.

Schweik was so sure he was in the right that he
didn't hesitate to shrug his shoulders disparagingly. At
this, Herr Altdorfer felt even more insulted. Since the
situation was becoming unbearable, he announced aggressively, "Well, I must say, sometimes you remind me,
if you'll excuse the comparison, of your namesake in

Prague. There used to be a certain Schweik there too, you know, although he must be dead and gone by now. You even speak almost the same dialect. Have you ever heard of him?"

"Yes," replied Schweik truthfully.

A sound of rushing water came from the background—a sign that it wouldn't be long before Herr Long joined in the conversation again.

Herr Altdorfer, stubbornly trying to make some headway with Schweik, finally said in desperation, "Let's take your janitor, for example. What if suddenly he were to come into a million marks—do you think that would make him more capable of publishing a pamphlet?"

"If he had to write it himself—not even with *two* million," Schweik replied, and seeing the janitor in his mind's eye, he broke into unconstrained laughter. Here at last was an answer to Herr Altdorfer's liking.

Herr Long, still buttoning his trousers as he approached the table, thought too that now at last they were on the right track.

"Very well, then!" exclaimed Herr Altdorfer hurriedly, so as not to let Herr Long take advantage of this promising beginning, "Then we are in agreement, Herr Schweik. At last you've grasped what I'm trying to say. Your janitor, even were he a millionaire, would have to have someone else write the pamphlet for him."

"Even then he couldn't do it," said Schweik.

Herr Long, relentlessly butting into their conversation, asked Schweik what he was implying.

"He couldn't publish a pamphlet the way Herr Altdorfer did."

"Why not?"

"Because the janitor—or for that matter any other

member of the common herd—would still not have been smart enough to think of distributing it at the main station, where most people congregate."

He had wavered at first between the station and the soccer stadium, Herr Altdorfer confessed, before realizing that not all the proletariat gathered in the soccer stadium, but only half: the men. Whereupon Schweik explained once more that to think of that you certainly had to be a lot smarter than a janitor. A janitor wouldn't hit upon the main station *or* the soccer stadium—he wouldn't hit on anywhere at all. He would just squander his money on food and drink and lose the last threads of his reason in the process.

"By the way, that reminds me of the 'White Rose' revolt in Munich,"* Schweik added after a brief pause. "There was a lecture about it on the radio. Those were intelligent people, too—students. Under the Nazis they dropped their pamphlets in the university courtyard, in broad daylight, so that they'd be sure to be seen—the pamphlets, I mean. No one else had hit upon *that* idea either."

The "White Rose" was a godsend for Herr Long, who, viewing the matter with the eyes of a philologist, was prepared to enlarge upon it.

"Are you acquainted with the text of those pamphlets, Gentlemen?" he began. "A German style, I tell you—excellent! There are no more than two or three sentences which need polishing. Of course . . ."

At this moment the cell door was unlocked from

---

* The medical student Hans Scholl and his sister Sophie led a student conspiracy against Hitler while they called in the "White Rose." On February 18, 1943, they distributed pamphlets calling for a revolt of German youth. Four days later, on February 22, they were executed, together with four others.

outside. Herr Long fell silent. The door opened, and in
the doorway stood State Attorney Zollner. Zollner's gaze
fell tenderly on Schweik. The guard behind Zollner remained outside, as the State Attorney, with a friendly
greeting meant only for Schweik, crossed the threshold
and closed the door behind him.

Karl Zollner seemed to have grown years younger.

Herr Long and Herr Altdorfer had sprung to their
feet and bowed. When they saw Zollner grasp Schweik's
hand and shake it warmly, they were seized with sudden
alarm, for this seemed to be conclusive proof that
Schweik was an informer for the State Prosecution.

Zollner asked Schweik how he felt.

"Not bad," Schweik answered thoughtfully. "The
coffee was a little hot this morning—but aside from that,
knock on wood, everything was fine. I've had my fill of
hot coffee for the time being."

Well, he could always set it in front of the window
to cool, replied the State Attorney with a smile—did he,
Schweik, have any further wishes?

Joseph Schweik saw in this question an opportunity
that should be grasped by the horns. He put his hand to
his cheek.

"If it were possible," he said, "I'd like very much to
go to the dentist here. I have a fine couple of cavities."

"Fine!" said the State Attorney, as if it had always
been the rule for prisoners of the SSD to be treated by
the dentist on request. "That can be taken care of."

Since the word "dentist" was a catchword for him,
he then added, "Apropos the dentist, can you recommend me a good one, Herr Schweik? I have to see one
too, you know."

Schweik hesitated.

"Mine is a celebrity," interposed Herr Long. "He teaches dentistry at the university. I suppose I needn't say more."

"No, that's quite beside the point," Herr Altdorfer now broke in jealously, so as not to miss his chance. "A mere theoretician, in other words! Mine is a practician, Sir, that's what matters. He began as an assistant, worked his way up by self-study. Those are the best—they have to fight for everything. Not long ago he earned his doctorate. And in *The German Dentist* he reported last year on his discovery that the German tooth, thanks to the higher calcium content of our water here, is harder, more resistant, and in general more valuable than the American tooth—which is true, however, only for the teeth in the GDR, not for West German teeth. He was nominated for the National Award."

Schweik had remained silent, for he didn't care what dentist's chair Zollner landed in. Hopefully one where he was properly tormented.

"And yours, Schweik? Don't you have one?" Zollner nevertheless persisted.

"Good grief, mine!" Schweik rolled his eyes. "Mine is an old bungler, usually drunk, not a trace of National Award or doctorate about him. He's no dentist at all, but a sort of tonsorial butcher, the kind we used to have so many of, who'll gladly open an abscess and heal it with horse-piss, but . . . ." Schweik trailed off, signaled Zollner with a conspiratorial wink to come close to him, and whispered in his ear, ". . . but he learned under the Empire."

"I shall think it over," said Zollner, looking from one to the other. "You can come along with me, Herr Schweik."

Five minutes later, in his office, Zollner took down the address of Schweik's master butcher, the one who always pulled two teeth instead of one, because there was seldom an hour when he didn't see every tooth he was asked to pull, double.

"Good," said Zollner, putting the address in his breast pocket for safekeeping. "I thank you, Herr Schweik."

"Think nothing of it. It's my pleasure, Sir."

"By the way, what do you make of those two idiots in your cell?"

"Long's not so bad," Schweik replied, turning thoughtful again. "He's a born scholar and his parents, things being the way they are, probably talked him into it. So he can't help it. But Altdorfer! No one forced him to become such a self-educated half-wit. People like that have only themselves to blame for their stupidity; for them there are no extenuating circumstances. I can't tolerate people like that. I can't help it, as you always say, Sir, I'm sorry to say, if you'll excuse me. How long do you intend to keep him locked up?"

"Who?" asked Zollner in some confusion, for as a young man he too had gone through the fire of self-education.

"Altdorfer."

"We're still not sure, Herr Schweik. Originally we didn't want to be too hard on either of them: three, four years perhaps. But now every day that we listen to their conversations in the cell, a couple of years are added. By the way, while we're on the subject, I must congratulate you, Herr Schweik. You handled yourself very well in those conversations; indeed admirable, if I may say so. You scared me a couple of times, but—elegant, elegant,

the way at the last moment you carefully avoided the
pitfalls! I take my hat off to you, dear friend!"

"If you keep your wits about you," Schweik said
with a modest smile, "you don't succumb to the stupidity of those eggheads, those brainy, educated idiots."

"You're right about that," replied Zollner, letting
Schweik in on some professional expertise. "I've always
had the easiest time of all with professors. I've never
counted, but it wouldn't be much of an exaggeration for
me to claim that I've procured a thousand years behind
bars for professors. And I took very little trouble with
them. In that respect, I find the profession very likeable.
I can leave the office earlier when they're around. Doctors and writers are not unpleasant, either. They enjoy
talking about their professional ethics, and out of sheer
ethics they stumble from one trap into another. That's
something you won't find with streetcar conductors,"
Zollner added, his expression hardening somewhat. "Or
with mailmen either. They're beasts, I can tell you."

State Attorney Zollner looked angrily at his cigar, a
"Potemkin," whose attractive label did the name proud.

Schweik did not want to let his own profession
pass unmentioned.

"Railroaders," he supplemented Zollner's remarks,
"are no gentle breeze either, I hope. I imagine they've
already given you many a tough nut to crack, Sir?"

"Railroaders are sickening, Herr Schweik. If you see
light still burning in my office at midnight, you can be
sure I've a railroader on my hands."

"I'm glad to hear that," said Schweik, selecting a
Potemkin from the cigar box on the desk. "It's nice to
be able to pride one's self on one's fellow workers."

State Attorney Zollner apologized to Schweik for

having forgotten to offer him a cigar. He gave him a light and then added that Schweik must not misunderstand him when he said railroaders were sickening. There were always exceptions—one, anyway.

Schweik put him at ease by confessing that he, Schweik, was not so sensitive that a State Attorney need worry about upsetting him.

The two men made a very picture of harmony, of mutual understanding, an image of idyllic human sympathy.

"And now I have another happy announcement to make to you," said the State Attorney. "This morning I was able to release your housekeeper, Frau Lehmann. I've satisfied myself that she is innocent. So far as her health goes, she's a wreck, if you'll pardon the expression, Herr Schweik."

"Did you question her?"

"I had to," sighed Zollner. "I can't release anyone until I've satisfied myself of their innocence. Frau Lehmann had the flu, and fever . . . But that was the least of it . . ."

The State Attorney fell into a troubled silence—a silence dictated by discretion. But Schweik only asked with his habitual candor, "Did she ruin your carpet?"

State Attorney Zollner nodded as remorsefully as if *he* had been the one who had done the deed. Schweik seemed to sense the pricks of Zollner's conscience, for he said, "Chin up, Sir. *You* weren't the one who messed things up."

"It's on account of the proceedings against you, Herr Schweik," Zollner replied bashfully.

"What about it! That kind of thing doesn't upset me in the least," Schweik said disdainfully. "I'll survive this like other people survive a train journey, when there's a draft from a window that won't shut. I always say to myself that if you want to learn something about life, about the cold hard world we hear so much about, especially from the mouths of our parents and teachers when we're young—then later, as a grown-up, you have to be at home in a courtroom. Not just as a spectator or a lawyer, like you; that's no feat. If you haven't sat on the defendant's bench, you don't know much about life. So you can go ahead and look me in the eye, Sir, and as for this little matter of a trial, just you leave that to me."

Zollner's eyes remained lowered in spite of this encouragement, and then he said in barely a whisper, "Don't be alarmed, Herr Schweik, I beg of you. They want to make a precedent of you."

"A what?"

"A precedent."

"What's that?"

"An example: a case which is supposed to set an example for many others."

"And *that* weighs on your conscience?" Schweik leaned over the desk and patted Zollner's meekly folded hands. "Don't be silly! That's something new, for a change. That's never happened to me, to be pointed out as an example for others, like an exemplary person, so to speak. It really does me good to hear that. I wish my Oberleutnant Lukasch, from World War I, could see me now. I tell you, he'd fall on his knees and beg my forgiveness for all the things he always accused me of. That proves how mistaken you can be about a person, he would say with tears in his eyes, you'd hardly think it was possible. Why, if that's all it is, Sir, you and the

Dresden State Prosecution really don't have any reason to feel embarrassed."

"I'm glad," said Herr Zollner, raising his eyes at last, "that you're taking it so well. I can't thank you enough for being so obliging, if you'll excuse me, I'm sorry to say. I shall try in spite of everything to see that you are released until your trial and can return to Frau Lehmann. Only I have to take all precautions, because you are a special case. There are still consultations to be held. It is now . . ." He pushed back his coat sleeve and exclaimed, "*Holy Jehosophat!* It's already ten after nine! And the consultation was set for nine. Come on, Schweik, we have to wind this up. You'll hear from me again today in any case."

At the door, Zollner parted from Schweik with the words: "Keep up the good behavior and be guarded in your cell. Let the others do the chattering."

"Those eggheads—you can have 'em," said Schweik with conviction.

FREE AGAIN

***** State Attorney Zollner kept his word. He actually did call on Schweik again that day. In fact he informed him, his face beaming with joy, that the warrant for Schweik's arrest had been suspended. "Orders from the very top, if you'll excuse me," he announced rather grandly.

When Schweik returned home, Frau Lehmann was not in the apartment, but Schweik knew his housekeeper's habits well and merely tapped a broom handle against the kitchen ceiling. A moment later Frau Lehmann dashed breathlessly through the door.

"Herr Schweik!!"

"That's what I like! Back home from prison, and where's my housekeeper? Sitting gossiping in other people's apartments."

"But I didn't get back myself until today," said Frau Lehmann, not without pride. "You haven't got anything on me there, Herr Schweik . . . But I never thought things would go so quickly for you," she added, covering her face with her hands. Now, with each word her uneven voice dropped to a more tragic pitch. "I cried all my handkerchiefs soaking wet, Herr Schweik. I couldn't have endured losing you for much longer. It would have been the death of me."

Schweik, who meanwhile had pulled open all the drawers in the kitchen without finding what he wanted, obviously overheard these words of love, for he rejoined, "Haven't you got anything to eat in the house? My stomach is growling. Down there they toss you out of prison in the twinkling of an eye and think what a favor they're doing you, instead of giving you a decent bite to eat and keeping you there a little longer. Now *that* would be decent of them, not the other way round."

Frau Lehmann went from drawer to drawer, closing them gently, and said in a soft voice, "There's nothing here."

"Then go fetch something at the store."

Frau Lehmann's voice grew still softer, "I haven't got any money, Herr Schweik," she said wretchedly.

"Why not? The day before I was arrested I gave you housekeeping money for two whole weeks."

"I spent it. I had to live too," Frau Lehmann answered with a sob, but Schweik, smelling a rat, shouted gruffly, "Don't lie to me! Most of the time you were in prison yourself—so what did you do with the money? Out with it!"

"I . . . I . . ."

"Think of the Eighth Commandment, Frau Lehmann! God punishes nothing more severely than when you add insult to injury by lying to someone who's fresh out of prison."

"I . . . spent . . . ," Frau Lehmann stammered out, "spent . . . it . . . at . . . the newspapers.' "

"At the newspapers'?"

"For . . . want . . . ads."

"For want ads?"

"For . . . per . . . son . . . als."

"For personals?" Schweik, taken by surprise, repeated his housekeeper's words for the third time.

"Yes, Herr Schweik." At least Frau Lehmann was now speaking coherently again. "I knew I couldn't bear the pain of losing you for long. So, you see, I had to see about some way of getting over it."

Schweik reflected for a moment and concluded, "Then you have no choice, Frau Lehmann, but to go to the store and get something on credit. I'm flat broke."

Frau Lehmann sighed and lamented and said she'd rather jump from the roof of the Dresden dungeon— the tradesmen were so vulgar when you asked them for credit; they looked at you even more coarsely than a sailor eyes a woman after a long sea voyage. As Schweik remained immovable, Frau Lehmann added that she must take care of her flu; she had to go to bed, and the sooner the better; prison had ruined what remained of her health.

As Schweik pushed her out through the door, Frau Lehmann was still crossing herself in alarm at his dreadful oaths.

Schweik's hopes that Frau Lehmann would be successful were, frankly, not very great. Credit was part of the capitalist system, where the buyer was exploited with all sorts of cunning tricks. Not so under the Socialist system, which had no mind to seduce the buyer into over-consumption.

Schweik undressed down to his shorts and washed himself thoroughly. He was returning through the adjacent hall, in which there still hung two photographs of Stalin—an early one and a later one—when the doorbell rang.

"Forgotten the key again, the silly fool," murmured Schweik, opening the door. What met his eyes, however, was not Frau Lehmann but a stranger of middle height and commonplace appearance, with a blue peaked cap on his head. "I'm here to read the gas meter," he said brusquely.

"Fine," said Schweik. "I'm happy to hear that. Who do you work for?"

"The Public Utilities."

"Then please give them my best regards and tell them I'm sorry, I would have been glad to oblige."

The stranger cast a quick glance down the stairway behind him, then he asked, "What am I to make of that, Herr Schweik?"

"That I don't *have* any public gas. We have a different kind of apartment, with propane gas, which we buy ourselves as and when we need it."

"I must speak with you anyway," blurted out the stranger, and he pushed Schweik nervously into the apartment, closing the door behind him. "I admit I don't come from the Public Utilities, but you've just come from prison, Herr Schweik. Am I right?"

"So that's it," sighed Schweik, who now saw the situation clearly. "It was all a mistake. You've come to fetch me again, have you?"

"Not at all, Herr Schweik! You're entirely mistaken." The stranger looked around again and continued, "Are we alone, Herr Schweik?"

"Yes. But . . ."

"No buts! I'll be quick about it. I come from

Gehlen's West German Secret Service. We don't lose much time. Don't stand there looking as if you'd just fallen from the moon, Herr Schweik. We also have our footholds here, unknown to everyone—just as the Communists have their footholds in Cologne or Munich or Bonn, naturally above all in Bonn, even in the Bundestag itself, unknown to everyone. Things get pretty hot for me in my work here, as you can imagine. We have our connections everywhere. Therefore we also know that you are fresh out of prison, Herr Schweik. And for the same reason we assume that you are willing to work for us. That you are willing to fight for freedom, right?"

"For what, did you say?" asked Schweik, to gain time.

"For freedom—or the dignity of man, whichever you prefer."

Schweik, still trying to gain time to figure out what secret lay behind the mysterious visit of this remarkable meter-reader, explained that he had already fought for many things in his life, beginning with the Austrian Royal Family, and that his ten fingers wouldn't be enough to count all the things he had fought for, mostly in uniform as a tried and tested soldier. As a rule he had only needed one thing for fighting.

"What did you need?" asked the meter-reader.

"A command."

"We can't give you a command," said the meter-reader regretfully. "You must realize that. With us you *must* sign voluntarily."

At the word "voluntarily" it struck Schweik with a flash: Now I have it! They're testing me. They've disguised themselves and they only let me go so they can test whether I follow them voluntarily, no matter what they ask of me. They think that way they'll get me after all.

Schweik had already reached the right decision when he said, "Who cares anyway? Where do I sign?"

"Bravo!" exclaimed the stranger, for whom things were getting pretty hot. "No one before you has ever come around that fast. So now you are one of us. You are bound to us, for better and for worse. Strictest secrecy and extreme discretion are in your own interest. On the dotted line, please."

The meter-reader pointed to a scrap of paper which he had conjured up out of some pocket or other, indicating where Schweik should append his name. Schweik duly signed, thinking that the stranger might as well go ahead and tell him what he wanted, for he, Schweik, had long since figured out what was going on behind the scenes, only he must not show it.

Meanwhile, the meter-reader had been praising the advantages of voluntary commitment, although, as he said, his experiences with involuntary commitment had also been quite pleasant. "And best of all," he added with a smile, "are our experiences with commitments which are both voluntary *and* involuntary. I therefore request you, Herr Schweik, to take note briefly of the fact that while we couldn't order you to work for us, we nevertheless had the pleasure of discovering several dark spots in your past, before we contacted you. At the moment I should only like to mention one of them: your housekeeper has two illegitimate daughters, who are being brought up by their grandmother in Leipzig. With these daughters, who in addition to everything else also come under the jurisdiction of the Law for the Protection of

Minors, you, Herr Schweik, in spite of your age—or because of it—have already deceived your housekeeper several times. But that is only a secondary matter . . . what were you saying, Herr Schweik?"

"That you certainly spoke the truth when you said, 'with us you *must* sign voluntarily.' "

The meter-reader's features lit up in a self-satisfied smile as he answered, "We choose our words carefully.

"But now I must go," he continued, getting to his feet. "You will hear from us again. Your code name for the present is 'Uzbek.' And one last question: how are your finances at the moment?"

"Terrible!" Schweik exclaimed spontaneously. "Why do you ask? Are you going to pay me damages for my arrest?"

A second later he could have bitten his tongue, because now he had let on after all that he knew what was going on behind the scenes. But the meter-reader only smiled again and said that he found Schweik very amusing.

As he spoke, he handed Schweik a hundred-mark note, and had him sign a receipt, dropping the word "advance."

"An advance is better than St. Vitus' dance," said Schweik, imprinting a kiss on the hundred-mark note, "not to mention ants in the pants."

The meter-reader smiled again, but at the same moment noticed the two photographs of Stalin on the wall, which he had overlooked in his nervousness. "Are you crazy?" he shouted.

'What do you mean?"

"That's *not* allowed!" barked the meter-reader, his eyes shooting back and forth between Schweik and the photographs. "You are one of us now, Comrade Schweik. That means that you mustn't deviate another centimeter from the Party line, do you understand that?"

"That's not hard to understand," said Schweik. "If I am one of you, then I'm not allowed to deviate another centimeter from the Party line, not even a millimeter—I see that as plain as day."

"Then you know what you have to do," said the meter-reader. He pointed at the photographs and departed.

When he was gone, Schweik held a brief conversation with himself, in which he admitted that the hallway was indeed an unsightly little cubbyhole, in which no real reverence could find expression.

After this monologue, Schweik hung the photographs of Stalin in that corner of his combination kitchen-and-living room which the Christian deity had formerly occupied. Shortly thereafter, the doorbell rang again.

"Didn't I say the silly fool had forgotten her key?" murmured Schweik. He went to the door and, to his surprise, found himself once more face to face, not with Frau Lehmann, but with a second stranger, who showed a remarkable resemblance to the first one, blue peaked cap, a briefcase, middle height, commonplace appearance.

"I'm here to read the gas meter," said the newcomer.

This coincidence was the most astonishing of all. Schweik sighed and remarked that he could hardly wait to hear what would come next.

The second meter-reader gave him a questioning

look and said, "What am I to make of that, Herr
Schweik? What are you trying to say?"

"I am trying to say, first of all, that I don't have
any gas, and secondly . . . "

"You don't have any gas?"

"If you don't mind my saying so—no."

"Goddammit!" swore the second meter-reader, rubbing his nose. "That's typical. They send you around
to read gas meters and don't bother to find out beforehand whether the people even have gas."

This meter-reader, who was in many ways so similar to the first one, was, however, distinguished by one
essential difference: he was not the least bit nervous; in
fact he was the very soul of calm.

"Oh, well, it doesn't matter how they send you
around," he continued calmly. "The meter-reading was
only supposed to be a means of making contact. Let's
begin right away *in medias res*, as the Latinists say when
they think they've talked enough cra . . . pardon, Herr
Schweik. I come from the Secret Service."

Schweik nodded and said, "That's fine. I was about
to say I suspected as much. But please do step inside,
Comrade. There are too many curious ears at the front
door."

Although Schweik's words seemed rather mysterious to him, the meter-reader said, "You're quite right,"
and let Schweik lead him into the kitchen, whence
Schweik offered him a chair, with the comment that it
must still be warm from his predecessor.

"I don't follow you, Comrade Schweik," said the
meter-reader. "Can't you be more explicit?"

"If you had come five minutes sooner, you would

have met the other one on the stairs," remarked Schweik.

"What other one?"

"The other one of your guys."

"You were too slow," Schweik continued regretfully, as his visitor stared at him in astonishment. "I can't help you, I'm sorry to say, as a friend of mine always says—a jerk. That makes you sit up and take notice, huh! Yes, it's true all right, the other one has gone and grabbed my signature from under your very nose, Comrade. That's probably why he was in such a hurry. Blond, like you, but just a shade darker. And he was quicker. He must have been about one or two years younger than you. What vintage are you, if I may ask? Nineteen eighteen, I would say."

"Seventeen," said the meter-reader with his extraordinary calm, but then he blurted out in spite of himself, "Goddammit! That lousy, god-awful joint! That's typical. That's what happens, when everyone's supposed to keep his tabs on everyone else. The result is, nobody ever tells anyone anything—not a flicker of coordination."

"I know what you mean," said Schweik, although he was confusing coordination with subordination, which he had been taught in the army. "I know all too well. Without coordination you might as well go hang yourself, as our old recruiting sergeant used to holler."

The meter-reader leaned his head on his hands, murmuring, "Let me think that over," and he looked so woebegone that Schweik, sympathetic soul that he was, said helpfully, "You know what? I'll give you my signature, too. All you'll have to do is to keep your mouth shut about my telling you that the other guy came here first. That's as simple as can be."

"That's a possibility," replied the meter-reader with restored composure. "But suppose they demand an explanation from you?"

"Because of this mix-up, I think that's unlikely," said Schweik with candor. "But if they should, then I'll defend myself by explaining that, after I signed the first time, I felt so bound to secrecy that I kept it a secret even from you. Then they'll even have to praise, and maybe even promote me. Can I now have my hundred marks?"

"What hundred marks?"

"My advance. The other one paid me, and you have no choice but to follow suit—if you want everything to look convincing, from A to Z. Otherwise your superiors could suspect me of letting slip the fact that the other guy was here and left a hundred marks."

The meter-reader understood from this twisted logic that he had no alternative but to submit, and while Schweik signed a paper committing him to the Communist Secret Service and kissed it twice, the meter-reader sighed several times and said that all this was the fault of the system. Whereupon Schweik asked, "Which system?"

"The quota system. Every one of us has to produce the signatures of two new confidential agents a day. Can you imagine what that means? We leap at every person who is released from political arrest, because the political cases are the easiest for us. We've got them in the palm of our hand. We can put pressure on them, although it seldom comes to that, because the political cases want to prove they've changed their convictions and are almost glad of the opportunity we offer them. Did my colleague have to put pressure on you, Comrade Schweik?"

"Not at all."

"Fine. So then I don't have to bother with that, either."

The meter-reader shoved his chair back. "Your code name for the time being is 'Texan.' You'll hear from us again. Actually I'd like to sit here and chat with you for a while, Comrade Schweik. You're a likeable fellow, and it's not hard to get along with you. Besides, it's very cosy here. Only the photos of Stalin up there . . ."

He fell silent, motioned with his hand, and added, "Well, I guess you haven't had time to get around to that yet, since you've been home. Where's the door?"

Schweik showed him the way to the front door. The meter-reader's thoughts, as his parting words showed, were already busy with the future, for he quipped, "I hope at any rate the next one has gas."

"Why do you stick to that ploy?" Schweik inquired at the door.

"In itself it's not a bad one," the other confided. "We didn't invent it ourselves, admittedly. We only adopted it. Our foreign experts in Bonn discovered that the West German Secret Service has had great success with this method. But you must be discreet about that, Comrade Schweik."

"Don't worry, Comrade," said Schweik reassuringly. "You needn't have any fear on that score. I was in on that even before you came. In fact, your predecessor also mentioned the West German Secret Service, so it's not news to me."

"Then I can count on you, Comrade Schweik?"

"It's a deal," said Schweik, clasping the other affirmatively by the hand.

When Schweik was alone once more, he said aloud, "You can put my dinner under your pillow and sleep on it, Frau Lehmann. I no longer need it."

He slipped into his coat and was just about to go out the door, when suddenly he stopped and struck his forehead with his hand, murmuring, "I nearly forgot." What it was that he had come within an inch of forgetting revealed itself when Schweik took the two finest potted plants from the windowsill in Frau Lehmann's room and placed them under the Stalin photographs in the kitchen, commenting, "That should do the trick. If someone else comes along and starts finding fault with the décor, he can go to hell . . . And that goes for you too," he added, nodding at the two pictures.

At this moment the doorbell pealed yet again. With a start, Schweik involuntarily assured the two photographs, "Sorry, I didn't mean it that way," and waited to see if the doorbell would ring again, which it did.

"The third one," sighed Schweik, and he went to open the door.

Over the threshold stepped Frau Lehmann. "Oh it's *you?*" cried Schweik, confused. "Why did you ring?"

"Because I forgot the key. That can happen to anybody."

From the pertness of her answer, it seemed that Frau Lehmann felt well satisfied with herself, that she had the upper hand. Her eyes sparkled triumphantly. Why?

Frau Lehmann was hardly recognizable. The dejected wreck who had trembled before the vulgar tradesmen as she left the apartment was now transformed into a kind of Goddess of Victory. Under her arm she carried a large, full paper bag. Inside it lay the reason for her transformation. She went into the kitchen. Schweik followed her, whereupon she informed him that any man who had a housekeeper like her had better start counting his blessings. She placed the bag on the kitchen table and began emptying it. Schweik's eyes grew as big as saucers as Frau Lehmann pulled out a huge chunk of liverwurst—a whole one, as thick as Schweik's arm—then twenty rolls and, by way of climax, even a little box of cigars. And what cigars! Bremer Handelsgold! Then, putting her hands on her hips, she said with bittersweet defiance, "Well, what do you say to that, Herr Schweik?"

What Schweik said now was an expression of true modesty: "What amazes me is that the tradesmen gave you all that on credit. After all, they know me."

But Frau Lehmann knew better. "It's got nothing whatsoever to do with you," she replied, and continued with emphasis, "I'm the one they gave it to. And if you really want to know, Herr Schweik, they actually *gave* it to me, credit didn't come into it."

"They gave it to you?"

"This is how it happened," said Frau Lehmann, taking a seat. "First of all, I went to the butcher's, my knees shaking. And he promptly tried to throw me out, but I was ready for that, and right away I started crying and told him that you'd just gotten back from prison. 'What's that got to do with me?' he shouted. 'I've no time for enemies of the State!' Then he gave me the liverwurst and said that he'd give it to *me* and no one else, because I'm a poor, decent woman who has to put up with an enemy of the State and get mixed up in all kinds of things. 'Remember that,' he said, 'if anyone ever asks why I gave you a liverwurst.' Then the same thing happened at the bakery with the twenty rolls. And at the drugstore too . . .''

"At the drugstore?" asked Schweik in a surprised tone.

"Yes, at the drugstore. The proprietor is a fine gentleman of the old school. Listen, now: he had just come into the bakery to order a cake for his wife's birthday. He heard everything I said and then told me to wait outside for him until he was through. I waited and then he took me with him to his apartment—that's why I was gone so long, Herr Schweik—and there he gave me the little box of cigars, saying that the cigars are for me, for my personal use. I was shocked and said I didn't smoke cigars, so he said, 'Then it's time you started. Let Frau Sacher, of the Sachertorte in Vienna, be an example to you. Years ago she started smoking half a box a day.' And before I could say another word he had pushed me out the door again."

During her long recital, Frau Lehmann had sliced open one roll after another and spread liverwurst on each of them, so that her master wouldn't go hungry. And Schweik, ensuring that the wolf was kept firmly from the door, only uttered joyfully several times, his mouth full, "What a day it is! What we need is 365 of them a year."

When he was satiated, he tried the first cigar from the unknown druggist—not of course without asking Frau Lehmann politely, "May I?"

"Don't just sit there asking," said Frau Lehmann with a chuckle. "That clod of a druggist can't see us, after all."

Schweik, sniffing the aroma of the first clouds of smoke from his cigar, suddenly felt apprehensive. "I hope no one smells it on the stairway," he said.

His housekeeper's face took on a look of concern, and she remarked that nowadays one really should remember that it was better to smoke these Western cigars at night, when the rest of the house was asleep.

She went out into the hall to make sure that no one was on the stairs. Since there was no sign of life, her worries evaporated, and, after quickly patting her hair into place before the hall mirror, she returned to Schweik with other things on her mind. "You've put on your overcoat, Herr Schweik," she remarked with obvious disappointment as she reëntered the room. "Why?—Are you going out? We could have such a nice cosy evening together."

Schweik winced and explained that he was sorry but it wouldn't work out, because he had to visit a sick friend at the hospital, which was bound to take a while, since the friend was very severely ill.

He put on his hat, saying, "And don't expect me before closing time, Frau Lehmann."

SCHWEIK AS A WEALTHY MAN

✳✳✳ It has always been true that money has its favorites, whom it chases after, whom it becomes attached to, from whom it doesn't want to be separated, in whose care it multiplies of its own accord. And no reasonable person can hold all that against money, for the treatment which money receives at the hands of its favorites is entirely different from its treatment by those poor devils who have none. With its favorites, money dwells in high-class safes, in fire-proof vaults, or in thick wallets of fine leather, worn next to the heart. Among the favored, it is transferred by that noble contrivance, the check. Whereas the poor man's way of passing money is a hand-to-hand one—dirty fingernails to dirty fingernails. Nor do such people carry money, should it perchance have found its way to them, next to their hearts: they carry it loose in their trouser pockets. That speaks for itself. No wonder that in such surroundings money continually cries, "Let me out! Let me out!"

Schweik's newly acquired riches had no other aim.

Schweik furnished proof of this fact only a few moments after leaving Frau Lehmann in bitter disappointment—a proof which may truly be considered convincing.

If anyone had seen Schweik descending the stairs, imagining he was heading for the hospital, he might well have had the impression that for Schweik there was no greater treat than visiting a sick friend. He smiled, whistled contentedly to himself, taking two or three steps at a time, didn't feel his rheumatism, and said to the janitor, who asked him what was the matter and whether America was about to declare war on Russia or something, "I have to admit I hadn't thought of that yet, but it's just as well you remind me of such possibilities, old boy, for war brings inflation—and that's something you have to watch out for."

A couple of streets later the signboard of a drugstore reminded Schweik of something, whereupon he entered the adjoining shop, a State-owned property. The young salesgirl who approached him wore on her breast a medal with a red star and the inscription: FOR SUPER-SERVICE. "May I help you?" she asked.

"Three cigars, Sweetie."

"Is that all you want! Can't you open your eyes? What do you think our display is for? We only carry *umbrellas.*"

"Very well, then," sighed Schweik, a man who never tried to evade the whims of fate, "give me three umbrellas."

Armed with three umbrellas, which together had cost almost a hundred marks, Schweik was just about to leave the store when it occurred to him again that he was sure he could remember this being a tobacco shop

—and, returning to the counter, he said to the salesgirl, "I remember your carrying cigarettes and tobacco. I'd stake my right arm on it."

"In summer," replied the salesgirl much more politely than before—for Schweik's purchase had made a lasting impression upon her—"in summer we carry tobacco goods, that's right, Sir. But that's not the rule here, it's the exception. Usually, we're a regular umbrella shop. But in the summer, thanks to the demands for umbrellas, which are few and far between, we switch over to tobacco goods. In the winter we return to our real vocation."

"And what do you do in spring and the fall?" Schweik asked with interest.

"That depends on the weather."

"What imagination! Bravo!" cried Schweik generously. "That's splendid. That encourages me to give you a tip which has just occured to me. It would be smarter still, if in the summer you didn't bother about tobacco and such like."

"And instead?"

"Perhaps ice skates."

The salesgirl, who had been made pregnant by a passing sailor and didn't have the five hundred marks which a certain Dr. Falke, a doctor from the Vopo,* demanded for medical intervention, suddenly became very excited. She breathed rapidly, kneaded her hands, and asked Schweik whether he would insist on copyrighting his idea. Schweik indicated generously that he couldn't do so, at which the salesgirl raised her hands in a pleading gesture and said, "Then you consent to

* Vopo is a derogatory abbreviation for the *Volkspolizei*, or State Police.

my sending this idea to the newspaper as if it were my own, for publication in the column 'Ways of Overcoming Economic Bottlenecks'? There are prizes for good suggestions."

"Prizes?" Schweik repeated.

"But I'm sure that wouldn't interest you," added the salesgirl hurriedly.

"Not interest me?"

"I'm sure it wouldn't. You're swimming in money. I've never come across a customer like you before. A customer who makes such purchases must be swimming in money—good heavens, he'd spit on five hundred marks."

The struggle which took place in Schweik's mind ended as his gaze fastened on the young bosom before him and he asked what he would get for his generosity. The salesgirl laughed; she sensed that she had won. She said that she had heard this question often enough from men, both young and old. But she shouldn't underestimate him, replied Schweik. In this respect he could still compete with any medical student; for him, age was no barrier. And he clutched passionately at the salesgirl's hand, which lay on the counter, so that things rapidly reached the point where the salesgirl, in order to defend herself from Schweik, had to draw his attention to another gentleman, who, she said, had been looking in through the window the whole time.

Schweik let her go, and with the promise, "I'll be back, Sweetie," departed.

Snow clouds clustered in the sky. A little later, after a short stretch past three blocks, Schweik arrived under a new roof, at a haven which he liked above all others. This was the "Traube," his favorite tavern. The hospital visit could now begin in earnest.

Schweik had not noticed that the serious gentleman at the window of the umbrella shop had been following him the whole time. In this gentleman's coat pocket was a week-old copy of *Neues Deutschland,* and he now swore softly to himself. Arriving in Schweik's wake at the "Traube," he realized all too well that this engagement would be a protracted one. It meant that he must camouflage himself; he couldn't simply hang around for hours in front of the "Traube" without being noticed. So the serious gentleman crossed the street, opened his out-of-date newspaper, and pretended to be reading it eagerly. In actuality, of course, he was keeping watch by means of that traditional ruse—the hole in the newspaper.

Inside the tavern Schweik had taken a seat by the window, without suspecting that in doing so he made it easier for the serious stranger in the street to keep an eye on him.

It began to snow. The interior of the tavern gaped with emptiness. It was still too early for the evening guests. Schweik laid his umbrellas on a table, confessing, "I'm curious myself as to what I'm going to do with them."

In the serious gentleman's notebook, the last two temporarily suspended entries read: *14.44: S. buys* three *umbrellas*!!! And *14.48* hours: *S. touches bosom of salesgirl. She defends herself, but not decisively enough. Appears to be certain understanding (!) between them.*

It began to snow harder. Schweik waited. No one came. At last it was too much for him, and he shouted in a booming voice, "Hey! Does one have to die of hunger and thirst around here?" This *cri de cœur* brought the old, short-sighted cook—a Sudeten exile called Frau Mracek, who came from Schweik's homeland and spoke the local dialect—out of the kitchen. She padded into the room, grumbling, "You'd think I had a hundred hands! I'm supposed to cook, wait on the guests, take care of the rooms—is there anything I'm not supposed to do?"

"Where is Frau Gartner?" asked Schweik. Frau Gartner was the proprietor's wife. Instead of answering his question, the cook, who hadn't recognized Schweik until this moment, asked, "Aren't you Herr Schweik?"

"Who else?"

"Hmph, you're a fine one to come in here acting high and mighty like the Aga Khan," said the cook rebukingly. "What do you want? Not a cent in your pockets—but as for shouting!"

"Is that the proper way of speaking to me?" Schweik retorted with dignity. "I have just come back from prison."

Normally this information would have had a positive effect on the cook, but today she only replied irritably, "I don't give a hoot! You've just come back from prison, all right, but our Herr Gartner *hasn't!* And what's more, he comes first."

"What? Herr Gartner's inside?" Schweik exclaimed with surprise. "When did they take him?"

"Day before yesterday."

"And nobody mentioned it to me?"

"Does that surprise you?" said the cook, lowering her voice. "Around here it's already the other way around. Here people say to you, 'Have you heard? They *haven't* come for so-and-so.' "

"What did he do?"

"He drank too much and after the twelfth double he said that he didn't give a damn any more, but in his opinion the Russians wouldn't have won the war without Stalin."

"That's obvious!" Schweik exclaimed, shaking his head over the unfortunate Herr Gartner. "They couldn't let him get away with that. That's an insult to the Russians. The Russians win every war, even without Stalin. *With* Stalin they win or won the war in half the time—that's what Herr Gartner should have said, then nothing could have happened to him."

"With me, you can go ahead and talk like that, Herr Schweik—about your Stalin, you know that. You can count on me, every time."

Schweik concluded that here again was a case of typical female simple-mindedness, of illogical, scatter-brained chatter.

Three truck drivers now entered the tavern.

"Do you wish to order?" Frau Mracek asked Schweik in a matter-of-fact tone. Schweik's answer scarcely fell in line with Frau Mracek's expectations. "This evening for dinner," he said, "I would like steamed roast calf with buttered potatoes, French beans, and dill sauce. Following that I'd like a middle-sized portion of meat loaf with black bread-crumbs, something nice and well-cooked, and juicy, with horseradish. If you don't have these things on hand, you can still pick them up at the butcher's. Of course you'll have to pay black-market prices, otherwise you'll only get herring, which I believe is on the list this week. We have plenty of time, I'm in no hurry to eat. I had a large supper only half an hour ago. As for drink, you can bring me a bottle of champagne—from the Crimea, if you can't get hold of any

French champagne. The champagne right away, though
. . . is everything clear, Frau Mracek?"

Frau Mracek, who couldn't believe her ears, only
laughed at Schweik and asked in a low voice, "Have you
just come from prison or from the nuthouse?"

"I know what you're thinking," said Schweik quite
unperturbed. "But you can't offend me, Frau Mracek.
The situation has changed, as you can see for yourself . . ."

Now, Frau Mracek thought she was seeing things,
too. Suddenly, rustling bills had popped up between
Schweik's fingers. Frau Mracek rubbed her eyes, but the
bills remained.

"Are you satisfied?" asked Schweik.

"I beg you a thousand pardons, Herr Schweik.
You have money, after all. You're a decent person who
deserves to be appreciated and honored—not one of
those proletarians who are so popular around here. But
how could I have got wind of your sudden prosperity?
You'll get your meat loaf . . .".

Schweik was still rustling his bills, and Frau Mracek,
clasping her hands over her head, exclaimed, "Good
gracious, if only our Herr Gartner could be in on this!
He's never seen you like this in his whole life—nor has
Frau Gartner, for that matter."

"Where is she then?"

This seemed to be a delicate question, for Frau
Mracek bent down and murmured in Schweik's ear, "It's
a scandal. She's running around with that Müller."

"With that Müller?"

"Hmph, Herr Schweik, you must know him—that
sly, shameless young whippersnapper, who used to be
here often enough when you were at the regulars' table

yourself. He's not ashamed of making the others laugh by telling them that he's gotten hold of a job of national importance, which is not only pleasant but also easy. What he does is to satisfy the grass widows, he says, of all the people who are arrested. That always made our Herr Gartner laugh loudest of all."

"Ah," said Schweik, "is that the one who wears very tight pants—the crew-cut slob, a sort of reddish blond, who looks like an American?"

"That's the one, Herr Schweik." Frau Mracek fell silent and seemed to be lost in thought. Suddenly her face lit up, and she continued, "But now *you* could intervene, Herr Schweik. With your money you can do anything. Our Herr Gartner would be sure to pay you back somehow, if they ever release him."

"Are you thinking of Buchta and Co., Frau Mracek?" Schweik asked after a brief pause. He had already half decided to take up Frau Mracek's suggestion, for the sake of Herr Gartner who had treated him to many a glass.

"Yes, I'm thinking of them."

"Good. Then this is what I ask of you now: make me my steamed roast calf and meat loaf, so that I can hear the angels singing in Heaven, then we'll see about it—but only, as I say, if I can hear the angels singing. If I don't hear any singing, then the Buchta brothers don't interest me either. So it's up to you, Frau Mracek. You see how it is. So, off to the kitchen. Wait a minute! First of all, my bottle of champagne!"

Frau Mracek shot back and forth, as fast as her varicose veins permitted, but she was full of inner calm and self-confidence, as her parting words, "You'll hear the angels, Herr Schweik," demonstrated.

Buchta and Co. was not in fact a real company, it only went by this name in Schweik's neighborhood. It wasn't listed in the commercial register, nor did it fulfill any of the other requirements which legally acceptable companies have to meet. But its customers didn't care about such externals. For these customers, Buchta and Co. existed as a tangible reality. The papers, stamps, and signatures which would have identified the company as such were in the eyes of those customers mere super-fluous nonsense. It was a two-man operation. The owners were brothers, Emil and Rudolf Buchta. Their motto read: Trust for trust! Without this motto, the affairs of Buchta and Co. would have stood on very unstable ground indeed. The reader can gather more detailed information on this subject from the list of the Buchta prices, from which the following is an extract:

Simple bodily injury (Beating)	30	marks
Dangerous bodily injury (Beating to pulp)	60	marks
Defense witness (Incl. unpremeditated perjury)	40	marks
Defense witness (Incl. premeditated perjury)	80	marks
Spreading rumor harmful to business	5	marks
Spreading two rumors harmful to business (for every additional rumor, .50 reduction)	9.50	marks
Half slander	15	marks
Complete slander	25	marks
Political denunciation	according to size	

And so on . . .

Payment: 50% upon order, 50% upon completion of commission. 3% discount on cash payments. Long-term credit granted only to innocently victimized customers (i.e., prison inmates).

The above-quoted prices of Buchta and Co. were not fixed, but only so-called "suggested" ones. That will easily be understood by anyone who considers that they represent rates for very different kinds of work— depending, for example, on whether one is to beat up a Latin instructor or professional boxer. For commissions of the latter kind, Emil and Rudolf Buchta demanded a price increase of up to one hundred percent, and in addition they also charged their own hospital expenses to the customer. On the other hand, they also offered price reductions to Latin instructors, old men over seventy, and disabled veterans.

AN HONEST BUSINESSMAN

✳ ✳ ✳ Schweik did hear the angels sing! Old Frau Mracek was a culinary artist, like all cooks from the Bohemian neck of the woods. After an appropriate interval, she placed before Schweik his order of steamed roast calf and meat loaf with black breadcrumbs—with the result that after his meal Schweik made a proposal of marriage. His declaration of love was brief: "Frau Mracek, in this steamed loaf and meat . . . meatcalf I see that you are a real beauty. Is your free still hand? . . . hand still free?"

"Don't talk rubbish, Herr Schweik. You've had too much to drink. You can remember Buchta and Co. for me instead. You promised, now."

"Another bottle of champagne! That'll be the third."

"The fourth," said Frau Mracek.

"How . . . how so?"

"Just go ahead and count the empty bottles on the table."

Schweik stared goggle-eyed at the three empty bottles and said with astonishment, "But there are six!"

Frau Mracek sighed. She was concerned about Buchta and Co., so she suggested making Schweik a strong cup of coffee. "Western coffee," she whispered seductively. "I still have some from a cousin in Coblenz."

Schweik wasn't interested in coffee, not even in Western coffee. He said that nobody could tell him what to drink. He wanted and could pay for champagne— and that was that! He pounded his fist on the table. Frau Mracek's attempt to say something else seemed to revive military echoes in Schweik's befuddled head, provoking him to bark out, "Champagne, I say! About face! Forward, march!"

Frau Mracek departed, protesting that that's how it had gone her whole life through, one injustice after another. When she was gone, Schweik felt in the right mood for reading the day's newspaper. There was a copy on the next table, so he picked it up. First of all he read the want ads:

Urgently Needed, 3 sacks chemical fertilizer. Offers from 3/1/56–1/1/60 write Agric. Coop. Sandersleben, Hettstedter Strasse 14. After 1/1/60, telephone 439.

Workman formerly independent, seeks ammunition (for former WW II army pistol 08) in trade for inheritance claim.

Worker's hero, soon 65, 46 years Party member, seeks *at any price* for old age *Well-preserved armchair.*

To all horse owners! Slaughter-house Stendal requires slaughter horses to fill capacity (may be sick, export to North Korea). Horses to be delivered by owners personally. Slaughter-house trucks in repair until next year.

For Sale: complete apartment furnishings. *Do not plan*

to flee Republic! Second furnishings inherited. Offers in writing to Police Inspector H. Werner, Zella-Melis, Ober-hoferstr. 3.

Youth Initiation Dress, Size 12, worn once, will give away for collect postal charges. K. Gruner, formerly Halle (Saale), new address: Düsseldorf, Graf Adolf Strasse 26/II.

Bar Stool sought. Offers to District House of Culture, Berlin-Weissensee, Klement-Gottwald-Allee 125.

Men's shoes, size 12 (can be brown), urgently needed for wedding. Write Er 4610.

Seek used lighter (prewar fabrication) to trade for new radio (People's prod.). M. Gutbrod, Kustrin, Bahnhofstr. 3.

Socialist Help urgently needed! Party member seeks for immanent birth of baby relatively well-preserved *zinc washtub* at any price. Offers to Fr 9435 Dewag.

Now Schweik turned his attention to the lead article, of which the headline and first paragraph read as follows:

CRIMES OF THE PERSONALITY CULT

The cult surrounding his person, which Stalin not only tolerated but even encouraged, had the result that honest Communists were liquidated, while repulsive sycophants, who were not ashamed to call Stalin magnificent, immortal, even holy, climbed from rung to rung and reached the dictator's inner sanctum. The 20th Party Congress of the CP in Moscow has opened all our eyes. We shall never forget how our magnificent Nikita Sergeyevich Khrushchev called Stalin to account. If he were to die tomorrow, this fact alone would suffice to assure him a place in the ranks of the immortals of Marxism-Leninism . . . etc.

Schweik attempted to follow these interesting remarks, while the sentences, lines, and words swam before his eyes, with the following result:

The cult surrounding his tolerated, but even encouraged, had liquidated, while were. Who Stalin from rung to sanctum of the 20th Party Congress die tomorrow mag . . . magnificent in the ranks of the account. Opened all our tals Marxism of xism Leni surroundism assure of Marxism-Leninism assure . . .

Following this exertion, Schweik fell asleep at the table. He didn't wake up until a peddler of lottery tickets entered the tavern and tugged at his arm in an attempt to sell him six chances. "Why six?" asked Schweik with some curiosity, when he had succeeded in collecting his thoughts. "Because you talked in your sleep, Comrade," answered the lottery-ticket peddler, "and you let on that you're crazy about the number six. I've been listening to you for some time now. You said again and again, 'If I say it was six, then it was six and it's going to be six and not three, until the end of time. I refuse to hear any other number but six.' . . . That's it, Comrade, and so now I'm doing you the favor."

Politeness deserves to be rewarded with politeness, thought Schweik to himself, and he bought six tickets, naturally blanks. He then observed: "You are a man, as they say, who knows how to take an opportunity by the horns. I like that. Sit down. Would you like a bottle of champagne?" The peddler took this opportunity by the horns all too readily and drank not one, but three bottles of the marvelous liquid which until this moment he had only known of by hearsay. Unfortunately he hadn't eaten anything. Schweik, on the other hand, was now sobering up. His nap had done him good. Besides, by this time the very quantity of champagne he had tippled seemed to have inoculated him against any after effects.

"What are your tickets in aid of, anyway?" Schweik

asked his new friend, to which the peddler replied with sudden melancholy, "For the needy Communist Party in West Germany. But that's tough going, I can tell you. Everyone says the West Germans should pay for their own Communist Party—they're better off than we are, after all."

Schweik pointed to the tray of lottery tickets which the peddler had placed on the table. "Do you have any winners left?"

"I don't know, Comrade."

"You don't know?"

"How am I supposed to know? . . . I haven't been at this job long—barely three years in fact. All I do know is that I haven't drawn a winner yet."

The conversation lapsed momentarily, and Schweik's gaze wandered to the window, behind which the snow was falling in thick flakes. Catching sight of the newspaper-reader on the opposite side of the street, Schweik remarked, "That guy doesn't even notice how he's getting snowed in. Whatever he's reading must be very interesting. I bet it's today's lead article. I found it very interesting myself."

The peddler, however, who was one of those people whom alcohol makes pessimistic, was of another opinion. "Don't give me any of that crap about newspaper-readers, Comrade," he snapped. "They've got their eye on something quite different from newspapers."

"And what's that?"

"Well, you know."

"How am I supposed to know?"

The lottery-ticket seller suggestively winked an eye. Suddenly it all dawned on Schweik. "You think . . ." he began.

"What else, goddammit?!" muttered the peddler impatiently.

"Who do you suppose he's after, out there?" asked Schweik wonderingly a moment later.

"No doubt someone from one of the houses around here, Comrade."

"That's not an easy profession," said Schweik, launching into a more thorough examination of the situation. "Hanging around in the snow like that, your feet and hands frozen from reading the newspaper all day. How much do they get paid a month, do you think?"

"Plenty, the bastards!" barked the peddler, quaffing a glass of champagne to regain his composure. But this only triggered the fog in his mind. Over the third bottle, he said he felt like warbling the *Horst Wessel* song.*

"You need something solid in your guts," said Schweik in response to this drunken threat. "We should have thought of that sooner. Otherwise you'll end up flat on your back—and you'll have only yourself to blame."

By the time Schweik returned from the kitchen, where he ordered a boiled knockwurst from Frau Mracek, the peddler was snoring, his head on the table. Schweik woke him up. The peddler eyed the tray of lottery tickets in front of his nose. "What's that?" he asked. Looking around, he caught sight of Schweik and cried, "Aha—Can't you guys ever leave a fellow alone? . . . All right," he continued in a friendlier tone, "give me one more chance. But only one, I tell you right aw . . . away. I know you guys."

* The prime Nazi song.

The next glass was his last. Schweik had to eat the *knockwurst* himself, for the peddler suddenly grew white as a sheet and mumbled, "I need some fre . . . fresh air." Then he staggered out in the direction of the toilet, where apparently he expected to find a heady gust of fresh oxygen.

He did not return. After some time had elapsed, Schweik sent Frau Mracek to see what had happened to him. "He's all right," she said on returning. "He threw up everything—you can smell it, can't you? Now he's sleeping. You can hear him snoring through the door."

Schweik sat at the table and thought of a number of disconnected things. In Prague I went swimming every morning in the Axa Hotel, he mused . . . I'm glad I didn't live in Pompeii . . . I must say, I'd like to know whether the midwife cut my umbilical cord with a knife or a pair of scissors . . . What would my shoemaker say if I asked him to take my measurements for a suit? . . . Ruhr coal heats better than Saxon coal.

At this last thought, Schweik looked around cautiously to make sure no one could have seen it reflected in his expression. But there was no one else in the room except the three truck drivers, who had long since started playing cards and were completely preoccupied with the question, which idiot had played the ten of hearts.

Schweik continued his meditations. Now it was time for proverbs: It's an ill wind that catches the worm . . . Two wrongs can't teach an old dog new tricks . . . Early to bed and early to rise saves nine . . . A friend in need is better than two in the bush.

Schweik, his thoughts dwelling on the bush, even

invented an entirely new proverb: A black widow in the
hand is worse than two in the bush.

Although Schweik was alone with his thoughts and
there was no one to object to this last proverb, nevertheless he seemed filled with sudden agitation, for he
jumped up, hung the lottery-ticket peddler's wares
around his neck, grabbed the umbrellas, jammed on the
peddler's cap, and stepped out into the street with the
threat, "We'll soon see about that!"

Schweik's excitement was immediately transmitted
to the unknown newspaper-reader opposite, who began
asking himself feverishly what Schweik's behavior meant.
Schweik looked around. No sooner had he caught sight
of the newspaper-reader, than he headed straight toward
him. What'll I do? wondered the newspaper-reader even
more feverishly. It was up to Schweik to act. The newspaper-reader, if he didn't want to draw attention to
himself, could only keep up his act.

"A chance, Sir?" asked Schweik.

The other saw that there was only one way to
survive the situation without arousing suspicion, so he
said, "Yes, I'll take one."

Schweik passed him a ticket and added, "It's a good
thing you bought one. You're going to win."

"How do you know?" asked the other, tearing
open his chance.

"I feel it. Fate is on your side."

"Good God, so it is!—Here, see for yourself!"

The stranger was doubly pleased at this turn of
events. Now that the danger was past, he thought,
Schweik would continue on his way without having
gotten a definite impression of his person. But Schweik
took the ticket, on which it was clearly stated that he

had *not* won, out of his hand, examined it from both sides, studied the six-digit serial number, and exclaimed, "*What* did I say! You win!"

"I win?"

"This ticket number begins with a ten. Well, all numbers that begin with ten win, even if it says they don't. Our director didn't hit on this idea until after the tickets had been printed."

"I don't understand."

"The number ten indicates October—the tenth month of the year. Now, and as everyone knows, that was the month of the October Revolution," said Schweik calmly, and he handed the stranger the prize to which he was consequently entitled: an umbrella. "It's more of a parasol than an umbrella," Schweik added, "but just the same, it'll keep off snow. In fact, you couldn't have done better."

The stranger, speechless with surprise, took hold of the umbrella as if in a dream. Schweik reminded him to open it. The stranger, subject to the iron law not to attract attention and not to get "involved" in anything, meekly did as he was told. A single thought exploded in his mind: *What does this mean?*

Much later, he was still racking his brains frantically, but there was no solution to be found.

Back at the "Traube," Schweik ordered another bottle of champagne. He felt he deserved it. Frau Mracek stuck her head into the room, disappeared again, and after some minutes she brought not champagne but coffee. "This is to be drunk!" she said commandingly. "Otherwise who knows what you'll end up doing. And what's more, I've just sent the kitchenmaid to Buchta and Co.—five minutes ago—to fetch one of them. This coffee will help pull you together, so you can arrange things properly."

The girl who had been sent out was only twelve years old, but nonetheless not too young to be trustworthy and reliable. She returned in due course with Emil Buchta, the elder brother, who was considered the boss of the "company."

"Greetings, Emil!" said Schweik in welcome. "Today, it's just a job for some genteel peeping tom. Sit down!"

"What is it, then?"

Emil Buchta liked to settle business matters in a trice. His friends knew this and acted accordingly.

"Teaching someone a lesson, Emil."

"Who?"

"A certain Müller. A lady-killer, the bastard! I'll point him out to you."

"That's not necessary. I know the one."

"You know him?"

Buchta gave a scornful look, as he replied, "I reckon, anyway, that we have the same bastard in mind. The one I mean is like that too—he's had more women than a pastor. He lives in the Heinrich-Zille-Strasse."

"That's the one!" Schweik said, pleased. "How do you know him?"

"Business, business."

"Oh, shit!" exclaimed Schweik, his brow wrinkling with sudden concern.

"Why, what's wrong?"

"Maybe you won't take the job on, then?"

"I don't get you, Schweik. Business is business. Müller pays me for a lesson for someone else, and someone else, namely yourself, pays me for a lesson for

Müller. Could anything be more cut-and-dried, more businesslike than that? What can we do about Müller's tough luck? You used to be a salesman yourself, Schweik. Do I have to explain the business world to you?"

"Certainly not, Emile."

"All right, then! Let's get down to brass tacks: What kind of lesson do you have in mind? Or better, how much are you prepared to spend? Also, when do you want the matter dealt with? And do you wish to leave your card?"

"First of all, he must be beaten to a pulp. Second, as soon as possible. Third, leave a card inscribed: 'Greetings from Herr Gartner.'"

"Will do."

"It's for Gartner, the proprietor, or rather for his old woman—old bitch, I should say. So that . . ."

Schweik got no further, for Emil Buchta interrupted him. "That's none of my business," he said quickly. "You can skip all that. I trust you have good reasons for the mugging of young Müller, just as you trust me to do the job conscientiously. That's the only way—trust for trust! Just one more question . . ."

"What?"

"Who's producing the money?"

"What money?"

"The money for our services."

"I am."

"*You* are?" Buchta repeated disbelievingly. Whereupon Schweik demonstrated just how solvent he was. Naturally, that turned out to be a mistake. For in his mind, Emil Buchta immediately decided to increase his fee. He also asked Schweik which Dresden church still had such a well-filled poor box nowadays.

At Schweik's explanation that the money was easily but honestly earned, Emil Buchta laughed heartily. "All right, all right, Schweik, my boy," he said. "Do you think *I* would betray such a treasure trove?" Then he got back to business, saying: "The affair won't create any great problems for us. Rudolf and I won't have to disguise ourselves and make a surprise attack in a dark alley, because we have Müller in the palm of our hand, thanks to a job we did for him once. He can't inform on us. We'll go undisguised to his apartment. He'll open the door, recognize us, and even say, 'Gentlemen, what brings you down this way? Come on in. I'm glad to see you.' Well, he won't get around to saying the last part when he's heard our answer to his first question."

Emil's businesslike tone prompted Schweik to enquire in a similar manner, "How much do you want out of me?"

"Seventy marks, altogether."

"I thought the fee was sixty."

"The *suggested* fee, Schweik."

"Fine. But then in this case you'd even have to reduce it. You said yourself it'll be an easy job, no disguise and so on . . ."

"Superficially, Schweik. But you mustn't forget the other side of the coin. Business is business, I grant you, but just think how we'll shake the confidence of our old customer Müller. And that's not something you can turn up your nose at. Wouldn't you charge extra for a conning like that! Now give me an honest answer, Schweik!"

Appeals to Schweik's honesty were of course superfluous, and his reply was brief but to the point. "Forgive me," he said.

Emil Buchta had every reason to feel satisfied. He had succeeded completely. Schweik paid—and not just a deposit but seventy marks in full, so that, as he said, he'd be rid of the whole business. Buchta gave him a three percent discount without hesitation. Of a strong and stocky build, hands like frying pans, he was a hard-headed individual, born to his profession. Time and again he had earned esteem for his company. Buchta and Co. served as an impressive illustration of the Communist dogma that, in the Communist State, which instills all its citizens with love of the law and the joys of work, the penal code will one day be a museum piece.

Buchta's distinguishing characteristic was his missing left ear. Years before, he had sacrificed it to a helpless old lady, from whom he had accepted the job of beating her mean old St. Bernard, who terrorized her. "Schweik," he said, "let's crack a bottle over our agreement. Normally, we'd take the money from the discount we've allowed the customer." He glanced at the clock on the wall, gave a start, and continued, "On second thought, I'm afraid I'm pushed for time, sad as it is."

"Why, what's up?"

"I've still got to pick up my Disabled Worker's Allowance for this month. Today's the deadline."

"I understand," said Schweik in an earnest tone. "You mustn't miss that. What do they have you listed as?"

"As a chronic arthritic. I succeeded in convincing the doctors there that I have such bad arthritis and inflammation of the fingers that it's impossible for me to close my fist."

Schweik resolved to write down the name of this complaint, just in case. This kind of sickness is really

God-given, you could say. That is, if this sickness didn't exist at all, then it would be impossible to convince the doctors of it, and that would be one more disadvantage for incapacitated people, who have a hard enough time of it as it is.

"And what sort of application does brother Rudolf have?" he asked.

"Incurable insanity."

"Did he have a rough time with the doctors?"

"Depends how you look at it. He had to do everything imaginable, but on the whole the work was more mental than physical. The decision was made after they sent him to the psychiatric clinic. First the medical assistant held him under observation, then the resident physician, then the head physician. And my brother stood with his ear to the wall, the whole time, because apparently he heard something there. Finally the medical superintendent himself came to have a look at him. My brother was still standing there with his ear glued to the wall. 'Can you hear something?' asked the medical superintendent, a very friendly man. 'Psst' said my brother, putting a finger to his lips. That made the other curious and he put his ear to the wall too. 'I don't hear anything,' he said after a while. 'Me neither,' answered my brother. 'And just imagine, Comrade, it's been that way with me for three days now.' That was the decision I mentioned, Schweik. Ever since then, my brother has been an officially disabled worker."

"An intelligent method," Schweik commented with the voice of an expert. "With such an intelligent method they *have* to declare you insane. I heard of a similar case once in Tabor, where I come from. There was a sexton who, they suspected, might be normal after all. So they put him in with the real madmen for observation, to find out for certain how things stood. The sexton sensed the danger which threatened him and realized that no conventional ploy could save him—it would have to be an especially clever one. But luck was on his side. When the nuthouse door closed behind him—that was in the morning, and they had just finished putting in a new swimming pool—the sexton saw his opportunity immediately. He ran up the diving board and jumped head first from the twenty feet. Down below, a psychiatrist who was just passing by asked the sexton, 'Did you enjoy your dive? Did you find it pleasant?' 'Yes,' said the sexton, out of breath. 'And when they fill the pool with water, it'll be even better.' With that he lost consciousness and four hours later he drew his last breath. That was the snag in his intelligent ruse. But you must admit his success in convincing the psychiatrists that he wasn't quite normal. To this day, no one can deny it."

Emil Buchta's eye fell on the clock, and he realized that he would have to take a taxi, if he wanted to get to the Welfare Center before it closed. "Take a taxi!" said Schweik. "Business is good, you can afford it. You're no poor devil, like the official who'll pay you."

Emil Buchta did not question this, but he did draw Schweik's attention to the fluctuations in private business, which should always be taken into account. Schweik must be aware of that himself. "Just now," said Buchta, "we have such a huge fluctuation in our political denunciations as would bring tears to the eyes of any businessman."

"How come?" asked Schweik, little suspecting that for him an historic moment was at hand.

"You know why, Schweik."

"I know nothing whatever about it."

"Of course you do."

"I repeat: I don't know what you're talking about!"

"Well look here," said Emil Buchta. "You know roughly what our *political prices* are—beginning with ten marks for our overhearing an enemy of yours say in the tavern that the Mississippi is longer than the Volga, up to a limit of fifty marks for denouncing Stalin as a criminal. Well, overnight things have gone haywire, so far as this Stalin job is concerned. What can we ask for that *now?* Not enough to slip under a rat's toenail. No one thinks twice about how that's hit us."

"What?" was Schweik's only comment.

"Which 'what'?" asked Buchta.

"What did you say?"

"I said several things. What do you mean?"

"That business about . . ." Schweik fell silent and looked cautiously over at the truck drivers. But they were now completely engrossed in finding out which idiot it was who hadn't played the ten of hearts, so that Schweik felt obliged to complete his sentence. "Stalin," he said.

The clock ticked. Schweik didn't take his eyes from the card players. He coughed, in order to drown Buchta's answer. Emil Buchta looked at him and shook his head, saying, "Are you mad, Schweik? It seems to me as if you're still afraid to mention that jerk's name."

"Jerk!" repeated Schweik with horror.

"Schweik, you blockhead, listen here, what's the sense behind this absurdity. Explain yourself, otherwise I'm going. I don't waste money on taxis just to play guessing-games."

A torrent of words poured over Buchta. Schweik

told Buchta he couldn't just run off and leave a friend in trouble that way. In such uncertainty! He said that now, suddenly, everything was revealed in a new light: Secret Policeman Sand, Dr. Olbert, State Attorney Zollner, the two secret agents today in the apartment—they'd all talked so strangely that all he could do was to grin stupidly. But now Buchta and Co.'s prices had spoken, and that was a horse of a different color, a very different criterion! A price like that said more than a hundred State attorneys. Did Buchta really mean that in earnest?

"Mean what in earnest, Schweik?"

"That a Stalin-debunking assignment has fallen so much in value that you can't charge a cent for it anymore?"

"We'd starve!" Emil Buchta exclaimed irritably. "Get that into your head, Schweik! We'd starve to death if we had to depend on *that* sort of deadwood!"

This was the historic moment in which Joseph Schweik's de-Stalinization consciously set in. Schweik's need for exhaustive political information on the new situation was understandably so great that it could not be satisfied in the few moments which Emil Buchta had left. The immediate problem was therefore solved by Schweik's paying a compensation fee of ten marks to make up for Buchta's Disabled Workers' Allowance until the following day.

Then came the political enlightenment which Schweik was seeking; Buchta punctuated his exposition by repeatedly asking Schweik whether or not he had just fallen from the moon. Schweik wrung his hands. "Incredible!" he said, which was his comment upon nearly every sentence Buchta uttered. Finally he sighed, saying, "It'll take me a long time to get used to this political volte-face. I hope I may live long enough to do so."

Time passed. Emil Buchta spoke also of the wonderful years when it had been profitable to denounce someone as a Titoist. Another source of income down the drain! As the evening guests arrived, an old woman who wanted to treat herself to a glass of beer asked if there was a place free at Schweik's table. "Yes . . . Down with Stalin!" Schweik answered. As he said this, Schweik must have given the old woman a downright hypnotic look, for the poor soul involuntarily replied, "My pleasure." And in the same breath she declared that she had forgotten her purse and would have to go back for it. She never returned to Schweik's table.

Around seven, Emil Buchta suddenly declared with vigor, "I'm leaving now."

"Why?" Schweik asked, surprised.

"To get cracking on your assignment. You know, Schweik, we deal with things expeditiously. We owe it to our reputation."

Schweik said he would accompany Buchta to his apartment. They called Frau Mracek. As Schweik paid the bill, his agitated thoughts were still far away at Stalin's mausoleum, so that he didn't notice an unpleasant fact: his whole fortune had shrunk to a few marks. "Frau Mracek," he said, "take this peddler's stuff with you into the kitchen. I hold you responsible for reuniting the peddler with his wares, when the time comes. I don't want the fellow to come to grief on my account."

"Hurry up!" called Buchta, who was already at the door. "To hell with the peddler!"

Frau Mracek noticed with satisfaction the hurry

Emil Buchta was in. In her joy, she promised to beseech the blessings of her patron saint, the blessed Saint Genevieve, for the men's project. "And don't forget your umbrellas," she reminded Schweik attentively. "Our Frau Gartner, if I know her, would snatch them up the moment she returns home—which I hope will be soon."

Schweik put the umbrellas under his arm and hurried after Buchta. Outside, it had been dark for some time. In Buchta's apartment, the two men found the younger brother, Rudolf Buchta, snoring on the sofa, with a case of beer at his feet. When they wakened him, Rudolf seemed possessed of a thirst for knowledge: He asked at least ten random questions. Emil pulled the blanket off him again and again, saying for the tenth time that he couldn't help it, but there was work to be done. Rudolf swore and demanded that the least they could do was to give him a bottle of beer and a cigarette, otherwise he didn't give a damn. He was, he said, a proletarian to the core, who had the right to insist on decent treatment in this country, that in his veins flowed the blood of generations of workers and peasants.

After the second bottle, Emil told him of Schweik's commission: the improvement of Müller's morals. Rudolf's memory of Müller was hazier than his brother's, but he was quickly assured of the simplicity of the operation, which simply meant paying a visit to Müller's apartment.

Schweik listened to the two brothers, his lively imagination enabling him to identify himself so completely with the situation that he suddenly announced, "I'm coming with you."

He couldn't care less about that, declared Rudolf.

Emil, on the other hand, felt responsible for the company's future and told Schweik that that wouldn't do; he
knew Müller's apartment, and it hadn't room enough
for four people. A fourth person would just get in the
way. Even after Schweik assured him that he would make
himself scarce, Emil Buchta remained obstinate.

This verbal tug-of-war ended, inevitably, with a
compromise. It was agreed that Schweik would accompany the others as far as the front door and wait there
until the matter had been taken care of. "When do we
start?" asked Schweik. "When we've had one more for
the road," answered the Buchta brothers simultaneously.
But even with such reliable souls as the Buchta brothers,
this euphemism mustn't be taken too literally, as was
demonstrated by the fact that when the three men left
the apartment, the case of beer was empty.

They traveled to the Heinrich-Zille-Strasse by
streetcar, Emil Buchta being of the opinion that the
police would begin their search, if any, by asking all
the taxidrivers whether they had taken any suspicious
characters to the neighborhood. Müller lived on the
second floor of a house with a rear courtyard. The house
hadn't been painted for twenty years, and in this respect
all the houses in the Heinrich-Zille-Strasse were as alike
as peas in a pod. A typical GDR street, in fact. The
streetcar stop was in front of a paint factory, whose main
entrance bore a placard reading:

> *In this People's Production*
> *Plant the yield has been*
> *quadrupled since 1939. Long*
> *live the German Democratic*
> *Republic!*

Müller's light was on. "He's in," confirmed Emil Buchta with satisfaction. "We won't have to come back three or four times. Everything's going like clockwork."

It was still snowing. Before the front door, the three accomplices separated. The Buchta brothers disappeared inside the building, while Schweik slipped into the dark entryway, to get under cover. Immediately afterward he heard footsteps approaching rapidly on the sidewalk. A man, looking searchingly in all directions—a desperate undertaking in this snowfall—hurried by. In a flash Schweik recognized, not the man himself, but the umbrella he was carrying, and an exclamation of surprise escaped him: "What a coincidence!" The stranger heard Schweik—What should he do? Both men—Schweik's retort had come unwittingly—realized that only by extreme presence of mind and cold-bloodedness could they make the situation seem harmless. Therefore the stranger returned to Schweik's doorway and said with apparent surprise, "So it's *you!* An amazing coincidence, I grant you."

"Do you live around here?" rejoined Schweik in a casual tone.

"Yes. As it happens, just two blocks away. And you?"

"No, I don't live here. I'm only here by chance, because . . . because . . ." Schweik cast about frantically for an explanation, finally blurting out, "because I chanced by."

"Aha!" replied the other, not ironically, but simply to deprive Schweik of an opportunity to collect his thoughts. Schweik, on the other hand, found that this "Aha!" sounded more than sarcastic, and it was perhaps only logical for him to embark at once on a discussion of the unusual coincidences, hoping thereby to lend his last contention an air of credibility. "You can believe what I say," he began. "I'm a child of chance anyway, as the saying goes, I think. I've always had plenty to put up with in this respect. If there was more light here I could show you a scar on my head, where years ago a most unusual coincidence befell me. In fact, there are people who claim to this day that it was the deciding factor in my development. It was my first or second year at school, and during vacation a charitable lady with a little house in the country took me in as a poor city kid, so that I could milk her goats, she announced on the day after my arrival. I was big enough for that, she said, not just for eating, and I should make myself useful in return for her hospitality. So, out of sheer good-will—there's no limit to the silly things you'll do at that age—I asked why her oven didn't draw better. 'Because the chimney needs sweeping, dumbbell,' she said pleas-antly, and then left the room to answer the front door. I thought and thought and stared at the little iron door in the wall that led to the chimney. And after I'd thought long enough about how I could make myself useful, aside from milking goats, I opened the little door and stuck my head in to have a look around. You must bear in mind, my dear Sir, that I'd traveled 140 kilo-meters from Prague to the village where all this took place. I'd worn a piece of cardboard around my neck, upon which my name and address and place of destina-tion were handsomely inscribed, and in spite of every-thing I'd arrived at the right place and smack on time. And just what had I got there in time for? So that just by chance, at the very moment I had stuck my head in-side the chimney, the chimney sweep whom the charitable lady had gone to let in could let his iron ball crash down on it."

The stranger, who for some time now had been at a loss as to what to make of Schweik's discourse, again interposed with the single comment—simply for the sake of saying something—"Aha." I haven't gotten anywhere, Schweik said to himself worriedly. He said "Aha" before, too. I'll have to try again. And while he and the stranger stood facing each other in suspended animation, Schweik treated his wayside companion to another anecdote from his anthology of gripping coincidences.

"Our teacher in the twelfth grade once showed us that it's wrong to say, 'That can't be a coincidence.' Even the most incredible coincidences are possible. It's even possible to have several at one blow. Just listen: one day our teacher came into the classroom and explained what a 'relief' is. A relief is a geographical reproduction according to nature, with real heights and depths, mountains and valleys. That's what the teacher explained. In the corner stood a heavy map of all Europe, rolled up and reaching almost to the ceiling. The teacher paced back and forth, and was so absorbed that he didn't even notice he was hitting the map with his elbow. The map fell, knocked him to the floor, and the lower part, the south, rolled down just long enough for the teacher to end up lying lengthwise under the Alps. That was the first coincidence. Our teacher, unconscious, didn't move a finger. Only one thing moved—namely, the bump that was appearing on his head where he'd been hit by the map. And can you guess where that bump swelled up, in relation to the map? Right under the peak of Mont Blanc: it pushed it right up, because as you know yourself, a bump like that swells pretty fast

if you don't hold a knife against it. And how were we
kids supposed to have the right sort of knife on us? We
only had our sharp jackknives, which you don't carry
around to flatten bumps, but to protect your honor. So
the teacher's bump went on swelling up right under
Mont Blanc—which was the second coincidence. This
was how we first encountered the highest mountain in
Europe; I'll never forget it as long as I live. I tell you,
nowadays kids don't get things explained so vividly as
we did then, and by such a conscientious teacher, even
though teachers today earn twice as much as they used
to."

Meanwhile, the Buchta brothers had rung Müller's
doorbell, after which they had stood a long time in front
of Müller's door. Eventuallly they heard movements inside and a muffled voice ask "Who's there?"

"The telegram delivery boy," said Emil Buchta.

"A telegram?—Where's it from?"

"From a girl in Gorlitz."

"Just a minute. I have to get dressed."

This "just a minute" lasted for several, which
seemed an eternity to the Buchtas, waiting in the silent
stairway and praying that no one would come along and
recognize them.

"Has the guy gone to bed already?" Emil Buchta
asked nervously, turning to Rudolf. "You two sleepy-
heads would get along fine."

At last Müller's footsteps could be heard again, approaching the front door. Care and anxiety were forgotten. "We can begin!" Emil Buchta affirmed joyfully.

It was at this very moment that Schweik was in the
midst of telling the stranger down in the entryway that

the teachers of today could take a lesson from his old one.

"Do you think so?" said the stranger.

"I think so all right. Don't you think so?"

"I think so too."

During this snatch of dialogue the two men over-heard the first crashes and muffled groans which escaped from the house above them. The noises got louder and climaxed as a window was torn open and a shrill woman's voice shouted, "Hellp! Hellllp! Hell—."

The cry broke off—not voluntarily, it seemed, but because of some violent interruption. The window was slammed shut and other muffled noises could be heard.

"What was that?" asked the stranger, paralyzed.

"What?" Schweik looked at the other with perfect composure, as if to say, "Don't get excited, my friend! Nothing is more harmful for modern man than unnecessary excitement."

"Somebody just shouted for help," croaked the other.

"Who?"

"A woman." The stranger's paralysis vanished. "Now don't try to tell me you didn't hear that."

"To tell the truth," Schweik replied with a heavy heart, "I did hear a little something. But I wouldn't pay much attention to it. Women are unpredictable, that's no secret. It occurs to them all of a sudden to scream for help when a spider creeps over their hand or their husband beats them. You mustn't get upset about that. Come, let's go for a stroll."

But the stranger ignored Schweik's suggestion. He stood rooted to the spot, opened and closed his umbrella nervously, and declared repeatedly that something must be done.

"What are we supposed to do?" asked Schweik, pulling at his sleeve. "You're not going to deny a husband the right to teach his wife manners. Let us not forget the Russians, our models, how they beat their wives! I imagine that's why Russian women all have such ample buttocks—that's called defensive adaptation, as another teacher once told us . . . Anyway, there's nothing going on up there now," he said after a short pause. "So we need have no conscience about going."

Schweik's observation that the din upstairs had ceased was true enough, but soon there followed the sound of people running down the stairs. Seconds later the front door flew open, and two figures leaped into the street, where they disappeared lickety-split into the snow. Out of one of the many windows which had been thrown open in the street, an intelligent voice called, "They were the ones." And inside the entryway, the stranger declared once more, under the weight of these impressions, that something must definitely be done. The striking contradiction between the stranger's words and his deeds could be explained by the official regulations for secret policemen engaged in following suspects. Nothing, according to these instructions, was more important than to avoid attracting attention or getting involved. Anything which might reveal their connection with the Secret Police must be avoided. A secret policeman who let his mask slip might just as well dig a hole in the ground. For this simple reason, the stranger had had to restrain himself from asking Schweik where his two buddies had disappeared. To satisfy his curiosity, he would have had to reveal that he had been following the three of them for some time.

"Well, what about it? Shall we go?" asked Schweik. He had barely spoken when in the distance a police siren started wailing.

In a flash the siren solved all the problems which had been plaguing the stranger. Obviously some action was now about to be taken. "Yes, well," he muttered, then, dropping his umbrella, he leaped out of the shadow of the entryway into the street. At long last Schweik was alone again.

"There's another one!" cried the same intelligent voice from a window. Then again: "There's a fourth one, a fourth one!"

The "fourth one" was Schweik, who had now also emerged from the entryway. He stood in the street waving the stranger's umbrella in one hand, while grasping his own two in the other, shouting across the snow: "Your umbrella! Your umbrella! Come back! You've forgotten your umbrella!"

Schweik was still standing there shouting when four policemen with drawn pistols surrounded him, their officer roaring out: "Hands up! Shut up! Give me those damned umbrellas!"

Schweik lost no time in asserting it was all a mistake and the matter would be cleared up of its own accord, that a police raid had never picked up anyone more innocent. "Search him!" the duty officer ordered his henchmen. But this undertaking ended in failure. Since Schweik was found to have no other suspicious objects on him, the policemen's suspicions were now concentrated upon the three umbrellas.

An hour and a half later, everything was over.

Schweik sat handcuffed in the police truck, which was to deliver him this time to the headquarters of the Municipal Police and not the Security Police. The lengthy report which the duty officer carried in his breast pocket contained, in addition to routine information concerning the scene and time of the crime and all available personal data, the following statement:

. . . the victim of the attack, who had four missing teeth, a dislocated arm, and several broken ribs, would disclose nothing *more* than the fact that he had not recognized the perpetrators of the crime. His intended bride, a married woman named Cosima Gartner, corroborated this upon demand. The crime was complicated by the fact that the perpetrators also violated the paragraph concerning malicious gossip, since they disturbed the victim, as he claimed, in the fulfillment of his premarital duty. The fact that his light was on did not by any means indicate the contrary, for he is, as he claimed, a man of high standards. Furthermore, the victim's statement on this matter may be considered proved by the fact that his intended bride ran naked to the window, where she cried for help and was seen very clearly by two adolescents from the opposite building, Young Pioneers with bright, sharp eyes, who later described the incident in detail to the police.

Further:

The bride-to-be's scanty dress was retained as evidence until the arrival of the police and is herewith committed to the files. As she was torn away from the window, Frau Gartner suffered abrasions as well as slaps in the face. The unknown perpetrator of the slaps also made himself guilty of the misdemeanor of intentional insult, since he did not hesitate to call the victim of his maltreatment a damned whore.

Meanwhile, the two accomplices kept watch in the

entryway of the house (see attached sketch), conversing in an apparently harmless manner in order to camouflage themselves further. This fact was observed through a ground-floor window near the entryway by a pensioned gamekeeper, whose hearing has been well-trained in his eighty-three years. The above-mentioned harmless conversation of the two accomplices distracted him, so that he did not suspect what was brewing only one floor above him. After the deed, all were able to flee, with the exception of one, whose mysterious, very suspicious manipulations with an umbrella —one of three that were found in his possession—made him lose time, so that it was possible to catch him in the act and apprehend him. He denies having anything to do with the crime, but when cornered, had to admit his conversation in the entryway and thereby his connection with that perpetrator who fled at the approach of the police. The complicity of the suspect in custody can therefore be considered proved. A further proof of the connection of the two suspects in the entryway is their possession of three absolutely identical umbrellas, two of which belong to the suspect in custody, whereas the third, according to the suspect's statement, belongs to the accomplice who fled.

Shortly before his removal to Police Headquarters, the suspect indirectly committed still another misdemeanor: insulting an officer. This occurred as follows:

The man from the opposite building, who upon hearing Frau Gartner's screams had notified the police by telephone, appeared before the undersigned and demanded the refund of his telephone charges. Whereupon the undersigned declared himself incompetent to deal with the request since no such authority is granted him in the regulations. One word led to another, but no direct insult to an officer had been spoken, when the suspect under arrest interfered and declared that he found the man's claim absolutely justified and that he was against wronging anyone with a just claim. Thereupon he refunded the telephone charges to the contending party out of his own pocket. This conduct set in motion the insult of an officer. One could almost say that the suspect had also made himself guilty of incitement. For

the man claiming the telephone charges immediately threatened all the policemen still at the scene of the crime, in-
cluding the undersigned, with his fists, shouting that our
poor victim had set us an example that we should do well to
follow. He begged the suspect with tears in his eyes for
forgiveness and promised him that in a similar case he would
never notify the police again. Finally, he even refused categorically to accept the refund of the telephone charges and
shouted, "That would be a real Judas' reward!"

Since by now other bystanders had begun to take the
side of the arrested party, the undersigned, according to the
new duty regulations concerning the handling of the public,
stipulated since the 20th Party Congress, gave orders for the
immediate departure of the Riot Squad, as soon as this report had been completed.

> Attested by
> M. Hornig
> Duty Officer

During Schweik's transport to the Municipal Police
Headquarters, he tried in vain to draw the duty officer
into conversation, by asking him whether he was married. The Riot Squad Lieutenant stared stubbornly into
space and didn't open his mouth until the trip was over,
whereupon he said: "When you take him in, watch out
that he doesn't nab one of those umbrellas."

There was enmity between Schweik and the regular
—as well as the political—police. This enmity had been
fed for the main part by incidents connected with
Schweik's dog trading, which he had practiced in Dresden after the war until the day when he too had, as it
were, been nationalized. So it wasn't only State Attorney
Zollner and his associates from the political executive
who could claim that Schweik had crossed their paths a
great number of times already, but also the examining

officials of the regular police. It was only natural, therefore, when on the following morning Schweik was
brought before a certain Herr Pike, official expert for
crimes of violence, the latter could not suppress greeting
Schweik with heavy sarcasm.

"Top of the morning, Herr Schweik. Back to pay
us another visit?"

"If ever a man was innocent, then I am now, Herr
Pike," answered Schweik earnestly, exhibiting the un-
compromising line of defense he had determined to adopt.

Herr Pike had a long, pointed nose, which turned
white at the tip when he was annoyed, as was now the
case. "Schweik," he replied, the tip of his nose whitening, "don't confuse us with those tomfool police, under
the shoddy old Hapsburg Empire. I'll finish with you in
no time, I guarantee it. A Schweik like the one in Old
Prague is unthinkable here, you can stake your life on
that. Mark my words! It's no longer a matter of proving
your guilt, I can tell you that right away. Your guilt is
already established. The Lieutenant did a good job."

To lend emphasis to his words, Herr Pike picked
up the duty officer's written report from his desk and
waved it about in the air. "Was the Lieutenant already
acquainted with you?" he went on.

"Unfortunately not," said Schweik. "He didn't even
want to tell me whether he's married. Nor was I acquainted with any of the others. I imagine the reason for
that is that those gentlemen are all quite young and have
only been on duty in the Heinrich-Zille-Strasse, where I
have never been arrested before. I see in that a further
proof of my innocence," Schweik added abruptly.

Pike now decided once and for all to remove any
remaining doubts about the situation. "Schweik," he said

sternly, "I refuse to waste another word with you about your guilt. The only thing we want to hear from you now are the names of your three accomplices. That's the main thing, then everything else will take care of itself. So out with it! Don't provoke me, Schweik! It's in your own interest to do what you're told. So far as your motive is concerned, we still have plenty of latitude. We can assume you planned a simple robbery, or we can decide on robbery and attempted murder, from which only the woman's screams for help deterred you. I surely don't have to explain to you, of all people, what that means. So out with it, I tell you again, in fairness to yourself. *Who* were your accomplices?"

In reply to this short sermon, full of cheery prospects for Schweik, the latter only said stubbornly, "I know nothing about accomplices. I have never had an accomplice and shall never have anything to do with one. I lead a life free of accomplices."

"Schweik, you are incorrigible. You . . ." The tip of Pike's nose turned snow-white. He threw a file on the floor and roared out, "I *order* you once and for all not to treat me like an idiot. Do you think I'm half-witted?"

"I don't think anything of the kind," replied Schweik, who saw in Pike's question a chance to ingratiate himself. "On the contrary, I think you're a very intelligent Pike, much more intelligent than another Pike."

"What's that supposed to mean?"

"That means I've already heard of another Pike. One day, the selfsame Pike went into a hotel and asked for a room. The receptionist asked, 'One with running water?' and that Pike said, 'No, that's only my name.'"

"Schweik!!!"

This scream said more than many a sermon. The guard standing outside thought it was high time to intervene and burst into the room.

"Take him away!" ordered Commissioner Pike. He was breathing hard, and his entire nose, from the tip to the base, was snow-white.

It's an old truth: the bigger an apparatus, an administrative body, an organization gets, the harder it is to keep track of. The resulting situation is best described by that well-known saying that one hand doesn't know what the other is doing. Now if that can be said of merely two hands, how much worse must it be when dozens of hands, so to speak, are involved! It is necessary to keep this image in mind when one tries to imagine the police apparatus of a People's Democracy and its ceaseless activity.

There are:

I. *The (normal) State Police, or Vopos* with the following divisions:
   (a) The Municipal Police (for the security of the population)
   (b) The Traffic Police (in charge of traffic)
   (c) The Morals Squad (in charge of other traffic)
   (d) The Railway Police, the Water Police, the Air Police, the Mountain Police, the Valley Police, the Building Control Police, the Health Control Police, the Sickness Control Police (also called Pest Police), the Fire Police, the Criminal Police (with its own well-known underdivisions, from the Board for Petty Violations all the way to the Murder Commission) . . . etc., etc.

II. *The State Security Police* (against the security of the population) with the following divisions:
   (a) DIPO (= Division for Investigating Political Opinions)
   (b) ADPPIC (= Active Division for Processing Politically Investigated Cases)
   (c) CDCPOIPPIC (= Central Division for Control of Political Opinions' Investigators and Processors of Politically Investigated Cases)
   (d) ASD (= Anti-Sabotage Division)
   (e) ACD (= Anti-Conspiracy Division)
   (f) ACRD (= Anti-Counterrevolution Division)
   (g) CDCASDACDACRD (= Central Division for Control of Anti-Sabotage Division, Anti-Conspiracy Division, and Anti-Counterrevolution Division)
   (h) SDSAS (= Special Division for the Suppression of Anti-Stalinists. In February, 1956, the Capital A [Anti-Stalinists] in the name of this organization was erased and replaced by a capital S [Stalinists]. Further upheavals could be avoided. One of the tried and tested officials of this organization was the well-known Dr. Olbert
   (i) DEBJCCJM (= Division for Elimination of Blue Jeans, Crew Cuts, and Jazz Music)
III. *The Secret State Security Police* with the following divisions:
   (a) SDECA (= Secret Division for the Enlistment of Confidential Agents. One official from this division was the second meter-reader, who had done his duty with Schweik)

(b) SDIPCA (= Secret Division for the Infiltration of the Population by Confidential Agents)

(c) SDADCA (= Secret Division for the Assignment of Duties to Confidential Agents)

(d) SDOFGOEP (= Secret Division for Observation of False or Genuine Outbursts of Enthusiasm by the People)

(f) SSSDSC (= Secret Super Special Division for Self-Control. This organization was generally considered *the* high point of the development of the Secret Police)

Many underdivisions have doubtless been neglected in this survey, but those registered here should suffice for the reader. They give an impression of the system and, what is still more important, of the gigantic extent of the apparatus, of the endless variations of the same task, the labyrinth of the boards and divisions, which must escape the attention of even the most astute observer.

There were so many people continually wriggling in this net that the individual was no longer noticed. What does that mean in concrete terms? That as Pike's prisoner Schweik had not the smallest prospect of coming to the attention of State Attorney Zollner or any other official. And this fact had important consequences.

Part II

SCHWEIK'S
REHABILITATION

DR. OLBERT STRIKES AGAIN

***** The telephone jangled. The noise
jolted Dr. Olbert out of a deep sleep. It was the middle
of the night and Dr. Olbert lay in his hospital bed in
the clinic. The telephone, which had been placed on his
night table, showed that here was a person of importance, one who had to have ready means of contact with
the outside world, even in the hospital.

On the telephone was a man named Groener, who
informed Dr. Olbert that no matter how he tried he could
continue no longer. "Why not?" asked Dr. Olbert sleep-
ily. He had had such a delightful dream. In fact, in his
dream, he had succeeded in triumphing over State Attorney Zollner with a correct judgment of that politically suspect character, Schweik. Dr. Olbert knew that
Zollner was responsible for Schweik's release from political arrest. In addition, several confidential agents who
spied on the State Prosecutor's office for the police had
informed on Zollner. Zollner had been heard to voice
Olbert's methods several times already, and had also used
the term "Stalinist." Dr. Olbert, accordingly, knew that

he had to be on his guard. Thus he had arranged, from his sickbed, to have Schweik shadowed following his release from political arrest. And now Dr. Olbert had just dreamed that the plan of shadowing Schweik had borne the most marvelous fruit: Schweik had suddenly been unmasked. In a debate over Molotov, that great fighter for Socialism, unequaled genius in foreign affairs and faithful Old Guard Bolshevik, Schweik had declared that so far as that guy was concerned, the last word had yet to be spoken.

Dr. Olbert rubbed his hands in his sleep. Now *he* was no longer the one in the soup, but State Attorney Zollner, Schweik's friend. It was in the midst of this beautiful dream that the telephone rang.

Herr Groener, who was on the other end of the line, was Olbert's best man on outside duty. He was the one who had followed Schweik to the Heinrich-Zille-Strasse, from where, at the approach of the Riot Squad, he had as a precautionary measure finally taken flight. In his official report the next morning he had kept silent about his near-disaster; instead, he had simply written that he had lost sight of Schweik in the heavy snowfall outside the "Traube."

When the shadower loses the scent of his prey in this way, there is only one way for him to pick it up again: he begins shadowing anew at the home of his quarry. And that is precisely what Dr. Olbert had ordered Herr Groener to do. Olbert was in a rage over Groener's failure and had ordered that he, Groener, was "to stand in front of Schweik's apartment until contact has been restored with him . . . I don't care if it takes a week!"

This was the bitter outcome for the ill-starred Groener, caught in his own web of lies.

In answer to Olbert's question as to why he had given up the chair, Groener replied in a quivering voice, "Because my knees are giving way, Comrade Dr. Olbert. I've been standing for eighteen hours. And I haven't had a thing to eat the whole time."

Olbert, still half asleep, countered Groener's lament by pointing out that in his day the men on outside duty had done much tougher things without batting an eyelash. He himself had once shadowed the chairman of a vegetarian club, who had traveled incognito to his brother in the country. The brother had slaughtered a pig, and he hadn't seen hide nor hair of the vegetarian for two days and nights. What did Groener have to say to that?

"Comrade Dr. Olbert," Groener said in a tremulous voice, "at least you knew for certain that the vegetarian was staying in the house you were watching. Or did you doubt it?"

"Of course not."

"That's what I mean, I do."

Dr. Olbert was now wide awake. "What are you trying to say, Groener?"

"That Schweik hasn't been home at all since I lost sight of him in front of the 'Traube.' "

"Is there any sign of life at his place?"

"There's life all right," Groener answered with a sigh, "plenty of it. People are coming and going all the time. But it isn't Schweik who opens the door for them, it's his housekeeper."

"What kind of people?"

"Men."

"*Men?*" Dr. Olbert repeated slowly. "What kind of men?"

"I don't know. In any case the thing looks peculiar somehow."

"Peculiar?"

Olbert already had his legs out of bed, and Groener, still anxious to earn a few points in his favor continued, "The men come from other quarters and districts. They don't know Schweik's house and house number, but find their way by means of an address on a piece of paper which they look at on the sly. Altogether, there have been eight such characters ringing the doorbell in turn. Seven of them came out again, after a spell. The eighth must still be in there, though. So far, he hasn't shown up again, Comrade Dr. Olbert."

Should the reader have concluded from Dr. Olbert's unsuccessful hearings with Schweik that the former was lacking in energy, toughness, and decisiveness, he was mistaken. Dr. Olbert now only barked into the telephone, "Stay where you are! I'll be there in ten minutes!" and he leaped out of bed with the lightness of a feather, forgetting the pain in his eyes.

Once arrived at Groener's vantage point, after a hurried taxi ride, Dr. Olbert was informed that the suspicious characters had all looked around cautiously at the door, especially when leaving the house again. His hunting fever rose even higher, and whistling through his teeth he commanded, "Let's go!"

The two men's patience was put to severe test before they gained admittance, although Dr. Olbert did not stop shouting, "Open up! Police!" Finally, they stood face to face with Frau Lehmann, who shook from head to foot and answered the question as to whether she had lost her mind, keeping the police waiting so long, by stammering that in her fright she hadn't been able to find her slip. She had found everything imaginable, even a lost photo album—but no slip. She burst into tears, folded her hands, and begged a thousand pardons for everything.

"Your slip doesn't interest me," said Dr. Olbert, cold as ice. "I regard that as an excuse. You know who I am. I warn you, don't underestimate me. Whose hat and coat are those on the hook?"

"Herr Schweik's," lied Frau Lehmann, horrified. That this was a lie did not become apparent until later. Dr. Olbert, in any case, saw the hat and coat for the time being as proof that, contrary to Groener's information, Schweik was in the building. "Lead me to him!" he demanded in a grandiloquent tone, as if he were searching a palace with a hundred doors.

"To whom, Your Honor, Sir?"

"To Schweik, goddammit!"

"I'm afraid I can't do that."

"Why not?"

"Because Herr Schweik isn't here," said Frau Lehmann, but she was shaking even more violently than before, and that was enough for Olbert. Again he only said, "Let's go!"

Groener dashed through the nearest door, which happened to lead to Frau Lehmann's bedroom. Frau Lehmann collapsed into a chair, and a few seconds later Groener could be heard shouting from the bedroom, "Aha!"

"Have you got him?" called Dr. Olbert, without taking his eyes off Frau Lehmann.

"No. But another one, Comrade Dr. Olbert."

Dr. Olbert let Frau Lehmann go and hurried into

her bedroom, where a surprise awaited him. The closet door, which Groener held, was open. And in the closet, bent over and terrified, was an elderly gentleman whose state of dress would have left much to be desired in any social gathering. He had nothing on but his trousers— and they were back-to-front, suggesting that he dressed in a great hurry. Dr. Olbert stood as if nailed to the threshold, his gaze fixed on the closet. The elderly gentleman was so terrified that it needed several attempts before Olbert could bring him to speak. "How did you get in there?" was Olbert's first searching question. His next question was equally penetrating: "What are you doing in there?" Since both questions went unanswered, Dr. Olbert warned the stranger not to underestimate him.

An indirect answer to these questions was given Dr. Olbert by Frau Lehmann, from the front room. She cried out complaining that she couldn't survive this disgrace—she was no longer young and healthy enough to bear such excitement like a sixteen-year-old. She appeared in the doorway and asked if she could go to the bathroom. "Go! In heaven's name, go!" cried Dr. Olbert, wincing. Then at last he directed a straight-edged question at the stranger in the closet. "Who are you, anyway?" he asked.

The man said his name was Wohlraab, Herr Wohlraab, that he was a baker, Party member, and the father of four children. He gave this information haltingly.

"So, you're married!" said Dr. Olbert cynically. "You know the best place for people with morals like yours?"

Wohlraab said nothing.

"Paris!" exclaimed Dr. Olbert with emphasis.

"Come on out of that stupid closet and put your pants on properly. You're in Dresden now, not in Paris."

Herr Wohlraab did as he was ordered. Meanwhile he admitted shyly that the recent circumstances didn't reveal him in a very favorable light, but that nevertheless he was a good father who took care of his family conscientiously, and that he was specially fond of his four children. He also loved his wife, but she was sickly, which explained why he was here.

"How long have you known Herr Schweik?" Dr. Olbert asked him, still clinging to the hope that he was tracking down a nest of political conspirators.

"Which Schweik, please?"

"The owner of this apartment?"

"I don't know him at all."

"But you know Frau Lehmann!" Dr. Olbert shouted indignantly. "Or do you want to deny that, too?"

Wohlraab shook his head.

"How long have you known her?"

"Since this evening," stammered the baker, looking shamefacedly at the floor, and, feeling that he must somehow tone down this bald fact, he reiterated that his wife was sickly—had been for years now.

"And a creature like that is a Party member!" thundered Dr. Olbert with a great surge of bitterness. Then he fell silent. The pause was interrupted by Frau Lehmann, who apologized for her delay in the bathroom. "How long has this man here known Schweik?" Dr. Olbert asked her sharply.

"Herr Schweik? . . . He doesn't know him at all."

"And how long has he known you?"

"Since this evening," replied Frau Lehmann, lowering her eyes to the floor.

Dr. Olbert said she should be ashamed of herself, especially at her age, and then shouted in rage at Wohlraab, whose allegations had proved to be true, "Get lost, you whoremonger!"

Wohlraab, pleased as punch at having gotten off so lightly, grabbed his hat and coat like lightning from the hook in the front hall, and with a polite, "Excuse the intrusion, Gentlemen," dashed out of the apartment.

"Aha! So that was Schweik's coat and hat! Why do you lie to me?" said Dr. Olbert swooping on Frau Lehmann like a hawk.

One more remark like that, Frau Lehmann protested, and she'd have to go to the bathroom again. Realizing his hands were tied, Dr. Olbert got the better of himself and said much more mildly, "If you tell the truth, nothing will happen to you. Now, you allowed seven other men into this apartment today. Who were they?"

They had all been just like Herr Wohlraab, answered Frau Lehmann.

"Whaaaat?" cried Dr. Olbert in utter astonishment.

This innuendo, however, was stretching things too far. It appeared that the other visitors had resembled the baker Wohlraab only insofar as they had each sought out Frau Lehmann. All seven had been attracted by Frau Lehmann's marriage ads. At the front door, as Olbert's plain-clothes man had correctly observed, they had shown unmistakable signs of timidity. Everyone who imagines he has just escaped some danger by the skin of his teeth, looks around timidly; that is a natural phenomenon. The baker Wohlraab, however, had not shrunk from danger. Indeed, he had not been led to Frau Lehmann by the desire to marry, but had long since reached the point of seeking love where it could be found most easily. Understandably enough, he was accustomed to fare forth on these expeditions without his marriage ring on his finger.

"Do you know that that fellow has been married for years?" Dr. Olbert asked Frau Lehmann.

"Married?"

"And that he has children?"

"Children?"

"Yes, indeed! Four! . . . That's all news to you, is it?"

An old truth was confirmed once again. The love of a woman turned in the twinkling of an eye to hate. "I won't shed any tears on his account," said Frau Lehmann. "I wouldn't have taken him, anyway. Do you know what he said to me? 'I may be a Party member,' says he, 'but that crap they churn out at our People's Production plants—why, the world's never seen the likes of it before.' That's what he said, he did."

"In what context?"

Suddenly realizing she had overshot the mark, Frau Lehmann started stammering. But Dr. Olbert was not to be deterred: it transpired that baker Wohlraab had been agitating against the springs of Frau Lehmann's new mattress.

"Write that down," said Olbert to Groener. "And remind me of it when I'm back from the hospital." He then ordered Groener to search the other rooms of the apartment, while for his own part he continued his interrogation of Frau Lehmann.

"Stick to the truth," he repeated to her, "then nothing will happen to you. The denunciation you have just volunteered is a move in the right direction. But now I ask you once again, where is Schweik?"

Schweik had disappeared without a trace, Frau Lehmann informed him. He had last been seen in the "Traube," where he had rung up a bill fit for a multi-millionaire. Where the money had come from was a complete mystery. His last words, as he had left the apartment, were that he was going to visit a sick friend. But in fact, he had gone to the "Traube," where he had been served by Frau Mracek, the cook. Frau Lehmann had been able to find out all this without too much difficulty, but the riddle as to how he had come by so much money had remained unsolved. Frau Mracek had no idea either where Schweik had gone after leaving the "Traube," nor did she know when he had left and whether he was alone or accompanied. She had seen and heard nothing, that she could swear to. She would sue anyone who claimed otherwise. What was more, the twelve-year-old kitchen girl had said the same thing.

When this torrent of information had ceased, Dr. Olbert shouted at Groener, asking whether he had found anything yet. "Yes!" answered Groener, hurrying back. "In the kitchen, on the wall. Here look!" In his hands he held two photographs of Stalin, an early and a more recent one. Both of them were accepted by Dr. Olbert with a sigh of gratitude. "Well thank God —that's something, anyway!" he said with some relish.

Frau Lehmann immediately claimed that the pictures were not her responsibility. She didn't want to denounce Herr Schweik exactly, but on the other hand she couldn't sacrifice herself for him. That would be asking too much of a housekeeper.

She was improving visibly, declared Dr. Olbert, and

having decided not to postpone his departure any longer, he merely turned to Frau Lehmann at the front door with the comment that were she to pass on to him at once everything she might hear from Schweik, she would exonerate herself completely.

Back in the clinic, he pestered the night nurse, who had to bring him pills for severe smarting of the eyes.

CARP IN
PIKE'S POND

* * * Commissioner Pike, official expert on crimes of violence, and now in charge of Schweik's case, sat in his office. For perhaps the tenth time already, he read through the report of the Riot Squad that had arrested Schweik in the Henrich-Zille-Strasse. The battle between Pike and Schweik had shown no progress to date. The clearest indication of the tenor of Schweik's hearings was the frequent whitening of the tip of Commissioner Pike's nose.

A new week had begun. On Mondays Commissioner Pike was always particularly energetic. He underlined various things in Schweik's report with a thick red pencil. Finally he rang for his secretary. She knew right away who was meant when Pike greeted her with the announcement, "Today I'll put an end to him," and she nodded indifferently. "You can take down every word right from the beginning, when I get to work on him," Pike continued. Another indifferent nod was the secretary's only reply. Her apathy stood in striking contrast to Pike's vigor. "What's the matter, dear?" he asked her.

"Don't ask stupid questions!"

"Oh that!" said Pike mildly, at once guessing what was on her mind. "*That* again. But, Baby, don't drive both of us crazy with *that*. After all, it's only fourteen days. With my wife it's often been three or four weeks, and it always turned out to be a false alarm. . . . Come on," he added, since the girl neither spoke nor altered her dour expression. "Don't make such a face, Baby. Laugh a little. Let's hope for the best. *Look* at me!"

But he only mustered a rather uncertain smile, and even this evaporated when the secretary retorted, "If you were in my shoes you'd soon wipe the smile off your face. All your kind is fit for is passing the buck. We're the ones who get stuck with the baby."

"Just a moment, Baby," said Pike with an aggrieved voice. "You have no right to talk like that. You always did plenty of passing yourself."

The secretary sniffed audibly a couple of times, so that he quickly exclaimed, "No tears now, I beg of you! Don't dramatize things! I'm sure it's nothing but a false alarm. I've experienced them often enough with my wife." In fact, he went on to say, his marital experience had made him believe in false alarms wholeheartedly. They had come to be a delightful habit, as it were.

"You'll see," said the secretary. Pike shrugged his shoulders and, considering the discussion closed, gave orders on the telephone for Schweik to be brought up. Soon, someone knocked at the door. It was a guard, who announced that the prisoner Joseph Schweik had asked him to report that he was declaring a hunger strike to prove his innocence. "Fetch him!" Pike commanded.

"Son-of-a-bitch," he began aggressively as Schweik appeared, greeted him amiably, and asked him how His Honor had enjoyed the weekend. "What business is that of yours? . . . I see you're still as bold as brass. But that's all going to change now, you can stake your life on it. I've got several things in mind apropos of your case."

"I don't know what you've got against me today," Schweik retorted. "Today is Monday. On Monday the proper thing to ask people is how they've enjoyed their weekend, and whether they've had a good time. But what do you have to say? That I'm as bold as brass. Perhaps I should have asked you something entirely different, maybe something that's got nothing to do with the weekend? Something like 'Good morning, Sir. Why was the Apostle Paul going to Damascus?' Then of course you'd have had good reason to complain and ask me if I was crazy. But it wasn't like that. My greeting was different. I know how to behave."

Since Commissioner Pike had long since learned what came of letting oneself be drawn into a discussion with Schweik, his response was terse. "So you want to go on a hunger strike?" he demanded.

"That's right."

"And what do you expect to gain by that?"

"To prove my innocence, Sir. No more and no less. That's all that's necessary. Look here, for the second time I've been sitting around for days, and we don't seem to advance an inch with each other. My housekeeper has no idea where I am, and up to now you haven't even allowed me to write to her. You don't know her; she's not very bright and therefore needs continual guidance. When in the twinkling of an eye we hear that this month there's no butter ration, but a choice of two pounds of flour or four pounds of apples, she's unable to make a quick decision. She needs hours to make up her mind, and then she just pulls a long face and gets nothing at all—because of course by the time *she* gets to the store all the apples and flour have been sold. We've often been left in the lurch like this with our ration cards. Naturally I bawl her out whenever that happens, and so she always tries to ask my advice beforehand. But *how* is she supposed to ask me when she doesn't have the faintest idea where I am —like now, for example? Not a soul knows where I am, aside from you. And this situation has got to be remedied!" Schweik said with emphasis. "For this reason I'm going on a hunger strike."

"So?"

"I insist that I have no desire to insult you or anything like that, Sir. Far from it. I don't want to get personal, as they say. I know how to behave. Naturally I'm very grateful that you've given me this opportunity to explain myself. I hope, now, you won't misunderstand what's prompted my hunger strike. It starts tomorrow, incidentally."

"Why not today?" asked Pike. It was apparent that his annoyance with Schweik had given way to amusement. "Is tomorrow a special day in your life? Some sort of anniversary?"

"It's always the anniversary of something," Schweik replied calmly, without a trace of irritation. "Even if it's no more than the fourth anniversary of the year the painter painted the kitchen. But my hunger strike has nothing to do with anything like that. I'm starting it tomorrow because today—so the guard tells me—there's meat on the menu, whereas tomorrow all we're getting is cereal. You follow me?"

"I follow you all too well, Schweik! How long do you intend striking?"

"Until my innocence has been proved and you set me free again. You'll soon see for yourself that I am innocent and without accomplices. This will come home to you, sure enough. Were you to let me starve to death, there'd be an inquiry and you'd have to take the rap. So you see, Sir, the length of my strike depends entirely on you."

"How come?" Commissioner Pike felt like asking, but he inquired instead: "And what if we feed you by force, Schweik?"

"Like they do in the West, you mean?"

"That sounds like them all right," answered Pike, smiling. "And all that big talk about freedom! . . . No, no, Schweik, don't worry. Here no one will force you to take nourishment. Here," he burst into a chuckle, "you can tighten your belt until you're literally gassed. Understand?"

"Are you asking me if I understand the expression 'tighten your belt,'" Schweik answered. "Of course! I know it from the army. Although I must say I don't know which regiment introduced it or which century it was. That's something you'd have to look into. It's an idea though—perhaps it will come in handy before my hunger strike convinces you that I'm innocent."

Commissioner Pike exchanged glances with his secretary, who at first had conscientiously taken everything down in shorthand, but had soon given up. Schweik's eyes followed Pike's. He noticed that the secretary was very pale, a fact that had escaped the Commissioner. Schweik asked himself what could be causing her pallor.

Pike, on the other hand, was occupied with an entirely different question: how he could give his interrogation a new twist and catch Schweik unawares. "Schweik," he said suddenly, like a shot from a gun, "what is a fingerprint?"

In spite of his direct aim, however, he had to repeat the question twice, for Schweik's whole attention was now fastened on the secretary. "You look very poorly, Fräulein," said Schweik. "You've got rings under your eyes. You're pale. Don't you feel good?"

The secretary said nothing, but she raised her handkerchief to her mouth.

"What did you eat for breakfast?" Schweik asked her, and then, without further ado, "Do you throw up a lot?"

While Schweik once again waited in vain for an answer from the secretary, Commissioner Pike recommenced his attack. "Didn't you hear me," he rapped. "I asked you what a fingerprint is!"

Schweik, however, was not to be diverted from the secretary. "Shall I get you the wastebasket, Fräulein?" he asked pleasantly.

Although the girl shook her head, since she considered the wastebasket unsuitable for what Schweik had in mind, Schweik nevertheless rose and prepared to put his idea into practice. At this, Pike banged his fist on his desk. He had no intention of being deprived of the pleasure of hearing Schweik's definition of a fingerprint. "Schweik, goddammit, I'm asking you for the last time!

What is a fingerprint?" he shouted, his nose whitening.

Deciding that for the time being there was nothing more he could do for the secretary, Schweik became aware once more of his interrogator. "Fingerprints," said he, "are what a criminal, if he's dumb or a beginner, leaves behind at the scene of a crime, when unthinkingly he fumbles around without gloves on. If he's unlucky, maybe the police will find them."

I'll pay you back for that "maybe," thought Commissioner Pike, as he demanded, "What is it that no two people ever have alike?"

"Fingerprints."

"Precisely. And what do you suppose we found on your accomplice's umbrella?"

"Probably his fingerprints," Schweik answered unperturbed, at once adding, "Excuse me, Sir, but how often must I tell you that that gentleman was no accomplice of mine, but a decent citizen, unknown to me, whose specialty is a love of reading newspapers."

"Son-of-a-bitch! Don't give me that fairy tale. We'll find that fellow—when we've gotten someone's fingerprints we always get our man. So my advice to you is to confess straightaway. It's your only chance of squaring yourself with us."

From the corner where the secretary was sitting there came a sound of choking. Schweik looked round at the secretary. "I've just said something to you, man!" shouted Pike, who had eyes and ears only for Schweik.

Schweik didn't reply; he was in suspense, and all of a sudden things went very quickly for the secretary. She had no time to run out of the room, and the result was that Schweik's idea with the wastebasket turned out to have been a useful emergency precaution. For his part, Commissioner Pike had no more thought for fingerprints. The whole room reeled before his eyes. Recognition of the terrible reality which lay behind the secretary's nausea struck him like a blow from a club. Good Samaritan Schweik had raced over and was holding the secretary's head. Pike sat paralyzed in his chair; Schweik had to prod him to fetch a glass of water for his girl friend.

"For my *girl friend?*" exclaimed Commissioner Pike, completely beside himself at Schweik's knowledge of this secret.

"Good grief!" sighed Schweik, "Does that surprise you? All the prisoners know that! Prisoners always know more than one thinks, you ought to have grasped that by this time. Aside from which, it's common knowledge the world over that every boss who isn't dumb kills two birds with one stone—his secretary *and* his girl friend. That's why all elderly bosses have young secretaries. The arrangement wouldn't make sense otherwise. The bosses have old women around them at home, but at the office things have to be different, otherwise no boss would ever be tempted to work overtime and the whole economy or bureaucracy would suffer. The same is true of business trips. In the West they have the additional incentive of earning money. But here personal profit motive is unnecessary. What's the result? The twofold responsibility and importance of young secretaries."

While he lectured Pike, Schweik did not forget for a moment to carry out his second responsibility, that of holding the secretary's head. For this he was rewarded by the poor girl, who, in a brief respite which nature allowed her, said with emotion, "You're very sweet to me, Herr Schweik."

When the girl felt better, Commissioner Pike, who altogether had been sent to fetch three glasses of water in the corridor, received further instructions to empty the wastebasket into the toilet. This was his most complicated task, for none of the many officials and employees in the building could be allowed to see him. So Pike had to cover a distance with many obstacles, going from dark recess to dark recess and ducking for cover whenever anyone came by. As a result, he was out of the room for some time.

In the meantime, Schweik satisfied his curiosity. "Fräulein," he said inquisitively, "you're not going to go and have a baby on me?"

The secretary still felt pretty miserable; she lacked the energy to deny Schweik's suspicion, and only hung her head. The same happened when Schweik inquired, "From him?" Not until Schweik asked what his wife would say about that did the secretary reply very dejectedly that the wife was a stupid old-fashioned cow, egotistical and unfeeling, who clung to her husband, had no sympathy for pregnant mistresses, and wouldn't think of divorce.

"Then what are you going to do with the kid?" asked Schweik.

The flood of tears which was released by this question touched his sympathetic heart, and he said comfortingly, "Don't cry, Fräulein. Not long ago there was a program on television, in which it was stated that the illegitimate child is no longer a disgrace here, that the unmarried mother is as good as any, and that a child born out of wedlock is no longer a burden. Under

Socialism there are kindergartens where unmarried
mothers can send their children when they go to work,
so that they can contribute to the triumph of our system . . . Didn't you see that program?" he asked, as he
saw that the flood of tears had merely increased with
every sentence.

Tears were indeed the only reply that issued from
the secretary. Schweik realized that propaganda phrases
were not what was needed here. "Then you need an
abortionist or an abortioness," he added bluntly. "It
seems to me that you'd prefer that."

"Yes!" she exclaimed spontaneously. "But I don't
know of anyone! . . . Do you know of someone, Herr
Schweik?"

Schweik's answer did not lack diplomacy. "Fräulein," he said quietly, "I beg of you, where do you think
you are? I'm a *prisoner* here, and you work for the
police. You mustn't forget that!"

A shimmer of hope crossed the secretary's face.
Her tears ceased. In her need she grasped at every straw.
She begged Schweik to be human, to have mercy. His
answer had betrayed to her that he did know someone
—otherwise she'd kill herself, and then he'd have that
on his conscience.

"Fräulein, I must draw your attention once more
to the fact that you work for the police and I . . ."

The secretary quickly abandoned the tactic of
mere pleading and began looking for a cigarette in her
purse, which she duly offered to Schweik. Schweik took
a cigarette, and a moment later she pressed the whole
pack into his hand. She invited him to smoke. Schweik
submitted, but asked as he lit the cigarette what the
Commissioner would say when he came back. The secre-

tary made a gesture of contempt. "Don't be silly!" she said. "If he thinks he can tell me anything . . ."

"What's he doing all this time?" asked Schweik, to which the secretary retorted that she hadn't missed him. What was more important to her was being able to talk undisturbed.

"I understand what you mean," rejoined Schweik, examining the cigarette in his hand. "But it's not as easy as that. Let's assume I do know the address of someone —mind you, I'm not saying that that is so. Well, there'd be no sense at all in my giving it to you. Why? Because abortionists have to be very careful. I would have to introduce you personally . . . that's if I did know of someone, as I've already said."

The secretary sensed that she would have to wager more than a pack of cigarettes to win Schweik's help, and said with sudden decision, "Very well, Herr Schweik. Then I ask whether you would be prepared to accompany me there, if I make it possible for you to do so?"

"If I am released, you mean?" replied Schweik, looking even harder at his cigarette.

"Yes."

"That would be a deal," said Schweik thoughtfully, finally calling the transaction by its proper name.

The secretary was now restless with joy. She stood up, took a few steps back and forth, sat down again and said that everything was clear, she thanked the Lord, and hoped the heavens would repay Schweik.

The relationship between Schweik and the secretary had reached this stage of development when at last Commissioner Pike, who had gotten himself more or less under control outside, returned with the wastebasket,

believing that nothing had happened in the meantime—
that he could shorten the reins again at the very point
he had left off when the secretary had become sick.
"Who do you think you are, Schweik?" he chided.
"Who permitted you to smoke? Where did you get
that cigarette? If ever again you have the effrontery to
suggest that I have a relationship with my secretary,
then Fräulein Ritter and I together will sue you for
libel, slander, and defamation. Understand!"

"If I were you I'd speak to Fräulein Ritter about
that first," rejoined Schweik cheerfully, confident of
the strong position of a girl friend and secretary in the
battle of the sexes. "Perhaps you'll think differently
then."

"What is that supposed to mean? Have you lost your
mind? . . . But of course!" Pike assured himself. "Of
course you have. Your hunger strike speaks for itself."

Schweik smiled. "I'm relieved of that now, to be
sure," he said dryly.

Pike now gave his secretary an involuntary, questioning look, upon which she made a sign to have
Schweik taken away. This could only mean that she
wanted to speak with Pike alone.

Schweik was led away, and Fräulein Ritter was no
longer the depressed, exhausted Luise Ritter with whom
Pike had been able to play the fool just an hour before.
Now she fought for herself like a tigress. "You and your
false alarm . . . what about that, you idiot? Do you
imagine I want to have the kid? No! A thousand times
no! And what about you? The scandal wouldn't do you
any good at the office, either."

He admitted all that, said Commissioner Pike, making his first concession. But he was a police official and

couldn't make common cause with a prisoner . . . no, never, that was simply out of the question. Fräulein Ritter asked him whether he could suggest an alternative, and when he had to reply in the negative she only said, "Well then, you fool?"

Commissioner Pike now made his second concession, by turning to the financial side of the problem and asking how much the thing—provided he were to agree to it—would cost. Fräulein Ritter's answer to this was equally unloving: "What do *you* care! I can't count on a mark from you, in any case. As always, I'll be stuck with the entire expense. You never have a cent in your pocket."

This was true. Pike had to turn over every penny at home, for his wife had been given this premarital advice by her mother: "The only way to guarantee a man's faithfulness is to keep him short of money."

Pike assumed a wounded expression and said, "Do you enjoy trampling on my feelings?"

Since this question brought no response, silence reigned until Pike sighed and asked to be allowed to sleep on the problem until the following day. Aware of how much he had already conceded, the feeling came over him that he had earned a reward. He looked over at the couch; for someone of his age his gaze became glassy in a surprisingly short time. He thought that his girl friend's condition had at least one advantage: one could put it to good use. Finally he said, "I'll call my wife and say I've been held up by work and she needn't keep lunch waiting for me."

"You can forget that!" was the brief, disappointing reply.

"But why, dear?"

"Your wife won't have to keep lunch waiting for you any more until Schweik is free again. Got it, sweetie?"

There wasn't much to "get." Lysistrata's famous weapon has been known to mankind since antiquity. The present case was only unusual insofar as it demonstrated fairly and squarely what could be attained by the proper apportionment of its blows. With this weapon it was possible in one and the same means to achieve two diametrically opposed ends: in the case of Dr. Olbert, it was instrumental in having Schweik locked up; while with Commissioner Pike it was serving to get him free again.

PIKE'S CHANGE
OF HEART

❋ ❋ ❋ State Attorney Zollner's first knowledge of Schweik's mysterious disappearance came when he received the two Stalin photographs Dr. Olbert had commandeered in Schweik's kitchen, with the following note:

Taken into custody during surprise night search. Pictures were hung on the wall and therefore in use. Ditto two potted plants serving to embellish the pictures. As evidence unmistakable. Housekeeper says she had nothing to do with pictures or floral decoration—apartment owner was responsible. Significantly, he himself has disappeared without a trace. Probably fleeing the Republic!

State Attorney Zollner read this announcement and grumbled, "Typical of that idiot Olbert! Now I'm supposed to guess who the fellow is."

With the exception of the word "idiot," this is exactly what he repeated on the telephone when he was connected with Dr. Olbert at the hospital.

Dr. Olbert had not meant to omit the apartment

owner's name from his note. That was a slip. At Zollner's rebuke, he blushed with embarrassment and hastened to repair his omission. "Schweik. Joseph Schweik," he said.

"Schweik?" exclaimed Zollner in surprise and immediately losing his temper. "Good God, man, why can't you leave the fellow alone?"

"Why?" replied Dr. Olbert, in the tone he felt Schweik's Stalin pictures permitted. "Or do you still insist that the fellow is all right?"

"Why not, may I ask? On account of the photographs? How do you know he is even responsible for them? You say yourself that the housekeeper told you . . ."

"That's right."

"And that's proof enough for you. Good heavens! Hasn't it occurred to you that the housekeeper would have told you the same thing even if it were really *she* who's responsible for the pictures?"

"Indeed it had," replied Dr. Olbert with unmistakable irony.

State Attorney Zollner, however, had already started on a criminological lecture with which, he decided, he would root out this irony once and for all. "How long has Schweik allegedly been gone?" he asked Olbert.

"Three days already."

"And you say that under the pictures were potted plants?"

"Yes indeed."

"Were they freshly watered?"

"What? The flowers?"

Now it was Zollner's turn to be ironical. "No, the pictures. Freshly watered pictures don't wilt."

There was a brief pause before Dr. Olbert said laboriously, "Sir, I don't know whether the flowers were watered."

"That's splendid, I must say. So you've neglected to confirm the fact. That's how you collect evidence—or rather, that's how you don't collect it! I'm sorry, but I can't help you. We'll have to confine ourselves to the mere assumption that the flowers had been watered. They must have been standing under the pictures for some time. Therefore, someone must have watered them regularly, otherwise this horticultural garland would have died off in no time. And who is that someone? Certainly not Schweik—at least not of late—for he's disappeared, you've said so yourself, Herr Olbert. *That's* what I call proof, Comrade. Not what you've served up!"

"But why has he disappeared?" asked Dr. Olbert, clutching at his last straw. But State Attorney Zollner's only comment upon this was that even the question of Schweik's whereabouts seemed to him to be in some doubt, and he therefore heartily recommended Dr. Olbert stop venting his rage on Schweik, for that would only distract the plans they had concocted for Schweik on a higher level.

This brought the telephone conversation to an end. Dr. Olbert was so depressed that he didn't react at all to the pretty young assistant nurses who entered his room and announced that the head nurse had sent them to apply the prescribed hot compress. Ordinarily he would have said playfully that if he had his way he'd apply a hot compress to *them*. But now he simply barked, "Go to hell with your hot compress! I have eye trouble. Only the devil knows who I'm being confused with in this joint," upon which the nurses, little surprised at their mistake, left the room again.

Such incidents were no exception. Confusion was the rule in Dresden hospitals, ever since Socialism had entered their doors.

Schweik's next meeting with Commissioner Pike took place on a Wednesday. If until now the tip of Pike's nose had turned white gradually during the interrogations, this time it was already white before the Commissioner uttered his first word to Schweik. This fact was significant. The Commissioner's nose betrayed him, although his words sounded friendlier than ever before.

"Good morning, Schweik," he said affably. "Please take a seat. How did you sleep?"

"The way one always sleeps in prison when one knows it's the last night—very well!" replied Schweik, sitting down. "Nice of you to ask."

"What do you mean 'the last night'?" asked Pike with such evident surprise that Schweik couldn't help rejoining, "Haven't you spoken to Fräulein Ritter? Where is she?"

Luise Ritter was nowhere to be seen.

"What am I supposed to have spoken to her about? She's my secretary. I dictate to her and she takes it down. This is what our conversations consist of, understand. Where is she today? On vacation. She still has three days left from last year." Before Schweik had time to interrupt, Pike added hurriedly, "Did Sergeant Hornig actually read this report back to you again in the Heinrich-Zille-Strasse, after he'd finished it?"

But it wasn't that easy to get Schweik to abandon the subject of Fräulein Ritter. "Does that mean, Sir," he asked, "that Fräulein Ritter has not yet spoken to you?"

"What in the world is all this nonsense about my secretary, Schweik! I told you she's on vacation. Very well then, what about the report?"

"How long has she been on vacation?"

"Since Monday. Immediately after your interrogation, Schweik, she went home, because she felt ill again."

"And you haven't spoken to each other since?"

"Not ten words," replied Pike ingenuously. "But now what about that report?"

Schweik still did not answer Pike's question. He only sighed and said, "Under the circumstances, then, I'll have to take back what I said about my last night in prison. As things now stand, the whole business has been postponed."

"I don't know what's the matter with you, Schweik. What's the point of all this chatter? You're talking in riddles. Now, am I to get an answer to my question or not? Did Hornig read you back his report or not?"

Pike's voice sounded impatient. It had lost much of its original friendly tone.

"No," replied Schweik after a long pause.

"No?" Commissioner Pike seemed extremely surprised and picked up the report from the table. "But you should have told me that sooner, Schweik. Perhaps I'd have seen certain things in a different light."

He fell silent and began to read the report, but soon found he couldn't give it his full attention. He was overcome by sudden irritation, shook his head indignantly, and threw the report down again, barking:

"That's incredible! That means that fellow Hornig has committed a clear violation of the regulations. I can hardly believe it. Did he really not read the report back to you?"

"Really and truly not," replied Schweik. "But that doesn't make a jot of difference. I haven't been accustomed to anything else for ages. And it's not necessary for you to get excited about it all of a sudden, Sir. I'm the one who should get excited, after all, but I'm not so small-minded. I'm generous, no one can deny that. Besides, this report here isn't important any more."

"Why not?"

"Too bad you haven't spoken with your secretary, or you'd know why by now."

"Don't start up about my secretary again!" shouted Pike furiously, the tip of his nose as white as a beacon. "I'm sick and tired of her. She is entirely irrelevant. But Hornig! Son-of-a-bitch, how dare he hand in such a report! What could have come over him? I ask myself. Why didn't he read it back to you? There's only one possible reason: the report was not irreproachable."

"I suggest," said Schweik, who thanks to his considerable association with bureaucrats was also familiar with their language, "that we consider the matter as closed, I've told you that already. Let's wait until your secretary's vacation is over. Until then, the best thing for you to do is to send me back to my cell, Sir."

It was obvious that the Commissioner was having great difficulty in restraining himself from striking Schweik across the face. The two men looked at each other, and it was now that Schweik at last decided he must say something about Pike's remarkable nose.

"Sir," he began, "what's the matter with your

nose? I've noticed it from the very beginning. Every few seconds it turns snow-white. During the war, in Russia, similar things happened. But it was cold there, in the winter. Was yours frostbitten too, perhaps?"

Pike's outward reaction to these comments gave a strong clue to his inward feelings. His face and even his nose suddenly turned a rich dark red—a process which caused Schweik to remark, "Now it's red again. I'm telling you, there's a continual back-and-forth coloration . . . In any case it's no drinker's nose," he declared in conclusion. "Only the younger prisoners suspect that, the ones who weren't in Russia during the war."

"By God, you're beyond the pale!" screamed Pike, "who the hell do you think you are? I won't put up with it! You can thank God"—he was screaming louder and louder—"for this report. Otherwise you'd have had it for good and all!"

He broke off, gnashing his teeth, and finally asked with superhuman self-control, "Maybe Sergeant Hornig blackmailed you?"

"He didn't ask me a thing, only the others—the smart alecks, of course, know everything."

"But he didn't read the whole thing back to you, you stand on that?"

"I have to, because it's the truth," declared Schweik, adding with a deprecatory shrug, "But let's forget about that. I don't want Herr Hornig to get into trouble. The report isn't worth it now."

"This report," continued Pike relentlessly, "represents a violation of the regulations. You should have told me that sooner, Schweik, then these hearings would have taken a different turn right from the beginning."

He picked up the unfortunate report from the table,

this time managing to read a few lines, then thrust it abruptly before Schweik, saying, "See for yourself. The red marks—I made them. Yes, I underlined some bits that made me suspicious long ago . . . Here, for example." Pike took the report back and read aloud. ". . . The two accomplices kept watch in the entryway of the house (see attached sketch), conversing in an apparently harmless manner in order to camouflage themselves further . . . etc.

"Schweik," said Commissioner Pike, letting the report fall on the table, "if only you had told me right away how this report came to be written, then I'd have questioned its veracity before—although the red marks do show that I had certain reservations at the outset. Now, what does this mean: 'conversing in an apparently harmless manner in order to camouflage themselves further'? I've underlined that very heavily, not because I wished to interpret it as proof against you, Schweik. On the contrary! In such cases the best camouflage is to hold your tongue altogether, to be as quiet as a mouse—am I right? Chattering, no matter the topic, is much more likely to be proof of genuine harmlessness than silence— am I right? Now do you understand what my red marks mean, Schweik? They are not directed against *you*, but against *Hornig*."

"Sir," replied Schweik, who had been trying repeatedly to interrupt the flow of words from the Commissioner, "you insist on worrying about something that's no longer of any concern. You want everything tied up in a neat bundle, it seems to me. You want to set right these inaccuracies, because with an exemplary report you can do me in—or at least I imagine that's what you have in mind. But report or no report, I am innocent.

You can verify that easily enough when your secretary returns from her vacation. Until then, I can only repeat, the best thing is to send me back to my cell."

"Schweik," asked Pike with a sigh, "how old was that gamekeeper, who allegedly heard you so clearly in the entryway?"

"Eighty-three, he told Hornig."

"*How* old?" repeated Pike, his eyes opening wide in astonishment. "*Eighty-three?*"

"That's what I said."

Pike gripped the report again, shouting, "Then that was no slip of the pen after all! And I was so sure that it was a slip of the pen that even when I read it the first time I automatically changed the 'eighty-three' to 'thirty-eight.' I just turned the number around, do you follow me? Son-of-a-bitch! That Hornig! Then he really did write this with complete conviction: 'This fact was observed through a ground-floor window near the entryway by a pensioned gamekeeper, whose hearing has been well-trained in his eighty-three years.' Good grief! And one has to work with such idiots. This is insufferable.

"Schweik," he continued, "there are no grounds in this report for locking a man up. That's now quite clear to me."

"Before you look for other grounds," Schweik started, but the Commissioner cut him short, saying, "Just a minute . . . wait! . . . I'll be right back . . ."

He left the room hurriedly, returned five minutes later and said, his face beaming with joy—in strange contrast to his white nose, "I have spoken with the resident judge, Schweik. You may go."

"Where? To my cell?"

"No, not to your cell, Schweik, or any other cell—go *home!*"

"*Home!*" cried Schweik in utter alarm. "But you haven't even spoken to your secretary yet!"

At that moment the last bands of restraint snapped in Commissioner Pike. "To hell with my secretary, Schweik," he bawled. "Get lost!"

BUCHTA AND CO. IN DANGER

*** "Frau Lehmann," Schweik announced to his housekeeper, who had heard him unlock the door and had come to meet him in the front hall, "here I am again. Heil Moscow! Has anything happened in my absence?"

"Good Lord, it's you, Herr Schweik! Where on earth have you been? And not a word from you the whole time! You must never do such a thing to me again! Every day I waited for a letter from you, telling me to follow you. But none came . . . Should follow you to the West," she added meaningfully, as Schweik gave her his hand.

"Why to the West, Frau Lehmann?"

"Well, we all thought that at last it's gotten to be too much for you. Dr. Hausmann has already been around to ask when the apartment will be vacant. It's quite normal, he said, all the vacant apartments we have here. Yesterday and day before yesterday, four on our street alone. That, he said, is why in the GDR we have no apartment shortage, while in West Germany there are millions of people without even a roof over their heads. One more proof that things are better here, he said."

"You and your everlasting West," said Schweik disapprovingly. "That's all you ever talk about. What would I be doing there? Here I'm a respected and honored member of the working class. What would I be over there? A lousy plebeian. And here? Here I'm something utterly different: a proletarian. Why different? Because here we have the *dictatorship* of the proletariat. Can't you grasp that, Frau Lehmann? Here we rule, over there it's the capitalists. Here everything belongs to *us*, the proletariat; over there it belongs to Krupp. Over there the proletariat is exploited, enslaved; here it is free. It's all perfectly logical. And because I belong to the proletariat, I too am a free man. Who knows what I would be over there?"

Frau Lehmann threw up her hands in disbelief.

"*What* are you here? A *free* man? It's too much! And that from a man who spends more time in prison than out of it."

"Only as a result of misunderstandings, Frau Lehmann. You mustn't forget that," Schweik said with dignity. "Up to now it has always turned out to be a misunderstanding after all, and every single time they've sent me home ahead of schedule, just the way they did today. That alone is the deciding factor. And such misunderstandings don't have anything to do with Socialism, Frau Lehmann. That's what you mean, isn't it—Socialism? Those misunderstandings aren't ideological or anything, they're whims of fate. That's the best way to look at it. Even in the old days, under the Monarchy, misunderstandings were as much a part of my life as daily bread. So it wouldn't do for me to blame them now on Socialism."

They broke off their conference in the front hall and retired to the kitchen, Frau Lehmann shaking her head. On the hotplate a saucepan was just boiling over. Frau Lehmann dashed over and removed it, while Schweik again asked her if anything had happened in his absence.

"Why, good heavens," she exclaimed with feeling, letting go of the saucepan. "It certainly has! I hope I can remember everything! They nearly broke the door down. I've already told you about Hausmann. Besides him, the Buchta brothers have been here almost every day to ask if I'd heard from you. And last Thursday a gentleman called, who wanted to speak to you. I asked him if I could take a message. No, he said, I should just remind you about the gas meter. What gas meter? I asked. You knew about it, he said, and he'd be back this week. That was on Thursday. And just imagine, on Friday another gentleman rang the bell and said exactly the same thing. I offered him a cup of coffee and said, 'You'll have to explain exactly what you want,' but he didn't have time for that. He was very nervous and in a terrible hurry. And just before that, State Attorney Zollner was here too, in person, and said you couldn't do that to him, fleeing to the West, because that would be his downfall—after he'd used all his influence to get you released. Dr. Olbert is just waiting for something like that, he said, his search of the apartment was proof enough, after all."

Schweik, who was on his way to the kitchen window to let the steam escape from the saucepan, came to a standstill between the table and the window. "What

search of the apartment, Frau Lehmann?" he asked
sharply.

"The one here, of course, by that pig Olbert,"
replied Frau Lehmann, her eyes filling with hatred. "In
the middle of the night he came, with another man.
There I was peacefully asleep, not hurting a soul, and
all of a sudden the bell started ringing as if the whole
house was on fire. In the excitement I couldn't find my slip
right away, so I opened the door there and then—and
who was standing on the doorstep? The two of them!
They turned everything inside out, but didn't find a
thing . . . only . . ."

She fell silent.

"Only?" asked Schweik.

"Only the two pictures of Stalin in the kitchen,
Herr Schweik."

"My God," sighed Schweik. "Didn't you toss them
in the garbage pail ages ago? Surely you could have
figured that out for yourself."

Frau Lehmann, sensing the intended insult in
Schweik's comment, replied that she didn't deserve a
lecture. On the contrary, she had been faithful to
Schweik. Dr. Olbert had told her to inform him immediately if she heard anything at all from Schweik. But now,
instead of betraying Schweik to Olbert, she had done the
reverse. And what thanks did she get? Insults.

Schweik patted her on the shoulder and said with
gentle condescension, "You get dumber and dumber
every minute, Frau Lehmann. Don't you realize that if
that's what's going on, one of Olbert's men must be
lurking in the neighborhood and has seen me come home?
So, forward march! Hurry, hurry! Tell him what he
wants to know, otherwise he'll be on your heels again

before you can say, Nikita Khrushchev. Give him my best regards, and you can also tell him from me that I'd like the Stalin pictures back. I want to hang them up again, so that . . .

"So that I have them in front of me as a continual reminder never again to fall prey to the *personality cult*. You tell him that, then everything will be all right. I'll call that ox Zollner myself, and tell him I'm back again and that this won't be his downfall."

Frau Lehmann had turned pale, and no wonder. Stalin behind her, Dr. Olbert in front of her, for the second time now—whose nerves wouldn't give way? Except of course Schweik's. She slipped hurriedly into her coat and shoes, fastened the latter with trembling fingers, and hurried off.

A few minutes later, Schweik too left the apartment. He went to the next phone booth and called State Attorney Zollner, to inform him that his fears were groundless. This reassurance put Zollner in an emphatic frame of mind, which he expressed with the exclamation, "Just wait! I'll show him! Scaring the wits out of me like that!" Whom did State Attorney Zollner mean? Schweik? Of course not! Dr. Olbert—he was the culprit.

After this brief telephone conversation Schweik set out to find the Buchta brothers. He considered it his duty, for he could well imagine the two brothers' un-easiness.

"Man alive! Schweik! At last! Come in!" said Emil Buchta in greeting at the front door. "Is everything all right?" he asked anxiously.

All this excitement seemed exaggerated to Schweik. "What's eating you?" he quipped. "Was there ever a time when everything wasn't all right with me, Emil?"

"Almighty God!"

Emil's pious exclamation preceded the two men into the kitchen, where a familiar scene met Schweik's eyes: Rudolf, the younger brother, lay snoring on a couch, with a half-empty case of beer in front of him.

"Hi, Rudi," said Schweik, but he received no answer.

"Leave him alone, Schweik . . . Are you thirsty?"

"Yes, I am, for a change."

Then he should help himself, Emil said, pointing to the case of beer.

Since it would have been pointless to wait for a glass in Buchta's house, Schweik drank out of the bottle, but nearly dropped it in the midst of a gulp, as a dreadful scream suddenly rang out in the kitchen: "Schweik, Schweik, what have you done to us?"

The accusing scream came from Rudolf. Apparently he was not awake, but had screamed in his sleep, for immediately afterward he resumed snoring. It seemed from this that there was but one explanation for his sudden outburst: he was having a bad dream.

"There you have it," said Emil Buchta reproachfully to Schweik. "All your fault."

"My fault?" said Schweik. "Just hold on a minute. What have I to do with his being stewed?"

"I got half-smashed myself, Schweik, thanks to you. Our nerves were done for."

"That's news to me, that of all people you two should be chicken," Schweik retorted ironically.

But when Emil Buchta had next spoken he saw things in a different light. "The bastards have sent us a summons to appear next week before the doctor, about our inability to work," said Emil.

"Whaaat?" exclaimed Schweik, leaping up.

Emil opened his mouth but said nothing.

"Are you kidding, Emil? Why can't they leave you in peace!"

The other clenched his fists, tongue-tied.

"All you ask is to be left in peace, Emil," said Schweik, his voice faltering.

"The bastards!" Emil choked out at last. "The bastards! The West is absolutely right."

The West, he explained, was absolutely right in saying that the whole damn trouble with Communism was that it was always interfering with people's private lives. But Schweik would not have been Schweik if he had not at this point given justice its due. "Don't exaggerate, Emil," he said. "Perhaps it's only this doctor, in other words just one individual, who's after your blood, not the whole Communist shooting match. I imagine that's it. The same thing could happen to you in the West too, under the capitalists."

Schweik should stop trying to drive him crazy, Emil declared irritably. When on earth would he get things straight? But Schweik wasn't going to turn a hair at Emil's animosity. He replied in a calm and friendly tone that it was now as clear as day that Emil's nerves really had been set on edge.

At this, Emil asked how long it was since Schweik had put up a good fight. "As regards this summons to the doctor, we said to ourselves that it must have been you who squealed to the police," he said angrily. "That's the real reason for our binges. What do you have to say to that?"

"What have I to say to that?" repeated Schweik, withdrawing his hand from reaching for another bottle. "Nothing. I don't have to explain myself. Just remember who you're talking to."

"There's a lot to be said for our suspicions."

"Stop insulting me, Emil, or you can drink by yourself. If I *had* squealed, think they would have stopped at a summons? Do you think they wouldn't have put you in the clink right away? Where's your common sense, Emil? If Rudolf's too smashed to think straight—there's not much in his head anyway—well, that's one thing . . . but you? You should be ashamed of yourself!"

"Then open up, man, and tell me how you soft-soaped those bastards into letting you go again. And drink up!" exclaimed Emil Buchta, half-convinced by Schweik's arguments. "Or go to hell. I can't stand pansies."

Schweik, conciliatory, did as he was bidden. "That they let me go again wasn't my doing," he explained. "You know me, Emil, I'm not the kind of guy who decks himself out in sheep's clothing. That's not my nature. So I tell you frankly that I have the patrol leader to thank for that, the one who nabbed me. Nasty son-of-a-bitch. In fact, his report wasn't entirely in order . . ."

"What wasn't entirely in order?" Emil interrupted in astonishment.

"The report of the guy who arrested me."

"And how come it wasn't 'entirely in order'?"

"Because afterward he didn't read it back to me."

"Because he didn't read it to you?" Emil looked more than flabbergasted. "Are you trying to pull my leg, man?"

Emil's tone prompted Schweik to describe quickly how Commissioner Pike had come to see his case in a more favorable light. But although he spoke with all his inborn eloquence and fire, nevertheless Emil Buchta only asked him in conclusion what kind of damned nonsense was that—not reading the report back! The Communist police!! There must be something else behind it, damn it all. And what? A clear case . . .

"They let you go, Schweik," continued Emil Buchta, approaching the window for a cautious look at the street, "so they can keep their tabs on you and see whether you contact your alleged accomplices. And what do you do, idiot? You fall for it, hook, line, and sinker."

"I don't think so," replied Schweik, with a smile of reassurance. "If that were the case, Pike would have held his cards closer to his chest."

In front of the house there was no one in sight except pedestrians—passers-by; no suspicious loiterers. This fact seemed to support Schweik's contention. Besides, Schweik had another argument up his sleeve.

"If you were right, Emil," he went on, "they'd have been around here long ago. What would they have to wait for? All right, then. Your nerves are really playing you up, old boy. The best thing for you would be to spend a couple of weeks at the seaside."

That was a fine way to talk, answered Emil Buchta grimly. Instead of going to the seaside he had the doctor on his back, and that was another kettle of fish. Even Schweik shouldn't talk such rubbish.

Their conversation turned to the nobility of toil, that nobility for which the official doctors so often carry out the knight-dubbing ceremony. The Communist nobility of toil took quite a beating.

"Cheers, Emil!" Schweik was to say often that afternoon in Buchta's kitchen. "This is the stuff to drown your sorrows in. You two certainly had the right idea."

For Emil this meant that his brother Rudolf's head start rapidly melted away. Schweik too did his best to catch up, and by the time the case of beer was empty, a harmonious relationship had been re-established between Schweik and Emil Buchta. Over a bottle of schnapps which followed, Emil called Schweik "old Comrade," and hoped he hadn't taken any of his remarks amiss. However, although Schweik assured him that everything was in great shape, Emil still felt he owed Schweik an apology. The guilty conscience of inebriates is not easily assuaged.

"I'll prove my friendship, Schweik," said Emil in a burst of enthusiasm, propping up his heavy head with both hands. "Do you have any enemies?"

"Not that I know of, Emil."

"And that . . . that bastard Olbert Schweik?"

"How do you know about him?" Schweik inquired.

"From that Lehmann woman of yours. She told me ever . . . everything, when I asked about you."

"He only does his duty, Emil. Frau Lehmann doesn't seem to grasp that," said Schweik.

Whereupon Emil warned Schweik not to threaten their future friendship by that kind of remark. Should the opportunity ever arise, Olbert would find out just who he was up against. Buchta and Co. weren't to be trifled with, even if they only showed their claws as a last resort.

Drunks say all kinds of things, thought Schweik to himself; the best thing is to let them prattle on and enjoy themselves and not contradict them. He left the apartment at the point when Emil Buchta started insisting rather heatedly that Japan was in Tokyo.

A LESSON
IN MANNERS

* * * Frau Lehmann, of course, had
been back from Dr. Olbert's for some time. She informed Schweik, upon his return, that there was certainly no doubt that he was smart, if he could even
figure out what the police were up to. In fact, Dr.
Olbert had already known about Schweik's reappear-
ance. He had been very ill-humored and shouted at Frau
Lehmann that she was an enemy of Socialism—he could
prove that she had had to struggle with her conscience
before coming to him, otherwise she could have been
there half an hour earlier. They were as sharp as that,
Frau Lehmann confirmed to Schweik, terrified at the
very thought of it.

On the way from Emil's apartment, Schweik had
eaten two helpings of potato salad and knockwurst at a
stand that was open twenty-four hours a day, a service
that was praised weekly by the Dresden Party newspaper
as a visible sign of the progress of Socialism. He now
felt fresh as a daisy again.

Frau Lehmann asked him whether he had yet heard

that Olbert, that scourge of humanity, was in the hospital.

"In the hospital?" said Schweik with interest. "No, that's news to me. I only know he had trouble with his eyes. Is that why he's in the hospital?"

"I don't know, Herr Schweik. I guess his eyes did seem a little irritated. But I didn't ask."

"You didn't ask?"

"Of course not."

"Of course not? What's that supposed to mean?" Schweik saw that there was another instance that called for his guidance. "Of course you should have asked him. After all, you weren't visiting some priest or other, whom it's better not to ask when his son's going to graduate. On the contrary, you were visiting a patient. As for the priest's son, you've no idea whether he'll graduate at all, so the question could cause you some embarrassment. Avoid questions like that, Frau Lehmann, otherwise people will say with good reason that you have no tact. But patients are different. They're just waiting for people to ask them what's wrong, where it's wrong, why it's wrong, when it started, what the first symptoms were, whether they were unpleasant, whether it's all due to overwork, and so forth and so on. Patients like those sorts of questions, because it shows them you sympathize. The exceptions that don't like them and dither—well, that's another matter. That means they've got something catching. Do you follow me?"

Although Frau Lehmann answered in the affirmative, Schweik did not seem convinced, for he continued, "Once in old Prague a bastard of a policeman arrested me—by mistake, I need hardly add. My crime was defiling public buildings, he imagined, because it was night-time and in the dark he could see that I paused in the shadow of a house, turned toward the wall and looked at it for a while, without moving, as if I were studying it. Further proof was not necessary, said the policeman to himself, and he didn't even bother to come closer. He simply waited, since I was heading his way anyway.

"Such circumstances are considered adverse, Frau Lehmann. But then I took up my defense all right—let me assure you. 'Lieutenant,' I said, 'I beg your pardon, but in my opinion you haven't enough proof against me. It is perfectly possible that on that wall there is one of those plaques we all are familiar with, on which is written that for example during World War I Mozart took refuge here on such and such a night from the Turks, and that this is where the idea for his *Fledermaus* came to him. Where now is your proof, Lieutenant, if you don't mind my asking?'

"Sure enough, Frau Lehmann, it worked. He was afraid of infringing the regulations. As soon as I saw that, I followed up my advantage. 'Lieutenant,' I said, 'I imagine it would be very unpleasant for you, if by chance I really had been studying a plaque like that back there and it could be proved that you made a false accusation against me.'

"Well, Frau Lehmann," said Schweik with a sigh, "what shall I say? In a sense it was a stroke of luck. There really was a plaque—I hadn't noticed it before. But it said, '*Vlasta Mirova. Chiropodist. Office Hours 8–12 and 2–5 o'clock.*' Mozart left me in the lurch, the—"

"And what did the Lieutenant say?"

"He was insulted, as you can imagine. In fact, he was in a bad mood altogether that evening. But that was partly because he wasn't feeling well. I could see that because on the way to the police station he had to disappear twice—first into a gateway, and then behind a tree by the Karls-Platz. And both times he groaned pitifully and mumbled something unintelligible. So I sneaked after him in the first place so I could hear what he was saying, and secondly, so we didn't lose each other."

"He was groaning? What did he say?"

"Mother of God, it burns like blazes."

"What burned like blazes, Herr Schweik?"

"That's exactly what I wanted to know, Frau Lehmann. 'Lieutenant,' I asked him, 'what's the matter? Have you got heartburn?' But that only made him even madder."

"How come?"

Schweik, conscious of the need for discretion, replied; "Because I missed the mark with heartburn, Frau Lehmann. We're now getting to the whole point of the story. You remember how it all started: I explained to you that there are patients who don't want to talk about their ailments. Well, the Lieutenant was one of those. He blew his stack and even threatened to push me around if I didn't keep my trap shut and stop sneaking after him, making his mouth water like this with heartburn. Make his *mouth* water? Well, that was his way of implying he hadn't gotten some infectious disease —huh!"

Schweik looked at the clock on the wall, and then said to Frau Lehmann, who was shaking her head over the ill-deserving policeman, "How did you find out Olbert's in the hospital, anyway?"

"I was at his office," Frau Lehmann informed him. "From there they sent me ahead. First they telephoned

in circulation, Herr Schweik. But not a bit of it! D'you
know what he said? That that's the last straw. And then
the doctor to ask whether he wanted to see me personally. I thought he might be pleased to be told you're back
when I tried to calm him down a little by asking about
the Stalin pictures, he just flew at me again. He hasn't
got them any more. They're at the State Attorney's
office, at your friend Zollner's, he said; you can pick
them up there. And when I left, he shouted after me that
the office isn't kept open every day just for the two of
us, we should remember that and not underestimate him."
Tears rose to her eyes and she exclaimed, "I can't take
it much longer, Herr Schweik. One of these days you'll
wake up and find me with a rope around my neck."

As her hopes of a shocked reaction remained un-
fulfilled, she sniffed loudly and asked, "Do you understand me? Apparently not . . . Why do you keep looking
at the clock? Are you all set for the 'Traube' again
already?"

"You couldn't have spoken a truer word," said
Schweik with a laugh of relief. He was, after all, a man.
And men hate a half-finished afternoon. To the mascu-
line way of thinking, half-finished afternoons have
always called for evenings to round them off.

"I haven't had a drop to drink all day," Schweik
added.

Frau Lehmann was indignant. "And your breath?"
she said unpleasantly.

"My what?"

"Breath."

"Breath? What about it? You get better and better,
Frau Lehmann. Now your imagination is running riot,
and on top of that you've got a persecution complex. A

man with a touch of alcohol in his breath—I ask you, does that mean he's been drinking!"

Schweik's insulting tone of voice was still ringing in Frau Lehmann's ears as she heard the front door being slammed below.

COMRADE GEBHARDT
FROM THE CSM

❋❋❋ In the "Traube," Schweik ran into a colleague from the railroad, an engineer from Berlin. The sprinkling of other people in the tavern were known to Schweik only by sight, so he had no one else to choose from. Schweik sat down next to the engineer with little enthusiasm. He didn't take the fellow very seriously, because during the war the engineer had only served his country in the reserves. For an old front-line fighter like Schweik, that didn't count. Aside from that, however, there was a much more down-to-earth reason for his not getting too chummy with the engineer: beer tended to loosen his tongue. And today he chimed in at once with the greeting, "Hi, Schweik, what do you know! So you're out again! Great! Come, sit down, how was the Walter Ulbricht vacation this time? Another quickie, huh? But I was ready to bet on that two days ago with some Party big shot in the ticket office at the main station."

If only he'd speak more softly, at least—but no, his voice boomed out over about five tables. Schweik said nothing and looked around for the waitress. The engineer, however, interpreted Schweik's silence merely as acquiescence and declared that he would let the Party big shot know this very day how lucky he was not to have taken him up on that bet.

"Let's talk about the beer," said Schweik. "Is it fresh?"

"What do you mean, 'fresh'?"

"That's what they say in Bavaria. I heard it from a Hungarian porter and he had it from a Rumanian sailor on the Danube, who had it from an American hitchhiker by the Bosporous. And he in turn had it from a Bavarian ski instructor in America, who was teaching his sister when she broke her legs. That's how small the world is. In Bavaria, 'fresh beer' means it's nice and cool."

"Sure enough, Schweik. Here, try it!"

"Perfect," said Schweik, after downing the proffered swig from the engineer's tankard. "There's nothing like a tavern. I drank a small bottle in private today, you know. But a swig in private isn't a patch on a swig in a tavern. They take better care of the stuff here."

In the kitchen door appeared Frau Gartner, the owner's wife, with a Band-Aid on her face. That, the engineer at once commented, was a revealing sign. He could scarcely wait for Schweik to give his order to Frau Gartner before hinting something about a well-deserved punishment for that female. Schweik didn't care one way or the other, but asked how he was doing at cards at the moment. He had been having lousy luck for weeks, replied the engineer, but the reason for that Band-Aid was much more interesting. Who had he lost to, persisted Schweik.

Schweik's reluctance to gossip about Frau Gartner

merely confirmed the engineer's impression that maybe Schweik thought she had merely slipped on the cellar stairs, and didn't suspect that there was quite some story behind that Band-Aid. "You know what, Schweik," he said provokingly. "That bitch got beaten for cheating."

Now there was no getting away from it.

"Cheating?" asked Schweik, his eyes wide in astonishment. "Did she, by Jove? You'd better watch it! That kind of rumor often gets around. In Prague once they even threw mud at the mayor's wife. That cost everyone who was caught a hundred crowns. The only extenuating circumstance was that they had the truth on their side."

"Imagine that!" chuckled the engineer. "And those dopes put up with it?"

Schweik didn't like to see his old acquaintances slighted in this manner. He decided that it was time to put the engineer in his place. "Cut it out!" he said sharply. "*You* would have put up with that too. You're no great fighter, otherwise you'd have spent the war somewhere else, old pal."

Since for Germans in particular the war still is an open wound, a well-timed reminder of it will silence even a Berliner temporarily. As a result, minutes passed before the engineer had recovered sufficiently to say, "Let's not quarrel about a bitch like that, Schweik."

"Why 'bitch,' may I ask?"

"But she is, man! They caught her, you know. With that fellow Müller, to be precise. You know him too."

"Müller?" Schweik seemed thoughtful. "Sorry, I don't know him."

"Of course you know him, Schweik. From the 'Traube,' here. That ladies' man."

"You're mistaken," Schweik declared emphatically.

"No, I'm absolutely sure, Schweik. I've seen you two standing together at the bar."

"You must have bad eyesight," said Schweik in a surprised tone. "And you an engineer! Good Lord, man, what if they find out about that!"

"Schweik, I don't understand you. You know the one! I mean the Müller from the Heinrich-Zille-Strasse."

"Heinrich-Zille-Strasse? Where's that?" asked Schweik vaguely.

This was too much, this was ridiculous, declared the engineer. Every *child* knew the Heinrich-Zille-Strasse. You just had to take Line 17 and it took you there straight as an arrow—no changes. And right next to the streetcar stop lived the famous Müller.

"For once and for all, will you please get it into your thick head," said Schweik weighing each word, "that I don't know him. I don't know anyone called Müller, I have never known anyone called Müller, and what's more I've no wish to know anyone called Müller! Do you know who you remind me of? Of the shepherd Freydl from Budweis, a violent individual, who once asked me at four in the morning if I knew Ksisch. 'No!' said I. 'Of course!' said he. 'Certainly not!' said I. Whereupon he said, 'And Krnc? Then you must know *him!*' Krnc? I thought it over. And do you know what I said to him then? 'No. I'm more likely to know Ksisch.'"

Schweik fell silent and regarded the engineer penetratingly. Then he exclaimed, "That's exactly the way *you* seem to me, with all your questions."

This was a victory for Schweik. The engineer returned neither to the subject of Müller, nor to the

Heinrich-Zille-Strasse, the owner's wife, nor the Band-Aid. Instead, after a while, he mentioned that he had night duty, that unfortunately he had to leave in half an hour. He was genuinely sorry about that, and sloshed down four more beers to drown his sorrow.

No sooner had he left than another man approached Schweik's table. About forty; well-nourished and well-dressed, by GDR standards, with a receding hairline. He pointed to the unoccupied chair next to Schweik and asked if it was free.

"Just a moment ago," said Schweik. "An engineer has warmed it for you. He had night duty. I'm glad I'm not traveling in that train tonight. Take a seat, Comrade."

"Just for one glass," said the other, sitting down. "How's it going, Comrade?"

"Not as often as it used to."

Instead of the expected laughter, all Schweik got in return was a pair of raised eyebrows. Schweik was a sensitive soul and immediately felt the other's disapproval, so he did an about-face and said elegantly, "Excuse me. My name is Schweik, Comrade. I'm a colleague of that engineer—I also work for the railroad. Formerly I was a businessman. Animal trading. But I was glad to give that up. I was glad to sacrifice it to Communism. I live in Dresden—my apartment is right near here—but originally I came from Prague. And what do you do, Comrade?"

"I am the Party Secretary of the CSM, Comrade Schweik. My name is Gebhardt."

Schweik now gave further proof of his social polish, for without batting an eyelid he replied, "I'm awfully glad you joined me. This is an honor that I'm the first to appreciate. What will you have, Comrade Gebhardt? Shall I call the owner's wife? She's probably back in the kitchen right now, helping out the cook."

"Ah, so then she is here?"

"Yes."

Then he should call her, Gebhardt told Schweik. It was fortunate that she was here and not in town, he went on, for she was the object of his visit. It was an official visit. The owner's wife knew nothing about it as yet. But first of all, he wanted to drink his beer in peace.

One became three.

His mission was difficult, he explained. He rejected the high-handed methods of many of his colleagues. He wished to influence people by persuasion alone. But that always had to be thought out carefully beforehand.

When Comrade Gebhardt outlined his occupation in such high-sounding words, he was not exaggerating. This membership of the CSM justified his attitude; it commanded his complete devotion. The initials "CSM" stood for the "Central Administration of Socialist Morality." The GRD bristles with such "Central Administrations"—typical Socialist institutions which capitalism will never succeed in imitating.

Party Secretary Gebhardt was one of the most active functionaries of the CSM. But he was not only exceptionally active, he was telling the truth when he said that he exercised tact in carrying out his duties. "You see, Comrade Schweik," he said, "I entered this tavern here and sat down right away at your table. There are free tables here, of course—but no! A man like me must seek conversation, otherwise he is neglecting his duty. I can't talk to a free table, or persuade it, or influence its politics. But with you I can do so, Comrade Schweik. I asked you originally how it's going. And how did you answer me? With an obscenity. Don't forget, vile language and thinking are symptoms of Western decadence. Any one of my colleagues from the CSM would have thrown that at you right away, I assure you. But I reject high-handed methods, as I've already mentioned. So I thought to myself, 'First of all, have a decent conversation with this individual, without obscenities or *certain jokes*. That sets an example which is convincing.' In the meantime, now, that's just what has happened. We have told each other who we are; I inquired about the owner's wife; somehow or other, I don't remember how, we came to speak of the longing of all boys to become engineers. Fine. In any case, we have had a decent, clean conversation, worthy of two citizens of our workers' and peasants' State. A conversation without obscenities or *certain jokes*—and you must admit, Comrade Schweik, that our beer hasn't tasted any the less good. Am I right?"

"A hundred per cent!" Schweik assured him.

Party Secretary Gebhardt, visibly satisfied with his quick success, announced magnanimously that Schweik's next glass was on him. Then he said that of all the battles he was forced to fight, the most difficult was the battle against those vulgar, dirty jokes men tell when it gets late. And yet there was no end of *decent jokes* to tell.

To show his benefactor that he hadn't wasted his glass of beer on anyone unworthy of it, Schweik said, "You're absolutely right there, Comrade Gebhardt. I can tell you a good clean joke like that—none of that smut, but just the kind you like.

"Once upon a time there was a gourmet restaurant with nothing but foreign delicacies. They needed a temporary waitress there—for vacation time, understand —and the waitress in question came from a beer parlor to help out. Right on the first day she forgot where she was, and because she had an itch, she scratched—but unfortunately not her face, which would have been excusable, but the opposite end, if you follow me. This promptly disturbed a guest who was present—a gourmet. He called her over and said touchily, 'Tell me, Fräulein, do you have hemorrhoids?' 'If they're on the menu—yes,' she replied."

Party Secretary Gebhardt looked earnestly at Schweik and said that one could debate about the "decency" of this joke, but in any case it allowed him the opportunity to mention that in those perverse Western restaurants they ate much worse things than that. That's why there was no place for such restaurants in the Socialist camp. There followed a cutting little speech about nudity in Western films and magazines, and on television and posters. It was that kind of thing, exclaimed the Party Secretary enthusiastically, that had sealed the fate of Ancient Rome.

Over the sixth glass of beer he came to his senses again and asked whether Schweik felt man enough to change over to hard liquor, since he had an urge for a schnapps.

"What can I bring you?" asked the waitress.

"Vodka of course!" exclaimed Gebhardt spontaneously.

"Excellent," he said after the first gulp. "I'd rather have it than whisky any day, Comrade Schweik. Vodka tops whisky, there's no doubt about it. That's symbolic of the whole world situation."

But Schweik's world at the moment was the

"Traube," and he felt no desire to look beyond its horizon, so he said, "I quite agree, Comrade Secretary—but what was it you said you had to discuss with the owner's wife?"

Gebhardt lowered his voice, although no one else was listening, and chattered a lot of nonsense of the kind which is conceivable inside the Communist world —where admittedly it is by no means considered unusual. He said it had been reported to his office that the owner's wife was violating Socialist marriage ethics while her husband was in jail.

"And it's not for that you lock people up, I can imagine," answered Schweik with rectitude.

Party Secretary Gebhardt stared into his glass and then remarked that the whole thing wouldn't be so bad if it were only an isolated case. "But this, of all things," he cried indignantly.

Schweik understood very well what Gebhardt meant, and in order to convey his grasp of the matter, he said, "You have a national problem on your hands, not just an isolated case, Comrade, I see that. One need only consider how many people are in jail, and if only half the wives take the bulls by the horns, as it were— well, you can kiss your ethics good-by, I assure you! I can imagine that if no one puts a stop to it, one fine day our good old Dresden will have to be rechristened 'Sodom and Gomorrah.'"

Party Secretary Gebhardt had never met anyone— an outsider—who had shown so much sympathy for the tasks of the CSM in so short a time. Schweik's obscenity was forgotten altogether; Gebhardt's regard for Schweik got the upper hand.

"Comrade Schweik," he said with warmth, "I am

happy to have made your acquaintance. You are the kind of citizen who is all too rare in our Republic. You have the right approach. And in spite of that you're also a man of intelligence, that's the amazing thing. You can grasp a problem, analyze it at once. Bravo! I repeat: you are an intelligent, enlightened man, Comrade. Drink! Whatever you drink this evening is on me."

"I have been enlightened since my fifteenth year," said Schweik, flattered. "Listen. When I was fifteen, one Sunday at high mass the priest gave a sermon in which he said that it is the duty of Catholic adults to enlighten their children before it's too late. I was afraid that at fifteen it might already be too late and turned for help to the second cook, whom I used to help out every afternoon in the tavern—a much bigger one than this one—peeling potatoes and fetching water and so on. She was a good soul, about thirty-eight, I recall, just the right age for enlightening a person who stands on the threshold of adolescence. She used to look at me for a long time—dreamily, I'd describe it today—and she always used to slip me a little something. This gave me the idea that she might be the one to enlighten me—she was such a good dutiful soul; however, I realized I couldn't very well broach the subject in the kitchen. It's a ticklish one and I thought we'd better be alone. So on the very same evening following the sermon I sneaked into her room and waited for her. It was winter, she took her time, I was cold. What did I do? I lay down in her bed—with my clothes on, naturally, so it wouldn't look as if I was already enlightened. Just for a minute or two, I said to myself, to get warm; when I hear her coming up the stairs I'll crawl out again quick and she won't notice a thing. But then what happened? I fell asleep. It was so cold I even had my head under the blanket. Suddenly I woke up, it was dark, and I felt Anuschka—that's what we called her—getting into bed beside me. I began to shiver. 'Well how about that—a visitor. Who is it to-day?' she said when she noticed me. 'Is it Jaro?' I lay quiet as a mouse, saying nothing. 'Rudi?' she asked. No answer. 'Wenzel?' Still not a word from me. Jaro, Rudi, and Wenzel were waiters. There was another one too: Jan, an apprentice waiter, barely sixteen.

"After a minute Anuschka said, 'Then it must be Jan.' That restored my courage a bit. 'It's Bepperl,' I said at last, 'and I would very much like you to enlighten me, please, Fräulein Anuschka.' For seconds she didn't move, then she laughed softly and said that it wasn't as simple as that. 'First of all you have your pants on, Bepperl. And secondly, for that kind of enlightenment words fail me. In the newspaper you can read often enough what a difficult thing it is; how even professors often don't know where to start, much less a second cook. It would be different, Bepperl, if you'd be satisfied with a wordless enlightenment. Judging by the way you're shaking it's high time you had some.' 'Fräulein Anuschka,' I said, 'if it's all right with you, please en-lighten me without words. Only one thing: I beg of you, do hurry, Fräulein Anuschka.'

"So then she did, until six in the morning. Later I was staggered about this, considering that the sermon had actually nothing whatever to do with Anuschka, since she was a Protestant."

Schweik took a big gulp, to moisten his throat, which had grown dry from so much talking, and then said to Gebhardt, who had made no comment through-out Schweik's long recital, "So that's how they enlightened me at fifteen, Comrade. And how old were you?"

Gebhardt decided to ignore this question. He considered various possible answers, among which were that this story exemplified the normal conditions in a capitalist kitchen. And so he promptly replied that it was typical of the capitalist system to regard kitchen boys as fair game for immoral purposes. He did not cease lecturing Schweik on this topic until the owner's wife returned to the table once more to bring more vodka. Gebhardt followed her with attentive eyes.

Then Schweik attempted to get the conversation started again by asking whether it was an enjoyable task to protect Socialist marriage ethics.

"Not at all, Comrade Schweik. One often gets into dangerous situations oneself," replied Party Secretary Gebhardt, who had by now arrived happily at his sixth vodka. "Let's take today, for example. That woman radiates something. Don't you feel it?"

"I don't know. Actually I think she could fill the glasses more generously."

Gebhardt's eyes returned to his glass. He stared into it for some time before asking Schweik huskily, "Do you think I should arm myself against her feminine charms when I speak with her?"

On that score Schweik was well able to reassure him. "No," he replied, "you don't have to worry about that, Comrade. So far as she's concerned, there's no danger for you at all. You see, you're baldpated and I happen to know she hates bald heads. Once in my presence she said as much to the delivery man from the brewery, who had a bald pate just like yours, Comrade. He'd asked her whether she could ever feel any love for him, just for a quarter of an hour or so. She gave him the full treatment, I'm telling you. 'Sure!' she said. 'With your bald head staring at me the whole time.' And she refused to give in, even though the beer delivery man wasn't a bit dumb—for a beer delivery man—and even assured her he could arrange things so she wouldn't have his bald head staring at her from in front, but from behind."

Party Secretary Gebhardt ably demonstrated his great self-control by replying, "Is that so?"

"Is what so?"

"That individual's opinion about, about . . ."

He stuttered and wanted to say "about men without hair," but Schweik cut him short with the uninhibited term "bald heads."

"And how!" Schweik continued. "Apparently she knew that the beer deliverer was a Party member, and she even threatened to report him to his superiors if he tried that one again."

Gebhardt's self-control weathered even this test. He emptied his glass, stood up leisurely, tugged his necktie straight, and said calmly to Schweik, "You know what? I see no reason for wasting time with anyone who is so hopelessly primitive. Why should I lower myself for that female? She deserves high-handed methods. I'll send her one of my colleagues."

He tossed some paper money on the table, nodded good-by to the perplexed Schweik, and prepared to leave. Schweik sprang to life. He noticed at once that the sum Gebhardt had left was altogether inadequate. "Comrade!" he called out. "That won't even cover your bill!"

"You pay for yours yourself! There's no damned reason why I should."

After he had left, the owner's wife came to the table to ask what had been going on all of a sudden and why the gentleman had departed so abruptly.

"It was his bald head," Schweik answered scornfully. "Some people are frustrated by such things. Apparently he was insulted at the mere mention of the term in his presence, seeing as how he sports one himself. And then he leaves me sitting on the bill, when he was the one who egged me on. That's manners for you! So you'll have to bear at least part of it, Frau Gartner—through no fault of my own, that goes without saying."

THE METER-READERS

✳✳✳ There are better feelings than waking in the morning to the knowledge that you are broke. But that's not the half of it. This sensation is inevitably accompanied by further phenomena which contrive to increase the melancholy or depression of the newly awakened individual. Anyone who has had one too many knows on the morning after that there is more than one headache in store for him; in fact several invariably pound at him simultaneously. Schweik had long been acquainted with this unfathomable quirk of fate. Thus, on the morning after his session at the "Traube," which once again had cleaned him out financially, he approached his housekeeper with the question, "Now then, what nice surprise have you in store for me today, Frau Lehmann?"

Frau Lehmann first wished him an aggrieved "Good morning," and then added, "The vacuum cleaner is busted."

This gesture by the vacuum cleaner was perfectly justified, for it was already a year old and came from a People's Production Plant. Nor was this the only bad news Frau Lehmann had for Schweik. Besides that, she reported, the dog had bitten a retired old-maid teacher and her niece from the house next door.

"What did you do?" shouted Schweik at the dog.

The latter, an intelligent schnauzer which found this kind of examination a great bore, especially in the early morning, lay on the sofa in the kitchen. Schweik's yelling grated on his nerves. He was not ready to get up. He looked away from Schweik with studied nonchalance, lying on his front paws to go back to sleep.

"He doesn't have a bad conscience. He must have been provoked," Schweik concluded.

"It's the same old story," said Frau Lehmann. "As far as you're concerned the dog is never in the wrong. He must have been provoked," she repeated sarcastically, and raising her voice added, "He wasn't provoked by a living soul! On the contrary, the old lady took no liberties at all—no more than anyone does with a normal dog! But then your beast is no normal dog."

Frau Lehmann's feelings about Schweik's schnauzer were all too obvious; her expression "beast" removed all doubt. And then there was the possessive "yours," by which Frau Lehmann completely disassociated herself from the creature which rivaled her place in Schweik's heart.

To be fair, it must be conceded that Frau Lehmann's opinion of the schnauzer had not been arrived at without good cause. This was indeed no dog of ordinary character and behavior, but an eccentric animal which almost never acted as one could reasonably expect of a dog. Its unpleasant encounter with the teacher had demonstrated this fact yet again.

The teacher had been walking down the street, holding her little niece by the hand, when suddenly Schweik's schnauzer, crouching in the middle of the sidewalk, barred their way. "In order to pass by, they would have had to step down into the roadway—that's what uneducated ignoramuses did without a moment's hesitation. Not so the intelligent teacher. She, who knew about the souls of animals, said to her little niece, 'Now don't be afraid, child. It's perfectly simple: One must never show fear to an animal. When an animal sees that one isn't afraid of it, it recognizes that man is superior, stronger. That is the animal's instinct, which God gave it. That alone is the secret of trainers in the cages of the most ferocious wild animals, child. Haven't you been told that at school yet? No? Well, I must say, how times change! I always taught that right away to my first-graders. But what do they teach you today? The day that peculiar Karl Marx was born. Now come along, Angela, don't be afraid of this mutt! Shame on you, you're trembling. There's a principle at stake here: The sidewalk, according to definition, is meant for us people, not for dogs. You see, he's growling already, but that doesn't matter. You mustn't let that frighten you. I always told my children to control their fear. Think of growling as no more than the first sign of barking. And how does one of our oldest German proverbs go? Dogs that bark don't bite. Now pull yourself together—in a moment he'll give way.'

"The intelligent teacher and her little niece paid for this last and decisive error with bites on their calves."

"On their calves?" asked Schweik, interrupting his housekeeper's report of the tragedy.

"Yes."

A smile of relief appeared on Schweik's face as he said, "Then they have only themselves to blame, Frau Lehmann. I can refuse to pay. Any court will concede that, if necessary. The bite wounds on the calves prove that at the last moment the teacher undermined her own theory; she *turned in flight,* as they say in the history book about the Romans at Teutoburger Wald. That provokes any dog, not just the old Germanic tribes. What did I tell you! It even provokes ganders—maybe an experience you yourself had as a child in the country, Frau Lehmann?"

And Schweik continued to see the matter in this light as he sat in the train on his way to work and retold the story, not without frequent exhortations to his listeners to take his side. At work, Schweik, who once again had been away for some time, was greeted with surprising equanimity. His colleagues were already accustomed to these periodical absences of his. So although they were glad to see him, they didn't make a big fuss about it. With his boss, it was quite another matter. "You must go and see him," they said, before Schweik even had his work clothes on properly.

The boss's name was Kullrich. Actually his employees managed to get along with him relatively well. But so far as his relationship with Schweik was concerned, he was firmly convinced that the devil himself must have cursed him with the fellow. And with this association in mind it was only natural that in his meetings with Schweik the word "devil" came to his lips more often than any other expression.

Schweik greeted Kullrich politely as he entered the office, but the latter immediately started shouting. "Why the hell won't the devil rid us of you, Schweik?" he bawled.

"I beg your pardon?" asked Schweik uncomfortably.

"Why don't you go to the devil? And where the devil have you been again?" exclaimed Kullrich, who was profoundly affected when Schweik stood innocent as a lamb. In fact, Herr Kullrich still believed that this was a deceptive tactic of Schweik's. He still couldn't concede that Schweik's behavior might be prompted by honest conviction of his own innocence.

"It surprises me," said Schweik, visibly hurt, "that you should ask me that. That sounds exactly as if you suspected me of not playing straight, as they say, and trying to shirk my job. Of celebrating sick leave, for instance—or something like that. But I wouldn't dream of it, you ought to know me well enough by now to realize that I don't show illness," he concluded in an offended tone. And after a short pause he then added with dignity, "So where could I have been then? Behind bars, naturally."

Herr Kullrich's chair could hold him no longer. He lept up and shouted, "You don't say! I never would have guessed it! In jail! That's something entirely new for you. How in the devil's name could that happen?"

Kullrich's irony was wasted on Schweik. Even the most obvious derision didn't touch the unfeigned consciousness of his innocence. Schweik declared emphatically, "That could just as easily happen to you. It can happen to anyone. Haven't you ever heard of an error of justice? There are errors of justice just as there is sand on the seashore, I can assure you."

"And what did they mistakenly accuse you of this time?"

"I am supposed to have been mixed up in attempted murder and robbery," replied Schweik disdainfully.

"In attempted mur . . ." Herr Kullrich's words stuck in his throat and he sank back into his chair. "Don't tell me you've taken to that sort of thing, too, Schweik? Up till now at least you only had political offenses on your conscience, and let the devil take the hindmost."

Schweik rose to his full height. "What political offenses? Not a single one, as it happens. Or didn't it turn out every time that I'd been unjustly accused? But aside from that, let me draw your attention to a slip you just made, Comrade Kullrich. You said, 'Up till now at least you only had political offenses on your conscience.' That sounds exactly as if in your eyes attempted murder and robbery are worse than political offenses."

This turn of the conversation left Kullrich speechless. Dumbfounded, he stared at Schweik, while the latter continued to admonish him. "You should try to avoid such mistakes in the future. With anyone else but me it could have unpleasant consequences for you, and that wouldn't do any of us any good, because you're a boss we've had enough scuffles with to get to know your weaknesses and adapt ourselves to them, whereas with your successor, if it should come to that, as the old saying goes, there'd be the devil to pay. Therefore I must ask you on behalf of the whole freight yard to be more discreet in what you say."

It took several moments before Schweik's director found the strength to answer. "By Lucifer, Schweik,

what has gotten into you?" he finally snarled.
"What do you mean?"

"Who the devil do you think you're talking to?"

"I only have your best interests at heart," said
Schweik mildly.

"Not at all! I know you."

"But if a stranger were to hear you express yourself
so awkwardly, he might get the wrong impression. *That's*
the point!"

Schweik put such emphasis on the word "that," that
he convinced Herr Kullrich it would be a serious mistake in the face of Schweik's firm behest to deny his
error any longer. That could only make matters worse.
Naturally anxious to put a swift end to the situation,
Director Kullrich finally told Schweik with a sigh, "It's
hell with you, Schweik. I wanted to tell you today that
it's high time you . . ." He waved his hand in resignation and groaned, "Never mind. There's no point in
mentioning it after all. You can go to the devil!"

"While I'm at it," answered Schweik with his
habitual resoluteness, "before I leave I would also like to
ask you for an advance."

Herr Kullrich was tempted to start shouting, but
then waved his hand again with even greater resignation
than before, and gave his assent to a fifty-mark raise in
salary.

"What happened?" Schweik was asked by his fellow workers upon his return. "Did he try to eat you
alive?"

"Just at first. Afterward we came to an agreement."

"What happened?"

Schweik's account delved unsuspected depths. He

did not stop at what had actually happened and what his boss had actually said, but also described things which hadn't happened and hadn't been said. Schweik performed like some great mind reader, telling his colleagues not so much what Director Kullrich had said to him, but rather what he had *wanted* to say.

"All the dolt wanted to say," Schweik began amiably, "was that things can't go on like this. That I can't have a job and be away all the time, leaving the work to my fellow workers. Where can that lead? For years now it's been the same old story. How can our freight yard, he wanted to say, ever fulfill a higher quota? Compared to the other freight yards, we've got a bad reputation as it is. At long last apply for a transfer, Schweik. It doesn't matter where, Schweik. And what could I, Schweik, have said to him again for the umpteenth time, Gentlemen? I could only have begun again, as on so many previous occasions, to explain the individual cases and how each one came about: how I was never responsible for deserting my job; how on the contrary it had only been fate and not of my making—because my horoscope is the way it is, I suppose. How when I was still a young fellow on a trek through Slovakia I had a pretty, dark-haired gypsy read my hand, during which all of a sudden she felt faint and let my hand fall. For what she saw in my future was too much for her. And right away came the first sample of what was in store for me. The gypsy's fiancé was standing nearby and probably got the impression that she hadn't let my hand go from sheer horror, but out of anger because maybe I'd tickled it with my forefinger, which to gypsies is more than just suggestive. He followed me to the next village, where fortunately for me another pretty gypsy crossed our path with whom he could cool his jealousy. Whereupon I seized the opportunity to go on to the next village. If you'd experienced something like that, Comrade Kullrich, I would then have said, you'd know what tricks fortune can play."

The eight or ten railroad employees standing in a circle around Schweik listened and laughed. One said that Schweik could go ahead now and admit that the gypsy fiancé's assumption had been right. He was one of the younger ones; the oldest of the group had other things on his mind.

"Schweik," he said, before they broke up to return to their duties, "just keep up the good work. That way we'll get rid of that damned quota increase of theirs. Let the old man go ahead and dream. He'd be hot for an increase, I'm sure—but not us! Before we swallow that increase, we'll do your work three times over, Schweik. Or do any of you guys think differently?"

"No!" "What do you think!" "Of course not!" "What an idea!" resounded the answers simultaneously.

It is a satisfying feeling to be appreciated by one's fellows, and Schweik was by no means insensible to it. Then the usual work routine began. For Schweik, however, it was soon to be interrupted again by a call to the telephone. He didn't recognize the voice on the other end. "Who are you anyway?" he asked, when the other told him without preliminaries that he must speak with him this evening—preferably at Schweik's apartment again.

"Your meter-reader," replied the other.

"No kidding! I would never have guessed. Are you the first one who came to see me, or the second?"

"The second."

"Then you're not the nervous one. Fine, that suits me better. And what do you want to discuss with me?"

The telephone buzzed with reproach. "You don't imagine I can tell you on the telephone!" was the reply.

"Is it important?"

"Comrade! What else? Jokes and idle chatter aren't what we're here for."

"Well then, fine. I'll be home after seven. But don't come any earlier because my housekeeper won't know what to make of all this meter-reading."

He would be there at half-past seven on the dot, said the meter-reader.

What a couple of clowns! thought Schweik and hung up. Perhaps he thought instinctively in the plural, as if he sensed what was coming. In any case, instinct or no instinct, that same morning Schweik received a call from the nervous meter-reader. He must speak to Schweik immediately, he said.

"When?" Schweik asked. "This evening?"

"No, I have another engagement this evening. Couldn't you manage it earlier?"

They made a date for lunch in an hour. Meeting place: a little restaurant not far from the station.

The meter-reader greeted Schweik appreciatively. "Where were you hiding yourself last week? Not even your housekeeper knew where you were," he began.

Schweik related his misfortune in the Heinrich-Zille-Strasse. The meter-reader, puffing at a cigarette and sliding anxiously back and forth on his chair, listened attentively. When Schweik had finished he remarked that now he understood everything. The affair in the Heinrich-Zille-Strasse fell under the jurisdiction of the ordinary police, not the political police. But his organization was geared only to report on everything in the political division. Until today anyway. Schweik's affair was an object lesson to them. From now on they would have to keep a lookout for contacts with the regular police, so that in the future Schweik—or others like him—couldn't just disappear like the sausage from the sauerkraut.

Schweik let this chatter babble past his ears, without paying too much attention. In the meantime he was musing over the fact that it hadn't actually been necessary for him to squeeze an advance out of Herr Kullrich after all. The thought of the meter-readers' fees appeared so attractive to Schweik that he was still only listening with half an ear when the meter-reader finally turned practical and said, "But now to get down to our first assignment for you. You work at a freight yard. That's all to the good. As to the purely technical proceedings there, we have naturally been in the know for some time. For example: How many trains pass through daily? Where do they come from and where are they heading for? What's being freighted? Naturally we already have all the answers. But—how shall I express it —the human factor! That's where we still have gaps in our information, understand! We know how many people work at the freight yard. But what's the political climate? What do they think of Communism? What do they think of the West? In case of war, would they commit acts of sabotage for the NATO powers? And here's another question: How would they react if an American pilot was shot down and parachuted onto their yard? These are questions enough for you to clear up, Schweik."

The only thing Schweik gathered from all this was

that the Security Service of the GDR expected him to spy on his fellow workers. He smiled. "Sorry, Comrade," he said. "With us none of these things are in question. Perhaps in every other yard, for all I know— but not in ours!" Then he stood up and said with emphasis, raising his clenched fist toward Moscow in Communist greeting, "And in *this* my colleagues are unanimous. One hundred per cent!" he added. "One hundred per cent, I repeat. Tough luck for the American pilot who lands in *their* midst!"

"Really?" The meter-reader ran nervous fingers through his hair. "Aren't you seeing things too pessimistically?"

"Too pessimistically? For the American pilot? I couldn't see things pessimistically enough for him."

It was hope which inspired the meter-reader to say once more in spite of everything, "But perhaps you are mistaken after all. Camouflage is very popular these days. Sound them out individually. The best thing will be for you to offer them a drink."

"If I could, fine," Schweik quickly interposed. He had reached his goal. Without mincing words, he described his financial situation—naturally as if Herr Kullrich and his advance were nonexistent.

The meter-reader's reaction to this was swift. He said the matter was urgent, since things were hotting up for him. Sitting around here in public, where anyone could recognize him, was insane. The waiter had just brought the soup. But regardless of this, the nervous meter-reader stood up again and said, "Anything else? I don't think so. Once more: you must sound out each of your colleagues to make certain. What you find out, keep in your head. No notes now! Nothing in writing.

Next week, on Friday evening, we will meet again. Then you will make your first report. Don't forget the date. I'll come to your apartment."

"When did you say?" Schweik asked thoughtfully. "Friday evening of next week?"

"Yes. Does that conflict with anything else?"

Schweik nodded. "Yes it does. It's the day of our freight-yard workers' fancy-dress ball."

"Oh, a damfool mardi gras!" groaned the meter-reader. But then suddenly his face lit up and he cried, "No, wait a minute! It's not so damn silly, after all. On the contrary, it's a blessing in disguise! It'll be *the* opportunity for me to meet you inconspicuously, without exposing us to any danger. On neutral territory. Excellent! And *the* opportunity to sniff out your colleagues for myself and find out whether you're taking too pessimistic a view of them, Schweik. Or . . ." A depressing thought made him wince. "Or don't you guys wear fancy-dress?"

"Yes, we do, indeed we do—and what's more, to the point of being completely unrecognizable. That's always been a firm rule with us, so that the show's guaranteed to be a real humdinger."

"Splendid," said the meter-reader breathing a sigh of relief. "What will you go as?"

"Guess!"

"Good God!" exclaimed the meter-reader indignantly. "Just when things are hotting up for me, you start trying to beat about the bush. Come out with it, man, I've got to recognize you at the ball!"

"As Liz Taylor," Schweik replied nonchalantly, as if this was a mere detail. "I had a conductor on an interzone train bring me a mask and a wig from Munich.

Now all I need is a couple of soccer balls, which I'll borrow from our football team."

The meter-reader had scruples. "I hope the mask is unflattering. I mean you should bear in mind that she represents, as it were, the typical capitalist woman of the West. Otherwise you might get sniped at by the Party press. For your own sake, Schweik, keep that in mind."

Idiot, blaring idiot, thought Schweik and he asked the meter-reader if he was serious about coming to the fancy-dress party, and if he was, what he would wear— so that Schweik could recognize him too.

"You will recognize me when I whisper your code name in your ear: Usbek . . . Good-by."

If this rendezvous with the nervous meter-reader should have required greater interest and deeper thought on Schweik's part, then this was even more urgently true of his meeting with the calm meter-reader in the evening.

In spite of Schweik's warning not to come too early, the second meter-reader rang the doorbell at seven twenty-five and was admitted by Schweik himself, who accompanied him into the living room. He turned down Schweik's invitation to take a seat. He was in a hurry today, he said. Normally this meter-reader was not the one for such uncivilized haste. Just spit out the dough, pal, thought Schweik, then you can get lost again as fast as possible!

"This evening I have my weekly game of craps, Comrade Schweik—that's why," the newcomer explained.

No professional considerations prevail against a game of craps—that is a natural law which now governed the ensuing conversation between Schweik and the calm meter-reader, whose mind was no longer properly on his work at all. As for Schweik, he had nothing but money on his mind anyway.

"I've brought you your first commission, Comrade Schweik," said the meter-reader, still standing.

"Second," Schweik corrected him.

"What do you mean, 'second'?"

"Your colleague spoke to me earlier this afternoon."

"What colleague?"

"The same one who beat you to it the first time too. I don't know what his name is. You guys never introduce yourselves. But that's understandable, in your particular line of business."

The meter-reader started complaining. That was typical of his miserable setup, he said. When would those self-important bureaucrats in their big stuffed armchairs start coordinating their poor tormented outside workers? Probably never! A puff on his cigarette restored some of his usual calmness. Also, he was suddenly reminded of his evening's craps. "Well," he concluded, "that sort of thing isn't my affair. Listen carefully, I'm in a hurry, as I've already told you. You will cover your place of employment . . ."

"I've already been assigned to that this afternoon," interposed Schweik.

"We are interested in your colleagues' convictions," said the meter-reader, ignoring him. "Do they really believe in the Socialist camp? What do they think of the West? If there was an imperialist attack on the peace-loving Socialist nations, who could be expected to perform acts of sabotage to the advantage of the West? Or what would . . ."

"Don't bother to go on," said Schweik in the midst of this familiar catalogue which, aside from some difference in diction, was little other than a carbon copy of the nervous meter-reader's. "Really, now, save yourself the trouble. All that's necessary is for you to pay my expenses."

"Money?"

"Yes, that's it. So I can treat my colleagues to a glass of beer, when I sound them out, because that's always the best way of going about things."

The meter-reader briefly considered this attack on his expense funds. "All right, that's perfectly true," he said. "Here, will this do for the time being?"

It was a hundred marks. "It would do," said Schweik magnanimously, accustomed to both meter-readers' open-handedness. There was no question of his going into ecstasies about it, of planting kisses of gratitude on crinkly hundred-mark notes. After pocketing the money, he said, "I'm afraid I can't promise you very much, Comrade. Up till now my colleagues haven't been guilty of the smallest offense."

"Is that so? And the missing quota increase?"

Schweik, wincing, groaned. Here was something new after all. "What quota increase?" he asked.

"At your freight yard." The meter-reader saw his evening of craps, which had been approaching rapidly, float out of reach again for minutes. He was annoyed. "Didn't that idiot tell you that this afternoon? That's a fine way of doing things—forget the most important item of all! Not even mention the point of everything. Good Lord! I'd like to meet that fellow. Dammit, I'll have to explain it after all.

"There's something rotten in your freight yard.

Less gets done there than in other places. And there's only one reason for that: reactionary thinking among some of you, maybe of a group. Your yard has never managed a real quota increase yet. Why not? Who's responsible? That's what we want to hear from you, Schweik. And that fellow this afternoon didn't mention it? A real pro, I must say. Why are you looking at me like that, Comrade?"

Schweik could only say that he was looking the way he always looked when he happened to be looking at someone.

"When are you going to meet the fellow again, Comrade Schweik?"

"Next Friday evening."

"Here at your apartment?"

"No."

"Where, then?"

Schweik told everything. And the meter-reader, when he had heard it, had a brilliant idea how to spoil the other's hoped-for advantage in personally feeling out Schweik's fellow workers.

"I'm coming, too. Then you can show me the guy, Comrade Schweik."

"How will I be able to recognize you?"

"I will make myself known by means of your code name: Texan."

That night Schweik dreamed of an unfortunate little dog that kept biting its own tail, while its master, a gigantic damned meter-reader, looked on and encouraged him:

"Seek quota increase, Schweik! Seek quota increase!"

At the Abortionist's

✳ ✳ ✳ Next day Frau Lehmann did her
weekly stint of ironing. As always when ironing, a task
she hated, she was not in the best of moods. This antip-
athy of hers derived from certain accidents which had
befallen her with nagging regularity. For instance, often
she would take a quick peek in the oven, leaving the
iron meanwhile on some garment or other and only
being reminded of it again by the smell of burning cloth.
This time, however, she had been ironing for four or
five hours already without any such mishap, having
taken the precaution of completely shutting down all
activity in or on the stove.

It's the easiest thing in the world, she thought to
herself, and now nothing can go wrong. She glanced at
the clock. Five to six. She was in the midst of ironing a
pair of Schweik's shorts. Increasing the loving pressure
with which she wielded the iron, she murmured happily
to herself. "He'll be here soon," she said. "Perhaps I
should fetch a couple of fresh rolls for his supper?"

Then the doorbell rang.

Frau Lehmann never let it ring more than once, if only out of curiosity.

Waiting to be let in was an individual who immediately aroused Frau Lehmann's dislike for three reasons: first of all, because she had red fingernails; second, because she was thirty years younger; and third, because she asked for Schweik.

"What do you want with Herr Schweik?" asked Frau Lehmann abruptly.

That's none of the old biddy's business, thought the other, and said: "He knows what it's about. Is he home?"

"He's still at work. Who are you anyway?"

"Excuse me. My name is Ritter. Luise Ritter. Herr Schweik knows me. And he is also expecting me."

"He *knows* you? And is *expecting* you?"

Both remarks sounded very reproachful, and Frau Lehmann was now fully determined, deep within herself, not to let this individual, "individual" in quotation marks, into the apartment.

"Could I wait for him?" asked the visitor. "It's already six o'clock, and he must come home soon. Or does he work late?"

"That's never certain with him. He often volunteers to fill a quota increase. I'm afraid I can't tell you anything."

The visitor was about to reply that she wished to wait in any case, but suddenly she said something entirely different: "Don't I smell something burning?"

"Good Lord! My iron!" shouted Frau Lehmann in horror and dashed into the living room, followed by the determined visitor, who seized this opportunity to get into the apartment. So now she was inside, and Frau

Lehmann would have liked to swat her in the face with Schweik's shorts, which she had snatched from under the iron, as the shameless individual even had the nerve to ask whether she might sit down.

No answer. Minutes of silence, broken only by the rustling of the ironing. On the wall hung a picture of a fire-spouting volcano with a stream in the foreground. "Is that the Elbe?" asked the stranger, in order to make conversation, since she felt that it didn't make a good impression to go on sitting there as if she were deaf and dumb.

Frau Lehmann, in considering what this individual could want from Schweik, had concluded that it was perfectly clear. What? Why, what all women want from a man: himself! And the younger they are, the more shamelessly they go about it these days. That would just fit that individual there!

So the question whether the stream in front of the volcano was the Elbe was shoved aside by Frau Lehmann, who said: "Fräulein, it's better that you should leave now and not detain me any longer. Who knows when Herr Schweik will be here? Sometimes he doesn't get home until midnight."

"Nevertheless I would like to wait."

This was said so firmly that Frau Lehmann went a step further in her thoughts: namely, that no one could be so shameless but a woman who already had some claim on the man in question, not one who was just setting her traps and trying to get a claim. But all is not yet lost, thought Frau Lehmann feverishly. For me all would be lost only if . . .

Arrived at this point, Frau Lehmann dashed up to

Fräulein Ritter and asked her point-blank: "You're expecting a baby?"

"Yes," admitted Fräulein Ritter, caught completely off guard.

So! Frau Lehmann staggered back, clutching at her heart, which gave a sudden sharp stab, and groaned that if that wasn't too much, she'd like to know what was. Then she began to cry, and just as Fräulein Ritter was about to say that she couldn't understand Frau Lehmann's tears, that there must be some misunderstanding here—just then they heard Schweik's key in the door.

Schweik was very surprised to see Fräulein Ritter and didn't even notice the tears of his housekeeper, who left without a word and retired to the kitchen, for it was clear as day that she no longer wished to be in the same room with two such people.

Fräulein Ritter greeted Schweik and said that Commissioner Pike also sent his best wishes. Hereupon she presented Schweik with a well-wrapped, longish, narrow package, which did not reveal what it contained, since it was wrapped in thick brown paper.

"For me?" said Schweik, in an astonished tone.

Fräulein Ritter answered that it was.

"What's inside?" Schweik asked.

Luise Ritter's answer recalled long-forgotten objects to Schweik's mind.

"Your umbrellas, Herr Schweik. Commissioner Pike forgot to hand them over to you when you were released."

"How is he?" Schweik inquired, rather touched at the sight of the package; indeed the umbrellas seemed fated to remain stubbornly at his side. "How's his nose?"

As he opened the package, Fräulein Ritter told him that Pike, thanks to his nose, had already come near losing his job altogether, or at least to being transferred to the traffic division. One of his superiors had once expressed the view that a nose like his was much too revealing in cross-examinations. For a clever and effective cross-examination, what was needed was a poker face and not a nose which shone like a signal. But fortunately for Pike, that superior had been unmasked just in time—after ten glasses of beer at an office party—as an undercover Titoist. With that, all his opinions were refuted—even the unpolitical ones such as those concerning the nose of a subordinate.

"Your Commissioner Pike's guardian angel did a cool job there, Fräulein Ritter," commented Schweik. "He was lucky the Titoist's unmasking came about at just the right time. Nowadays unmasking a Titoist like that wouldn't help him at all. But I shouldn't talk, I've had the same thing happen to me. Titoism was a real blessing for me too, back in the days when it was still a crime. Remember? At one time they had just condemned me, in spite of my innocence, to twelve years in the penitentiary. That could rightly be compared, I guess, to a transfer to the traffic division.

"But enough of that, it's all over and done with. Thank you for your trouble in bringing the umbrellas back in person, Fräulein Ritter. It wasn't necessary. And give Commissioner Pike my best salutations."

In plain language, what his last remark meant was: "Get lost, sweetie. Can't you see I'm hungry?" In this frame of mind Schweik was not the least bit impressed when Fräulein Ritter, instead of departing, said, "And now, Herr Schweik, to discuss the details."

"Discuss what?"

"Who is going to help me, of course," replied Luise Ritter, raising her eyes trustingly to Schweik. "You know."

For a moment Schweik looked nonplussed, then he suddenly struck his forehead with the flat of his hand and exclaimed, "Ah, now I remember! *That's* what you're after! But Fräulein Ritter, what has that to do with me?"

A short pause ensued, during which Luise Ritter prepared herself for battle. "You must be joking, Herr Schweik," she began in a voice gaining in firmness.

"Not that I know of, Fräulein Ritter."

"Herr Schweik, do I take it that you wish to forget the deal, as you yourself called it, between the two of us?"

"I forget nothing," said Schweik with emphasis. "But what kind of a 'deal' is that? In a deal, Fräulein Ritter, both parties have to do their fair share. Years ago, before Communism, I was a businessman myself. So I'm sure you won't want to tell me what a deal is."

"But I've already done my share!" exclaimed Luise Ritter in distress.

Frau Lehmann, her ear glued to the keyhole, was filled with exultation, because this female had run into resistance from Schweik instead of meeting with love or agreement, as Frau Lehmann had feared.

"Fräulein Ritter," Schweik retorted, "that's about the limit, I must say. Do you expect me to sit by and say nothing while you try to make an idiot of me?"

"I don't understand you, Herr Schweik," said Luise Ritter in a tremulous voice. "Who says I want to make an idiot of you?"

"You do, of course!"

"Why me?"

"You expect me to help you?"

"Yes!"

"In other words you expect me to give you the address you want, regardless of whether or not I'm landed in jail again—and, what's more, just when I've been released?"

"That was through *my* help, Herr Schweik! That's the fact of the matter. That's why you must fulfill your side of the bargain."

Schweik, on the contrary, knew perfectly well what had secured his release. "Fräulein Ritter," he said sternly, "don't waste any more of your time. It's no use trying to make me believe I owe you something. Let's stop all this nonsense, I'm hungry. Apparently your boss didn't show you Sergeant Hornig's report."

"Why should he have shown it to me?"

"Because it is his report that I have to thank for my release," said Schweik with complete conviction. "It was not in order."

"Whaaat?" shouted Luise Ritter hysterically. "Are you serious?"

Why shouldn't he be serious, asked Schweik with dignity. Commissioner Pike himself had brought his attention to the errors in the report.

"But that nitwit was just putting on an act, Herr Schweik!"

"Well, fancy that! Now don't try to pull that one on me, Fräulein. Not on me, of all people. How often do I have to tell you my housekeeper is trying to keep my supper warm?"

Luise Ritter had reached the end of her tether. Tears streamed down her face as she exclaimed, beside herself, "You wretch, you! But I don't give a damn now! Just as I forced the Commissioner to release you, I'll force him to arrest you again this very evening. Then you'll be sorry."

A new situation.

"Wait!" said Schweik to Luise Ritter, who was already heading for the door. "What's the hurry?"

"I'm going straight to Commissioner Pike."

"What do want to see him about?"

"I've just told you."

"There's no need for any hurry! Wouldn't you like to have supper with me first? I'm inviting you. We'll share whatever my housekeeper has prepared for me."

A new situation, thought Fräulein Ritter to herself, and she sat down again.

There's no need to describe how the two of them reached agreement during supper. "Then the best thing will be for me to introduce you to my *friend* right away this evening," Schweik said in conclusion. "When you've met him, you can decide between yourselves when to begin . . . treatment."

"That would be nice, Herr Schweik."

"You won't need me any more, after I've introduced you." added Schweik rising from the table.

Schweik's decisive, abrupt way of concluding the matter seemed sharply to remind his protégée of the ordeal which awaited her, and in a typically feminine way she seemed suddenly to shrink back at the very thought of it. She asked Schweik if the man was reliable.

"That's in his own interests," answered Schweik. "Of course he is. He won't mention it to a soul."

She hadn't meant that, she said. She was wondering about his professional ability. Schweik assured her that in that respect the man's very name was a guarantee of quality: among the initiated he was known as "Paracelsus." "And he," Schweik explained, "was a very famous doctor. Perhaps the most famous of all—aside from Dr. Eisenbart.* They named paratyphoid fever, which he discovered, after him."

Luise Ritter laughed dutifully, for she thought Schweik was attempting to cheer her up with jokes and calm her anxiety.

In the street they spoke softly, so that no one could have a chance of overhearing them. They covered the distance on foot, although it was quite far and the way led beyond the thickly settled suburban area where Schweik lived. Schweik's comments on the way were aimed to prepare his protégée for Paracelsus. He was a man one must not be scared of. He was vulgar and coarse —but as anyone knows, medical science seems to infect all its disciples with these characteristics.

After this priming, Luise Ritter could hardly accuse Schweik of painting her savior in too rosy colors. Schweik stopped before the garden gate of a modest-sized house and declared, "This is where he lives. I hope he's home. I don't see any light, but that doesn't mean anything, because he always keeps the shutters closed. That's so no one can see what he's doing inside. Take notice of the street and house number, Fräulein, so you can find your way alone next time."

Schweik's hopes were not disappointed. The door opened. The old tonsorial surgeon called Paracelsus, who was described earlier as usually being in a condition

---

* A seventeenth-century doctor and peddler of quack remedies, immortalized in a song: "My name is Doctor Eisenbart, and healing is my special art."

which made him see everything double (due to which he often relieved his patients of two teeth instead of one), was indeed at home. How big and heavy the real Paracelsus was does not concern us here. The Paracelsus we are talking about measured almost six feet and weighed over two hundred pounds. In other words, he was a very big, heavy man with big, heavy hands. He had a red face, from which a fleshy blue nose protruded. Blue noses can be a sign of severe winter; but our Paracelsus' nose was blue even in the hottest weather. It is of course common knowledge how such noses as his derive their coloring, and Paracelsus was no exception to the rule. He had been born and raised in East Prussia, the child of a fanatical teetotaler. An old law observes that one extreme is always followed by the other, and such was the case with the son of Paracelsus senior.

It was in a godforsaken hamlet between the lakes of Masuria that the little boy who was to earn the illustrious name of Paracelsus grew up. His father sent him as apprentice to a blacksmith. Here the boy learned to treat ill-conditioned horses' hoofs. Little did anyone suspect that this was to be the cornerstone of what would become a general medical practice. One day a tramp who had once enjoyed some higher education— the victim of a hopeless love affair in his youth—on passing through the hamlet fell sick, and chanced upon the young blacksmith. When the latter cured him of his high fever with cold footbaths, he rewarded him with the title "Paracelsus." This name stuck; it even followed its bearer to Dresden, where he had been driven after World War II.

"Paracelsus," said Schweik in greeting at the door.

"Hello. You can let us in without the code word. After all, you know me. I have a patient for you."

Paracelsus had only downed a mere half-bottle of home-distilled schnapps, and his sobriety seemed to be weighing heavily on him. Silent, ill-humored, without a word of greeting to his guests, he led them into a sparsely furnished room. On the table stood the half-empty bottle of schnapps. No glass. Not until all three were seated did it seem that after all Paracelsus hadn't lost his voice. "Schweik," he began with sudden verve, "here you are at last. I've been dying to give you a piece of my mind. You ass, what could have induced you to send me that . . . whatchamacallit . . . anyway?"

"Who?"

"That Zo . . . Zombie, or something like that."

"Zollner?" asked Schweik.

"That's the one."

"Why not, Paracelsus?"

"Why not? Are you nuts or something? . . . A State attorney! I shit on State attorneys, and don't forget it!"

Schweik sighed and asked, "Wasn't the idiot ashamed?"

"Ashamed of what?"

"Of letting you know he's a State attorney?"

"Nope."

Schweik sighed again. "How odd some people are! If I were a State attorney I wouldn't tell my own mother, for fear she'd disown me."

Paracelsus, temporarily cheered by this remark, declared, "But I took good care of him, I'm telling you! He won't come back a second time."

He took a hearty swig from the bottle, which helped

snap him out of his mood, and then he continued, "What's the trouble with this chick here? Don't tell me, Schweik, that someone's been having fun and games with her!"

"That's exactly what I have to tell you," replied Schweik with a smile.

"Then the two of you can just get lost again."

"That doesn't sound like the Paracelsus I know!" cried Schweik. "What's come over you?"

What Schweik didn't know was this. Just recently, Paracelsus had trouble with a female law student. When her treatment was over she had said, "You're getting no fee out of me. Go ahead and see if you can do so by legal means. As a law student, however, I can tell for a fact that you'd be wasting your time."

Thereupon Paracelsus had sworn, over two bottles of raspberry schnapps, never to touch another of those "damned, shitty females." He sat and drummed his fingers on the table. "Is the kid yours, Schweik?" he asked.

"Yes," said Schweik, the old tactician, quickly. He saw a chance of arousing his friend's sympathy.

Meanwhile Luise Ritter struggled to maintain her self-control. The two men's dialogue, however, was more than she could bear. At Schweik's "Yes" to Paracelsus' question whether Schweik was the child's father, she began to cry. Unfortunately that was a great mistake. Fräulein Ritter's tears reminded Paracelsus all too vividly of the law student. She had sat there just the same way, and had cried just as pitifully—before the operation, naturally! And afterward? . . . No! They can go to hell, every one of them once and for all, thought Paracelsus.

"What about it?" asked Schweik.

Paracelsus told him what he had just been thinking. Schweik sensed that he had suffered a reverse. All he could do now was to begin again at the beginning. "Paracelsus," he asked, "am I or am I not your friend?"

"Cut it out! You sent a State attorney to my house!"

"To hell with the State attorney!" said Schweik, getting heated. "We're talking now about this girl here. She's ready to jump in the Elbe."

"So what?"

"Are you serious?"

"Absolutely."

Poor Fräulein Ritter sobbed audibly and was momentarily on the point of dashing off and actually jumping into the Elbe. Schweik weighed up the pros and cons. What shall I tell him? The truth? That I'm not the father. That it's her boss, a married man? That he half-raped her? That he would have thrown her out if she'd stayed? That that's the way it is with all bosses? Useless. It wouldn't get him anywhere today with that bastard, said Schweik to himself, his eyes resting on Paracelsus in disappointment, as the latter once applied himself to his bottle, unmoved. Schweik was furious. Wait, he thought, I'll take care of you. I'll get things cracking in spite of the odds.

"Paracelsus," he began for the last time, "then you'll have to hear the truth. I'm not the father . . ."

"Obviously!"

"How come?" Schweik at once snapped back at him, since Paracelsus had used an insulting tone.

Sure enough, Paracelsus now laughed. "Because you couldn't have been, even if you had wanted to, you old gelding," he said mockingly. "Do you think I believed you for a second?"

Schweik felt very tempted to reply that no one should judge others by his own failings, and go strutting about like a young pasha; but he well knew how to restrain himself in front of a lady. "Enough of that," he said with dignity. "We can talk about that when we're alone, and you'll be amazed by what I have to tell you on that score. But not today. Today you've got to help this girl, dammit," said Schweik, now quite upset. "Don't make me mad—she didn't get pregnant voluntarily."

"Oho!"

"She was raped."

"Aha!"

" 'Oho, aha,' what's that supposed to mean? She was raped, get it?" snapped Schweik.

"Raped? Mishandled by her boss, you mean," jeered Paracelsus. "The same old story. I know it by heart. Nine out of ten give me that malarkey. The boss would have thrown them out, obviously, they wail. When all the time they've climbed into his bed just so he won't bawl them out. That's what's at the bottom of it, Schweik . . . Now just leave me alone."

Schweik gave Paracelsus a reproachful glance. "Who says she was raped by her boss?" he asked.

"You mean to say it was someone else?"

"Yes."

"Not her boss?"

"No."

"Just normally raped, according to the penal code —outdoors, so to speak?"

"That's right."

Paracelsus laughed and grabbed the bottle of schnapps. "Tell that to your grandmother, Schweik. No one has to resort to that anymore. Who rapes nowadays?"

Schweik's answer struck home. "Don't ask stupid questions! Haven't you ever heard of the Red Army?" he said vehemently.

"Damn!" Paracelsus sat up with a jolt. "That's quite another matter. Why didn't you tell me that right away?"

Schweik pointed at Luise Ritter, who at this turn of the conversation had even stopped weeping. "She asked me to respect her shame. She couldn't bear it, she said, if she was to have the kid after all and people find out that it's half-Russian."

The gynecologist Paracelsus gave Fräulein Ritter a friendly glance. The abortionist in him had come alive again and he suddenly smiled at her. Nevertheless Schweik, unnecessarily as it now happened, felt bound to press home her claim to sympathy. "Now do you understand her situation, Paracelsus? Many girls," he added with fervor, "have been in her shoes. They can't go to a health service and ask to be operated on in a clinic. When they explain what's happened, they're always reprimanded for slandering the Red Army."

To which Paracelsus only cried out again, "Why didn't you tell me this right away? . . . Those damned Russians!" he suddenly shouted. "I'm an old East Prussian! I'll show them! . . . How many months gone is it, honey?"

He gathered from her answer that they were not pressed for time. "Very well then," he said decisively. "Come back week after next, on Saturday night. Then you can rest here on Sunday, if that should be necessary.

Bring two-hundred marks with you. Even an old East Prussian has to live."

Some months later Schweik ran into Fräulein Ritter by chance, outside a movie theater. Naturally he wanted to know how everything had gone. Fräulein Ritter began to tremble and turned pale. "What's the matter?" asked Schweik in alarm.

"It was frightful," she groaned. "I don't know how I stood it. And in the end he wanted twice as much for it."

"Why was that?"

"Because I would have had twins, he claimed. It was an odd thing, he said, but for some reason *everyone* always came to him with twins."

* * * Schweik and Frau Lehmann had new roles: he as nurse, she as patient. Frau Lehmann had a fever, a high temperature, a devilish sore throat, no appetite, and a healthy desire to take Schweik to task. "Satan loves his children," she said—a pious saying she had learned to cherish in Schweik's service. "One person runs riot and doesn't catch a thing; the other takes good care of herself but goes down with a temperature of 104. That's what I call divine justice!"

Schweik, at his housekeeper's request, had warmed up some camomile tea in the kitchen, and now entered Frau Lehmann's bedroom with a big teapot, just in time for yet another lecture from her. "Won't you ever change the record, Frau Lehmann?" he said with a sigh. "You've served up the same old story ever since I got back from the 'Traube.'"

"You were out until two in the morning again!"

"The drinks were on someone else," said Schweik defensively.

Only a wife or someone who aspires to be one can appreciate this line of argument.

"Who was it this time? I must say I'd be ashamed to take advantage of a drunken man like that, Herr Schweik."

Schweik finally placed the teapot, which was burning his fingers, on the bedside table, and declared that the man in question had not been intoxicated, nor had he been in need of special consideration. He was—this took the wind out of even Frau Lehmann's contradictory spirit—only a visitor to Dresden.

"Where's he from?" asked Frau Lehmann, with a sudden presentiment as to what Schweik's answer would be.

"From West Germany. From Karlsruhe."

"Well, in that case you couldn't have drunk him into the poorhouse," said Frau Lehmann grudgingly. "With ten West German marks—changed on the Black Market—he could have treated everybody in the place."

He spent a bit more than that, said Schweik laughing. But the fellow had been more than willing to do so; he had considered it his political duty.

Frau Lehmann's mounting curiosity was so strong it even made her forget her sore throat. Everything that comes from the West, even if it's only shoelaces, always arouses keen interest in the East. Most of all, people. Frau Lehmann now inquired about the man's profession.

"He's a gardener," answered Schweik.

"Independent?"

"No. He works only for the City Park Service in Karlsruhe."

Schweik felt a sudden slight pang of remorse. Too late he now noticed the subversive note struck by his use of the word "only." Fortunately, however, Frau Lehmann was less observant and continued, "And why did he consider it his *political duty* to fill you with beer?"

Schweik took a seat, indicating that Frau Lehmann was in for another long recital. "That," he said, having made himself comfortable, "only came out in the course of the evening. At first he sat all alone in the corner, and his misfortune—if you can call his standing drinks all around a misfortune—was that he was reading the newspaper. It was a day-old copy of *New Germany*. We didn't know who he was—but obviously he was someone special, because no one here could have afforded his suit and shoes except a National Prize winner or high Party functionary who could do his shopping in West Berlin. 'Just look at the bastard!' my colleague Schlund kept repeating at the regulars' table, before we found out he was a gardener from Karlsruhe. We didn't discover that until just before seven. He had been getting more and more nervous and leafing excitedly through his newspaper. Finally he threw it on the table and got up, came over to us and asked if we'd allow him to join us—he came from Karlsruhe and was no enemy of peace. We were delighted, fingered the material of his suit, and then my colleague Schlund, who was especially anxious to make up for his previous remarks, asked him in a friendly way how he hit upon that bit about the enemy of peace.

"Then the gardener started talking about the paper, *New Germany*, saying that that was all he'd read about the West Germans. In eight pages alone, there were a dozen articles and news reports directed against West Germany. Sixty-four times—he had counted them—the expression 'enemy of peace' had recurred, and there were others in a similar vein. But then interspersed regularly between them, was this recommendation: 'Germans to the conference table!' or 'East and West Germans must solve their problems together.'

"Now we were supposed to explain how that made sense. After all, he was only a gardener. 'Comrade,' I wanted to explain to him, 'that's dialectics. What were Lenin's words? Essentially, dialectics is the investigation of the contradictions in the nature of things themselves.' As I say, I wanted to explain to him. But Schlund beat me to it with a simpler explanation, although actually it was more of a suggestion. 'Do what we do, Comrade,' he said, 'forget all that crap!' And when I interrupted, asking him to keep the conversation on a decent level, he told me to go to hell. With that kind of remark it's easy to silence an educated person, so I let him talk.

"Then we asked the gardener whether he'd counted up any other expressions. Yes, he said, and he gave us the results: 'warmongers,' twenty-one times; 'militants,' the same number; while 'fascists' and 'Nazis' each came up forty times. We checked out these figures and found them correct. That surprised some of us, and we told him we don't notice this kind of thing any longer in the newspaper."

"*If* we read it, Herr Schweik," interrupted the incorrigible Frau Lehmann.

"I *do* read it, Frau Lehmann, you know that! I neglected to read it on one occasion only. That was the day of the 20th Party Congress in Moscow, and you are aware what unpleasantness that caused me."

Frau Lehmann sensed that she was in danger of being sidetracked from the original topic of conversation. She said she still didn't understand why the gardener from Karlsruhe had considered it his political duty to treat them to free beer.

"Right," said Schweik, "we mustn't forget that. Well, he was so annoyed by the incessant enemies of peace, warmongers, militarists, and fascists—of which he as a West German was part and parcel—that he wanted to square the issue, to prove that he at least is a *friend* of peace like us. In the course of the evening we encouraged him to other expressions in *New Germany*, whereupon he gave us further examples: 'reactionary,' ten times, then 'capitalist slave,' 'provocationist,' 'anachronist,' and even 'obstructor of progress,' so that the whole regulars' table became more and more enthused about *New Germany*.

"With every fresh round the gardener ordered, Schlund solemnly declared his absolution from another accusation in the newspaper. He said his authority in such questions came from his position as acting leader of the Workers' Combat Group. Then the gardener asked several times to be nominated a member of the group . . ."

"And you told me the man wasn't drunk," said Frau Lehmann, once more interrupting.

"He wasn't, Frau Lehmann! Not even at the very end. At one in the morning he could still calculate exactly how he's going to die in nine and a half months. We laughed and didn't believe him, but then he told us that he'd been to see the doctor, and that the doctor found sugar in his urine, so much that he had said, 'My dear man, if you don't stop drinking beer, you have only a year to live.' The checkup took place two and a half months ago, which leaves the gardener only nine and a half months more, Frau Lehmann. If he'd been drunk, he couldn't have calculated that so precisely for us."

Suddenly the doorbell rang. Frau Lehmann asked Schweik to answer it, adding, "That'll be Frau Hauser bringing back my new broom, the one from my cousin in Coblenz."

"It could be someone else," rejoined Schweik smiling, after a glance at the clock.

"Who?"

"The gardener."

"Noooo!" cried Frau Lehmann with all the strength she could muster, despite her infected throat.

Schweik was not to be put out by this reaction. "He promised to visit me," he said smiling. "I asked him to, so that he doesn't go home with the wrong political impression, which he might well have gotten in the 'Traube.' I'll invite our Party agent Wegner up, so that together we can give him a better one."

Frau Lehmann was panic-stricken. She sat up in bed shouting, "Don't you two dare come into my room! I feel ill enough already. You can tell him anything you want in the kitchen."

Wegner, the Party agent, was alone in his apartment. His wife had taken the children for a haircut. Wegner leafed through the records of the HAS, or House Association. He was preparing an excerpt which he needed for lodging a complaint with the Buildings Administration of the CHA.* Since he was alone in his apartment as he wrote, no one was able to overhear the interesting, unarticulated sounds he produced. Comrade Wegner, in short, was in an hour of trial when Schweik appeared and informed him why he had come. Perhaps this was the reason Wegner did not give a very good

* CHA = Community Housing Authority.

showing in the conversation later in Schweik's kitchen, with the gardener from Karlsruhe.

Schweik's expectation that the "rich uncle" from West Germany would naturally bring something to drink had been fulfilled. When the gardener and Wegner had been introduced, Schweik pressed the former, saying, "Bravo, my friend! The rules of etiquette are more important to you than a doctor's opinion. Not everyone would be so dependable."

Wegner then asked the gardener whether the West German Supreme Court, which had passed such shameful judgments on West German Communists, still resided in Karlsruhe. The gardener answered in the affirmative.

"Have you already demonstrated against it?" asked Wegner. "Or at least formed a resolution?"

"No."

"When do you want to begin?"

"Who do you mean by 'you'?"

"You and your organization."

"I don't belong to any organization. Organizations can go to hell, that's the way I feel, if you don't mind my saying so," declared the gardener, who had already reached his usual state of agreeable intoxication. "The only one I belong to is a betting association for the lottery. Not bad, I tell you. We always win a little chicken feed. Do you have a lottery here?"

Since Comrade Wegner seemed temporarily unable to reply, Schweik helped him out. "We used to despise the lottery as a form of Western decadence," said Schweik. "But that was a mistake, just like Stalinism, which I'm sure you've heard about. About a year ago we realized that the money the State makes on the lottery only strengthens the Socialist camp."

At this, the gardener produced the sort of guffaw that could easily have put him behind bars, had he been a citizen of the GDR. It had to be silenced, so for tactical reasons Schweik asked him hurriedly whether he might offer him a little something to eat along with his schnapps.

"You may, my friend," was the rather grandiloquent reply. "What do you have to offer?"

He'd have to ask his housekeeper about that, said Schweik; she was sick in bed, by some stupid quirk of fate. He excused himself politely and disappeared. Frau Lehmann smartly told him, however, that he must have lost his wits, and he returned saying that unfortunately he had spoken too soon, the most he could offer was a couple of boiled potatoes. "But you won't have much appetite for them," Schweik added candidly, "because I'm an honest man and I'll tell you right away that these spuds are being used as a hot poultice for my housekeeper's neck and I'd have to remove them first."

The gardener, surprisingly, seemed delighted. "Actually that's just as well," he said. "I'm twenty pounds overweight as it is, from all that food back home. So I couldn't be happier about the six pounds I've already lost in the week I've been here.

"I tell you," he continued in a serious tone while Schweik and Wegner avoided his gaze, "it's sickening when you just don't know what to eat next. That's why I'm glad to be here, so that when I get home things will be twice as appetizing. Next year I'll come back with my two kids, so the spoiled little brats can learn to be content with a fishtail. Believe me, I was touched when I saw for myself how things are here. We're too overfed in the damned West—you're much healthier, my friends.

"It's the same story with heart attacks. Where do they come from? First you stuff yourself to the gills, then into the car and not another inch on foot, anyway not at weekends. I've felt sick at the wheel three times already, and that's a warning signal. And then all the nervous strain and annoyance over the tens of thousands of other cars you're squeezed in between. Every unemployed person drives a Volkswagen. When I see your streets here—well, they're like a dream come true. You have no idea how lucky you are, Comrades."

Now was the moment, thought Comrade Wegner. "Oh, yes we do, Comrade!" he exclaimed. "Look at people's faces here, how they beam. They shine with security, happiness, trust, and the consciousness that we are approaching a better future. Just look here," he went on, grabbing a copy of *New Germany* from the chair, "That's exactly how Walter Ulbricht put it only yesterday—here it is—in a message to the Obstetricians' Congress in Karl-Marx-Stadt. He said that even newborn infants have this same consciousness here."

"Because here we feed them peace from their cradles, and not atomic weapons," threw in Schweik.

New Germany proved once again to be a treasure trove of still other slogans for building political awareness. The most impressive text was accredited to Walter Ulbricht himself:

The West German peasants suffer, because they must succumb in the fight for survival against capitalist farming operations, which are equipped by their rich concerns with the most modern agricultural machines. The West German peasants are individually too weak, and their farms too small

to be able to make profitable use of modern farming tech-
niques. They suffer, because the State is not concerned about
them, and in the interests of stabilizing monopolist exports
floods the inland market with foreign agricultural products,
etc., etc.

Comrade Wegner's reading of this text from end
to end was received with spontaneous applause by the
gardener. "I can scarcely believe it!" he said. "Your
Ulbricht must have gotten that right from the West
German peasant leader, from Rehwinkel himself. He
gives two talks like that every week."

He motioned the others to come closer to him, and
when all three heads were nearly touching he began
again in a conspiratorial whisper, "But Ulbricht sure fell
for Rehwinkel there, all right! Listen, I can tell you two,
you're my friends. The damned peasants at home don't
know what to do with all their prosperity. They're a
pain in the neck for the whole country. I told you about
our roads before. Well who do you think jams them full
with the biggest cruisers? Why, those wretches of
peasants! So you're absolutely right to keep them on
short rations here."

These continual rebuttals were beginning to get on
Comrade Wegner's nerves. And besides that, for understandable psychological reasons, at this moment he was
reminded of HAS records. So he capitulated and suggested that they kept off politics.

"What else is there to talk about?" asked Schweik.
"Everything in life is politics. That's a basic axiom in
the Marxist world."

The gardener had a solution. "I could tell you something about my girl friend," he said. "That, I guess, is
not politics."

Politics or not, the gardener's lady was an inexhaustible topic. Time passed, the level of liquid in the bottles sank—and who knows, perhaps the three would have sat together until evening and dreamed of a certain young lady from Karlsruhe, had not Comrade Wegner suddenly remembered that his wife and children must have been back from the barber shop for ages and must be locked out of their apartment, since they didn't have a key. The thought of this situation brought on an acute spasm of conscience in the much-feared house agent. "You'll have to come down and stand up for me," he pleaded. "My wife gave me strict instructions not to leave the apartment. And now she's probably been standing outside the locked door for two hours. Oh, it's too dreadful to contemplate," he moaned.

Schweik, who knew Frau Wegner, turned down this plea to himself and his friend the gardener. "Tell her I made you come," he suggested. "Tell her it was your political duty to come along. What are you house agents for anyway?"

"Schweik, you can talk, you're not married. In marriage, politics and philosophy don't count—least of all to my old woman. She'd make mincemeat out of Comrade Ulbricht himself. Don't laugh, Schweik, you'll see how it is when that Lehmann woman finally nabs you."

Wegner slunk to the door, and Schweik called after him asking whether he'd get sunstroke in the middle of winter, imagining such nonsense about him and Frau Lehmann. As for the gardener, he often said in Karlsruhe afterward that in the last analysis even Communists are only human. He had witnessed it with his own eyes.

THE UPS AND DOWNS OF BUCHTA AND CO.

* * * Police Official Dr. Olbert realized that if he didn't get out of the hospital soon, he would lose his tug of war with State Attorney Zollner over Schweik's scalp. The effect of such a defeat on his personal well-being was equally clear to him. So he decided to become a malingerer—no common malingerer, to be sure, but a reverse malingerer, so to speak. The normal, simple malingerer pretends to be sick, while in reality he is bursting with health. That kind of malingerer is common enough. In peacetime they may be relatively few and far between, but in wartime they come up like weeds. For national heroes as such exist only on paper; in reality most of them are of a breed quite different from popular conception. Not the least bit eager to be sacrificed on the altar of the fatherland, often they pretend to suffer from sickness which will prevent their being sent to the front. Their battlefield is the bed of a military hospital. There they struggle with the enemy—the staff doctors. Victory is uncertain, for the military doctors themselves are hard-boiled individuals who

know their stuff. Nevertheless, they are outwitted time and again. That is just as well, for nations must go on living after a war, and it is thanks in great measure to the malingerers that they are able to do so. Those unfortunates who fall at the front are, on the contrary, powerless to shape the future.

The great army of malingerers in wartime assumes in effect the role of an army of antiwar demonstrators ranging themselves against the Latin motto, *dulce et decorum est pro patria mori.*

Dr. Olbert represented the entirely different type: the reverse malingerer. He could lay claim to singular uniqueness. For he was sick and yet he suddenly began to simulate health. Few humans are fated to achieve this. Staff doctors dream in vain of this kind of malingerer.

The battle of the reverse malingerer bears no resemblance to the battle of the simple malingerer. The battle of the latter is fraught with difficulties; it requires all he can muster in the way of cunning, intelligence, and dissimulation. The simple malingerers, in other words, can achieve their goal only with the greatest difficulty. For reverse malingerers, on the other hand, it's a cinch.

"How do you feel?" inquired the attendant physician during his visit to the patient Olbert, whose eyes hurt more than ever.

"Marvelous."

"No pains?"

"No."

"Not even when you read?"

"No."

"But you complained of severe pains yesterday?"

The previous day Olbert hadn't yet decided to become a reverse malingerer. "They disappeared overnight, Doctor," he answered with heroic stoicism. "I want to leave," he added abruptly.

"That seems rather premature to me."

"Not at all," said Olbert.

"I'm convinced of it," said the doctor.

The discussion ended with the usual doctor's punch line: "On your own responsibility." The whole thing had lasted less than three minutes.

On his way to the next room the resident physician said to his assistant, "A peculiar fellow. The inflammation has hardly receded at all, there's no doubt about it. And in spite of that the idiot suddenly pretends he's cured. Well, I don't care—he'll be back in the clinic before he goes completely blind."

After leaving the hospital, Dr. Olbert set out once more to ensnare Schweik. Up to now, he reasoned, I've been out to get him alone. But a man is known by the company he keeps—from now on I'll keep tabs on all his contacts. That way I'll nab him after all, so he'd better not underestimate me!

And where is the best, simplest, most accessible place to keep one's tabs on a man, provided he's not tied to someone's apron strings? In his tavern, of course.

There was a boisterous atmosphere that evening in the "Traube." The regulars' table was full, and who led the conversation? Schweik. He was on his favorite topic: intelligent people.

This is how it happened. One of the regulars was a certain Johann Wagner, a post-office worker, easily excitable in spite of his sixty-two years. When he appeared in the "Traube," somewhat late, he said to the others who were already there, "You'll have to excuse me. I was so excited I couldn't find my shoehorn."

"As usual!" laughed one. "What happened?"

"They came for the wife of our janitor and had to tie her by the hands and feet. I arrived just five minutes too late, but the others told me all about it."

"That's really something," admitted the other. "That would have gotten me excited too. Tying up a woman by the hands and feet isn't something you see every day, even here."

"Why?" asked several of the group simultaneously.

"She refuses to let her husband divorce her, so to solve the problem he denounced her."

This was Schweik's first opportunity to approach his favorite subject. "An intelligent fellow," he said dryly. "What did he denounce her for?"

"You'd never guess!" exclaimed the post-office worker. "She's supposed to have said to him that she doesn't give a hoot about de-Stalinization any more. What she's waiting for now is Khrushchev's overthrow."

"That's insane!" shouted Schweik, who was suddenly just as excited as the post-office worker. "Imagine thinking such a thing! She doesn't belong in prison, she belongs in the nuthouse. Now I see why they tied her hands and feet!"

As regards the subject of intelligence, the unfortunate custodian's wife could hardly be considered one of its higher representatives. Quite the reverse. However, it is a matter of common experience that in conversation one thing continually leads to its opposite, and Schweik was an old hand at switching course. Last summer on an excursion to the Saxon Alps, he said, he had met two rather more intelligent people. There was a truck driver, for instance, he'd have to tell them about. But first he'd have to fill in a little background.

"I went by train," he began. "But I couldn't come back the same way, because while at lunch I noticed that somehow I'd lost my return ticket—God knows how. So I decided to try to hitchhike. There was a pretty young thing from Bautzen who had the same idea. So we both waved, and right away a truck stops and I thought to myself, there's courtesy for you! Most truck drivers are just the opposite, rude, vulgar, and right away it's 'Go to hell.' That's what you hear all the time from truck drivers. So I stood there thinking about that while the truck stopped in front of me. But then the driver said, partly to me, partly to the pretty young thing, 'I only have room for one. You'll understand, now Comrade, the pregnant woman comes first.'

" 'Where to, Fräulein?' " 'Bautzen,' she said. And there she was inside the truck already, and before they drove away I heard the following dialogue through the window: 'Thank you, Comrade. That was smart of you, the way you managed it so the old duffer couldn't say "I was there first." Do you think he believed I was pregnant?'

"But they were wrong there. I wondered right away how he could have come to that conclusion, because, I tell you, the girl was as slim as can be and no more pregnant than I was pregnant. And then the driver said, with evident relish, 'Just wait till we get to Bautzen, Fräulein.'

"I couldn't hear the rest of the conversation, unfortunately, because at that moment the truck got underway. So there I was again waiting for the next one. Where was I? Oh yes, the truck driver. I don't mean the one going to Bautzen, although he was pretty foxy, but another one, who was considerably more intelligent and I haven't gotten to him yet. Just listen. There I stood waiting at the roadside. And before any more trucks showed up, another honey joins me—a real cutie this one, young and even slimmer than the first one. Well I am all ready to be taken for a sucker again, I thought, and because I wanted to prevent that I said to the girl, 'It's unfair of you to come and stand next to me like this, when you're pregnant. It'll ruin my chances.'"

"Well that really touched off an explosion, Gentlemen. How dared I be so insolent? Didn't I have any eyes in my head? She held her bare ring-finger under my nose. Did I think she was one of *those* women? 'What women?' I asked. 'Calm down Fräulein. The other girl didn't start yelling when someone said she was pregnant.' 'Which other girl?' She was shouting even louder now. 'What's she got to do with me anyway? I've a good mind to box your ears! I don't care a rap who's expecting. All I know is I'm not one of them.'

"And so on and so forth until I started feeling silly and began shouting, 'Just wait till you get to Bautzen!' 'What had Bautzen got to do with it?' she said. She was heading for Görlitz. Now she was in the picture, she said, I must have a screw loose.

"Well, thank God a car stopped right afterward and she climbed in, so things were peaceful again. It happened to have a Bautzen license plate. So I was right after all, I thought to myself as I watched the car disappear in the distance. Nevertheless, that female will be a lesson to me, I decided; when the next one comes I'll tell her right away I'm sure she's not expecting.

"Wait a minute, what was I talking about? The

truck driver, that's it. Now listen. In fact a third female did happen to show up, and naturally I said exactly what I intended to say to her. Well, holy Maria, the first two were jewels compared to her, I tell you! She started screaming for help, because *she* thought I was suggesting hitting the hay with her, most probably by force, then and there on the deserted highway. Just imagine, suspecting me of being a monster like that! I didn't know whether to laugh or cry. To judge by her accent the girl wasn't from Bautzen or Görlitz, but from Zwickau, I think . . ."

"In Zwickau," said one of the regulars, finally interrupting Schweik's endless flow of words, "they're all dumb. I was in the army in Hamburg, but our sergeant was from Zwickau. So you don't have to tell me about Zwickauers."

"I'm not through yet," said Schweik. "Well, I stood there for ages and had to endure a lot, before finally someone took pity on me and gave me a ride. And who do you imagine that was? None other than the truck driver I began my anecdote with. And a very changed man from the one who started all that business about pregnancy. A respectable, serious man, and quite likeable. And highly intelligent, what's more. He was a convinced Socialist, it transpired. As such, he kept pounding his fist on the wooden partition behind him as he drove. Wham, bam! Wham, bam! I watched this for a while, and then I asked him, 'Why do you keep doing that, Comrade? What are you trying to do?' 'To save gas,' he replied. 'To save gas?' I asked, as sharp as a tack. Then he started to explain. He drove for a big People's Transport Company with a big fleet of trucks, he said. He and his colleagues had to sign an appeal every week, on which it said that saving gas meant that Socialism will triumph sooner. That was why he kept pounding on the cabin wall.

"You still can't figure out what he was up to, I suppose. Well, he had an important cargo for export—actually birdcages full of canaries. They're so crazy about canaries in the West they don't care about the balance of payments and such like because it's fashionable to be an animal lover there . . . wait . . . Don't let me get off the subject again, it's the pounding bit that's titillated you, I know. Well then, this pounding on the wall was meant to make the birds fly about and thus lighten the load."

The laughter excited by this story of an intelligent, passionately Socialist truck driver left only one of the regulars unmoved: Emil Buchta. He didn't bat an eyelash, but sat there morosely, with a dangerous, not to say murderous expression on his face, as if he wanted to blast the whole globe to smithereens. The only thing he participated in was drinking. The reason for Emil's cutthroat mood was no secret to his friends. He had made this quite clear to them when he had arrived at the regulars' table with the tragic cry, "I've just got back from the official doctor's."

The only exaggeration in this *cri de cœur* was the word "just." Actually more than half a day had passed in the meantime, so that this inaccuracy had tragic undertones. Indeed it spoke volumes. It meant nothing less than that half a day afterward Emil Buchta was still totally shattered by the shock of the examination and its result.

But first another question: how could Emil Buchta, after the attack in the Heinrich-Zille-Strasse, where the

"Traube" owner's wife had been so ill-treated, dare show his face there at all?

This was exactly what Schweik wanted to know. He was horrified when he saw Buchta come through the tavern door, and he took him aside to ask whether he was out of his mind.

"Why, Schweik?"

"You can't provoke Frau Gartner like this! Before you're through she'll explode and we'll have the police on our necks."

"She'll forget about that all right, Schweik. I talked to her ages ago. In fact I informed her that it's entirely up to her whether the police find out that her friend Müller deals in American cigarettes from West Berlin."

"That's something, at least," said Schweik with a sigh of relief. "When you've gotten hold of a secret like that, you're on the long end of the lever, as the old Russian inventor Archimedev said. Then I don't have to worry about the two of you causing a scandal. She'll probably just stubbornly ignore you when she puts your glass on the table. But that's bearable, being ignored, as long as the glasses keep coming."

In fact they did keep coming, these refills. But in spite of this, Emil's mood remained equally morose all evening. "Good heavens, man," said the local mailman in an attempt to comfort him, "just forget about that doctor. Nothing's definite yet. I assume, in any case, that you'll be protesting against that idiot's decision?"

But Emil had lost all hope. "They'll take care of my protest, all right. And my brother's too," he said woefully.

"Did they decide that he's able to work too?" Schweik chimed in.

"They sure did!"

"Damn! Couldn't he act feeble-minded any more?"

Emil looked dully at the table and said, "He tried everything. Just imagine, he threw open the doctor's door, and ran into the room screaming, 'The Party is always right!' That'd do the trick, he was convinced, and so was I. But what happens? The jerk certifies him healthy, 'mentally normal.' Since then Rudi hasn't done a thing but lie at home on the kitchen sofa shouting every ten minutes, at the ceiling 'What *more* could I have done?' I admit," Emil concluded gloomily, "I can't answer that myself."

The whole regulars' table shook their heads in wonder at that freak of a doctor. What none of them knew was the fact that the doctor had had to fill a new higher quota. On that particular day he would even have certified as normal a man who proclaimed he was God Almighty. The laws of the quota know no mercy.

Emil Buchta took toll of the catastrophe. "Buchta and Co. is through, Gentlemen," he said with a crest-fallen air.

"As if this means everything's decided once and for all," said the mailman, trying once more to infect Emil with a measure of optimism. But in vain; Emil was resigned. "No, no, never mind. But they can go to hell," he bawled with sudden ferocity. "We've put up with them much too long here as it is. I'm quitting. And in the West . . . ."

Schweik interrupted him with a sharp poke in the ribs. "Hold your tongue! Or you've had it," he said sharply in an undertone.

The tavern door had swung open. Over the threshold stepped a stranger, a thin man whose red-rimmed, inflamed eyes, coming out of the dark, blinked under the lamplight. It was Dr. Olbert.

"Who's the beanpole?" asked Emil softly, warned by Schweik's poke in the ribs.

"He's from the SSD," hissed Schweik. "An old friend." Then he called loudly over to the blinking beanpole, "Are you looking for me, Your Honor?"

Disappointment spread over Olbert's face as he recognized Schweik. It would have suited his plans better not to have met Schweik here. Then he could have played innocent and laid his traps on the sly. But that was unthinkable now. Under the circumstances, Dr. Olbert decided to move to the other extreme, his habitual one: He would not play the innocent, but the satanic tyrant. Thus he would spread panic, cause confusion, achieve his ends this way. "I have the feeling," was his polite greeting, "that there must be a hundred years of prison service—political, of course—represented by this merry little group sitting here. Perhaps even more."

There was only one who dared give the proper answer: Schweik. "That depends," he said with quiet deliberation, "how you mean that, Your Honor. Whether you mean full, served years, or only unimportant ones, half-baked ones that only exist on paper and don't really count. Years of pardon—of amnesty, so to speak. Or the kind a person may have been condemned to, but that he never served, because it turned out in time that he was innocent. Those kinds of years just happen to be my specialty, Your Honor, as you know all too well. I've never counted them, but I imagine if ever I wanted to total them up—if it were worth the trouble, I mean—that maybe I'd come up with almost a hundred years single-handed. So how did you mean your question, Your Honor? You won't mind if we ask you to condescend to express yourself precisely, so we can give you an exact answer."

"Schweik, I warn you. Don't make the mistake of underestimating me again."

To prove that Dr. Olbert must have misunderstood him—if indeed he imagined Schweik felt any animosity toward him—Schweik got up and with an exaggerated gesture of courtesy offered his honored guest a place at the table. Olbert had hardly sat down when he began again, "How much time have *you* spent in jail, for example?"

This question was addressed to the mailman. But the latter was a man of courage and not one to be duped by mere appearances. He asked gruffly in return, "Who are you, anyway?"

Here again Olbert, out of sheer habit, warned his questioner not to underestimate him. After this characteristic preliminary, he demanded that Schweik tell his companions loud and clear just who they were talking to.

"With none other than Herr Dr. Olbert, of the State Security Service," said Schweik obligingly with a gentle smile. "But you mustn't be afraid of him. The gentleman is polite and reasonable. He doesn't bite. That's simply the first impression he gives. When he's convinced that you have a clear conscience he's glad to give in. I speak from experience. Otherwise I would be somewhere else and not here, Gentlemen."

"If I were you, I should be a little less cocksure," exclaimed Dr. Olbert angrily, in an attempt to correct the entirely undesirable picture Schweik had painted of him.

Emil sat and mulled over the name Olbert. So that was the guy Buchta and Co. had promised to help Schweik against! What an opportunity for the firm's swan song in Dresden! The longer he looked at Dr. Olbert, the more he warmed to the thought of killing two flies with one blow: first of all, by fulfilling his promise to Schweik; second, by revenging himself one last time on the whole regime, the whole lousy system embodied in Dr. Olbert. The guy was long, thin, emaciated; in short, nothing but skin and bones. Such people, as everyone knows, have to be careful about drinking. Alcohol makes short shrift of them. This fact must be emphasized here because it was to play a major role in Olbert's downfall.

Emaciated beanpoles not only have a low resistance to alcohol, but also have to run to the john after every glass they imbibe. Fat men are without these deficiencies. Medical pundits have come up with somewhat complicated theories about the important differences between the fat and the thin; while scientists have one very simple explanation: a big barrel holds more than a small one.

One more fact. A sudden change of temperature accelerates the rate of conversion of liquids in the body. Anyone can establish this for himself by jumping into cold water on a hot summer's day. Thin Dr. Olbert had entered the cozy, well-heated "Traube" from the wintry atmosphere outside. The difference in temperatures was considerable, so that he had in more than one respect succumbed to the laws of nature. After one sip of his beer he didn't even have time to repeat his question as to how often the mailman had been in jail.

While he was gone, Emil Buchta poured some schnapps into his glass.

"What are you doing?" asked Schweik in astonishment.

Emil gave a hard cold laugh and said, "You can see well enough."

"Why? The guy can't even hold his beer."

Emil's laugh grew even more merciless, and Schweik asked again with growing anxiety, "What are you planning to do, Emil?"

"I'm going to fix that bastard."

"In what way?"

"Politically."

"Emil!" cried Schweik. "Do you know what you remind me of? Of someone who wants to sell the Pope indulgences. He knows the trade better than you."

"Just let me get him stoned, then you'll see who knows the trade better all right, Schweik."

As if by command, all of the others except Schweik suddenly got up, pulling out their wallets to pay their drink checks. Emil Buchta interrupted his tirade to ask disapprovingly of the group, "Where are you all going?"

"Home. This is getting too hot for the likes of me," said the mailman, speaking for all of them.

Emil Buchta said good-by with a scornful "Damned fools!" and told Dr. Olbert, when he returned from the toilet and asked about the others, that their wives had planned a raid on the "Traube" just at this time.

Outside, Dr. Olbert had naturally given considerable thought to the best tactic to use on this table of subversive beer-drinkers. Naturally he was acquainted with the favorite topic of German drinkers—military service—so he had decided to start off by asking the assembled company whether they had fought in Russia in

World War II, and if they had, why they hadn't deserted to the Red Army. But now they had all vanished, except Schweik and the other guy. What was to be done? Dr. Olbert decided to stick to his guns. "Were you a soldier?" he asked.

A stupid question; it was addressed to Emil Buchta. What German male, with legs and arms and a head, has not been a soldier in his lifetime?

"Unfortunately, yes," replied Emil.

"Did you fight in Russia?"

"You mean did I take part in the invasion of the Soviet Union?" he said in reply. "Sorry, in all those years I only fought in the West, against Frenchmen, Englishmen, and above all against Americans. Right, Schweik?"

"Against those imperialist pigs," confirmed Schweik.

Disappointed, Dr. Olbert reached for his glass and quaffed down half of it in one gulp. For him, that would have been bad enough if it had been just beer: that this was not the case didn't occur to the inexperienced Olbert. He began to feel hopeful again when he heard Schweik say, "But they sent me all over."

"To the Soviet Union too?"

"All the way to the Volga," declared Schweik proudly, old soldier that he was. "The rest was no war, only a glorified maneuver. That's what I say."

Olbert rubbed his hands together under the table. In his delight he downed the second half of his glass. One thought raced through his head: If only I'd thought of asking about his military experiences sooner, during the cross-examinations in jail! Quickly, so as not to give Schweik time to think, he interrupted him. "It's understandable that you're proud of your time in the army.

The thought of deserting to the Red Army probably never occurred to you?"

"Nowadays I wouldn't hesitate. But not then, I admit that."

"Why not then?"

"*I'll* explain that," Emil Buchta chimed in. He felt it was high time he came to Schweik's rescue. "Because four weeks before the war he caught a severe headcold which bothered him all the time at the front. It even paralyzed his political foresight, which he would have needed for that kind of decision. Did *you* have that kind of political foresight, Sir?"

"Was I addressing you or Schweik?" said Olbert icily.

"Me," said Schweik. "But I couldn't have explained things better myself."

The waitress, who hadn't failed to notice Olbert's empty glass, brought a new full one—just in time for Olbert to wash down his annoyance over Buchta. But the latter, nevertheless, managed to conjure another schnapps, with which he deftly replenished Olbert's glass. This, too, soon flowed down the latter's throat.

In this way, Dr. Olbert's blood pressure rose rapidly, and after only one more drink, in stark contrast to his previous inquisitorial technique, he cried spiritedly, "What delicious beer!" He was in a hurry to knock back his drink—and in still more of a hurry to reach the john.

"It's going great," said Emil Buchta joyfully to Schweik.

"What, Emil?"

"Everything."

"You say that so strangely and if I understand you

correctly you don't just mean his springing another leak. What's going great, Emil?"

"The way we're taking care of that bastard," replied the other.

"Emil, come to your senses, I beg of you. That doctor has sent you completely off your rocker. Well and good, but don't get your fingers burned."

"Who's getting his fingers burned?" said Emil with cavalier abandon. "Not me! I'll clobber them one. I'm getting out soon anyway, as I've already told you."

"Emil . . ."

"But before that I'm going to keep the promise I made you, Schweik."

"What promise was that?"

"That I'll get rid of that Olbert for you."

"Glory be!" said Schweik, suddenly remembering. "So that's what you've been up to all this time! Good heavens, Emil, if that's it, I'll be glad to relieve you of your obligation this instant. In all conscience, I can handle Olbert well enough for myself . . . In my own way," he added, smiling softly, after a short pause.

At this, Emil Buchta reiterated that it would be like spitting in his own face if ever he made a promise to a friend, shook hands on it, and then went back on his word. Indeed, for a moment, the cloak of noble friendship covered Emil's thirst for revenge relatively well. His next words, however, revealed time overriding motive. "Nothing can save him now, Schweik," he said portentously. "You are about to witness the last heroic deed of Buchta and Co. You can regard me as a tool of fate."

Schweik sighed. "Of fate, eh? Well, there's no sense in pitching against fate, I guess. If you insist on getting fate mixed up in this, Emil, I'm not one to stand in your way. You know me, I'm the last person to meddle around with fate."

He fell silent, sealed his decision with a glance, and put his glass back on the table with the words, "Well, all right then. I'll leave him to you, Emil. God bless him, and let the devil take the hindmost. I wash my hands of the whole thing. How do you intend to go about it?"

"It's perfectly simple. I'll get him stone drunk, till he passes out. Then I'll denounce him for saying such and such when he was tight. I've no qualms about swearing to this on oath—you know Buchta and Co., Schweik. Got it?"

"But he'll defend himself in court."

"I guarantee you they won't let him open his trap, for the sake of the old revolutionary motto: 'Another traitor in the Party ranks unmasked!' You know how crazy they are about traitors in the Party ranks. It's a regular psychosis with them—you can hear it any day on the West Berlin radio."

"You know I don't listen to the West Berlin radio, Emil. But let me give you a good tip, as a friend. If you really have to do Olbert in, then don't report him to his own crowd at Police Headquarters. But to the State Attorney's office. There's a certain Zollner there: he'll be glad to listen to you."

While they sat waiting for Dr. Olbert, Emil asked what could be taking the SSD big shot so long. Maybe he'd fallen in and drowned?

When at last Dr. Olbert did re-emerge, he was of course totally unaware of the sinister trap that awaited him. "I'm thirsty," he said, taking a great gulp from his glass, and then he revealed an entirely new side of his personality by declaring that all Germans must stick together.

After the next gulp he began to sing—German marching songs, of course. That's how it always is, and woe betide the skinny man who, though normally abstemious, lets down his guard just once! For him, things go twice as fast. Three beers, fortified with schnapps, and then a fourth beer on top of that were enough to topple Dr. Olbert to his ruin. He appealed to Schweik and Buchta to regard him first and foremost as a German, to forget everything else. He was a *good* German, he shouted, pounding on the table, and he warned everyone within earshot not to think otherwise.

"What's a good German?" asked Emil Buchta.

"*You're* not!" he snapped back. "But Schweik is! A good German is one who fought in the East. Sorry I have to say that to you, Buchta."

He turned away from Buchta, looked at Schweik with an expression of comradeship, took a large sip from his glass, and then continued, "I was in Russia too, Schweik. You can trust me. I was an anti-tank man. We shot up T 34s like hotcakes. And what the T 34 was, Schweik, you explain to your friend here who did nothing in the war but sit on his ass on the Western Front."

"The T 34 was real sad, nobody can deny that," said Schweik willingly following Olbert's command in appropriate military language. "One time during a surprise attack one of these crates, whether you believe it or not, shot the plate I was eating from right out of my hands, just as I was about to take my first bite. The field kitchen upped and went and we saw neither hide nor hair of it for the next three days. In the meantime there was nothing we could do but pick our noses. Three days and not a thing to eat—I ask you, is that the proper way to conduct a war? Don't talk to me about the T 34!"

" 'Proper,' " chimed in Dr. Olbert. "Good grief, man, those guys conducting a war the 'proper way'!"

"But they sure did a proper job of cooking your goose once," said Emil Buchta to rile him.

"Where?"

"Well Stalingrad, for a start . . ."

"At Stalingrad there were only two things that stopped us," explained Dr. Olbert—long past the point of no return—with heavy emphasis. "The winter, and our allies, the Rumanians and Italians."

At no point had the Russian Army—that lousy rabble—been the real victors, he continued. The only thing you could give the Red Army credit for—and that, for God's sake, was precious little—was its size. "Excuse me, Gentlemen," he said interrupting himself after another swig of the vitriolic brew, "I must skiddoo to the john again. How do you two keep going without it?"

He didn't wait for a reply, however. He was in too great a hurry.

"Should I carry through my plan to the bitter end?" asked Emil turning to Schweik when they were alone. "After all, that louse is already done for. We can finish him off right away."

Schweik wanted to put in one last good word for an old comrade-in-arms. "Emil," he said, "must you? Shouldn't we at least give him credit for having suffered under the T 34 . . ."

Emil Buchta, however, cut him short mercilessly. "No! What we must do is put an end to that idiot with-

out further ado. Aside from everything else, anyone as
dumb as that doesn't deserve any mercy. As you know,
I originally planned to get him stone drunk and then
accuse him of statements he *didn't* make. But meanwhile
the half-wit has dug his own grave. He just tosses all
the evidence one needs in one's face. There'll be no
need for me to perjure myself in court, Schweik," he
concluded bitterly. "And yet just think—to top it all I'll
have to swear on oath to those bastards to something
that's true anyway! So far as I'm concerned, that just
about takes all the gilt off the gingerbread!"

Meanwhile Dr. Olbert, beyond all hope of rescue,
happened to think of a certain Manglitz. Manglitz was
a former corporal from his field unit. A highly decorated
daredevil who had never given a damn for anyone or
anything, he had also been a heavy drinker. The reason
Dr. Olbert was reminded of him just now was that in a
drinking bout Manglitz had never had to leave the table
either.

When he returned to the table Olbert immediately
asked, "Is one of you called Manglitz, by any chance?
Manglitz was one of our colonels, and so had a bladder
like yours. But except for that, you couldn't hold a
candle to him, I can assure you. In one day alone he shot
up seven of those damned Russian crates. It was a joy to
watch, until unfortunately he got knocked off by the
eighth one. God knows, a guy like that can only be
found in the German Army!"

He took a compulsive gulp in memory of Corporal
Manglitz. A very big gulp. Then he went on to declare
that the whole Red Army, "compared to us," had been
a laughable rabble. Every one of "our" privates had

licked ten Reds. "I can give you that in writing!" he shouted, pounding on the table again.

Emil Buchta could not let this opportune moment go by without making the most of it. Quickly he said, "But ten is surely an exaggeration!"

"Fifteen's not an exaggeration!" bawled Olbert with a wild look in his eyes. "And what's more I'll give you that in writing, too!"

"I might believe it in writing," said Emil Buchta retreating half a step. "But ten, mind you, not fifteen!"

In the end, Dr. Olbert scrawled the following words on a piece of paper he had the waitress bring, and he handed it to Emil Buchta:

> I here declare that EVERY German
> soldier licked TWENTY Reds.
>
> Dr. Olbert

And that really was the end, the end of it all.

Three days later State Attorney Zollner succeeded, in an extraordinary lightning trial of a "traitor in the Party ranks," in procuring not the four or five years with which an outsider would have been punished for the same offense, but ten full years for Dr. Olbert. "For every Red Army soldier allegedly licked, half a year!" Zollner demanded in his arraignment.

Traitors in the Party ranks are always eliminated in lightning trials, so that the sensation soon blows over. Emil Buchta declared as a witness for the prosecution that in the "'Traube" he had immediately guessed from Olbert's face what kind of creature had sneaked his way into the SSD. (In his arraignment, State Attorney Zollner substituted for the word "creature" the more colorful epithet "Trojan horse.") For that reason he, Buchta, had consciously and not just instinctively poured schnapps into Olbert's beer, in order to hasten his unmasking. His crowning success had been the declaration in writing, which the Court had before it as Exhibit Number 1, so that the accused couldn't later deny the charges leveled against him.

For his appearance in the witness box, Emil Buchta was accorded special praise and recognition by the Court. The next day the Party press also featured an article in its judicial section about a model "watchman of the Socialist camp." When Emil's deadliest enemy, the official doctor who had certified him fit to work, read this acclamation of Buchta, he realized with horror what a mistake it was to have this "model watchman" for an enemy, and reversed his attestation with all possible speed. "You see," said Emil Buchta afterward to Schweik, "good works have their reward. We have freed the whole city from a scourge. You, too, Schweik, did your part as a witness in court, even though you insisted on weakening your statement by saying you felt there were extenuating circumstances. Thank God they gave him the proper extenuating circumstances, all right! And thanks to all that, the official doctor has come to his senses too."

The final result was that Buchta and Co. did not have to transfer to West Germany after all but remained, much to the benefit of their customers, in their home city of Dresden.

THE FANCY-DRESS
BALL

* * * On the invitation to the freight
yard's fancy-dress ball were these words: "Anyone
whose true identity is discovered before the unmasking
at midnight will be rewarded with four unscheduled
Sunday shifts."

A most effective method of stimulating higher
achievement! In the Workers' State they knew better
than anywhere else how easily the fine bonds of philosophy can be discarded for the nobility of toil.

Schweik as Elizabeth Taylor was a huge success! He
was alone in his apartment when he donned his costume. Frau Lehmann had gone out to a café, thus lend-
ing substantial emphasis to her protest against his stun-
ning mask, which she labeled a "sin before God and
mankind." Most irritating of all, she was quick to notice
the two soccer balls squeezed inside his ensemble.

While he was dressing, Schweik treated himself to a
self-critical monologue. Since he was alone, he let himself go a little. The last snatch of this one-sided ap-
praisal—before Schweik parted from the mirror—should

give the reader a fair sample of the general tone. "Now only the behind is genuine," he said preening himself. "A do-it-yourself job, but one even the real Liz Taylor could be proud of."

Schweik's success with his costume began in the streetcar, where several passengers forgot their destination and continued one or two stops beyond it. A Party member, identified by his badge, nevertheless declared that a mask like that, from the "Western world," didn't deserve a single glance, unless it were one of contempt. But even he rode three stops too far.

The cry which flew from mouth to mouth as soon as Schweik appeared in the railroad canteen, now serving as a ballroom, also had its origin in the "Western world"—to be precise, "Sex bomb." The comments which Schweik's mask elicited from the other masks he passed proved beyond doubt that it was a railroaders' ball that was being held and not a chrysanthemum ball. "A bird like that," was one comment, "is something we— with our female tractor drivers—can only dream about."

"With a chick like that," said another, "you'd be reduced to a pulp in no time." "Who, me?" came the reply. "*She* would, you mean. She'd be begging for mercy on her hands and knees before I got through with her."

The first man to ask Schweik for a dance said, "You gorgeous mask, may I? I'm sorry the band can't play what you're used to."

"Too bad," agreed Schweik. "Dancing the polka doesn't exactly set one's blood on fire." Then as they danced Schweik said, "It's easy enough to see who I'm supposed to be, but how about you?"

"I'm Casanova."

"Imagine that! Then I can count on some fun and games, as they say?"

"Naturally," said Casanova, who in reality was a girl from the bookkeeping department of the ticket computation office.

They concluded their dance with the mutual assurance that they'd keep one another in mind. Then a bearded individual who claimed to be Robber Kneissl from Bavaria asked Schweik for a dance. But since Schweik wanted to have a good look around the room first, he turned him down. What was it that struck him most about the gathering? That as always those dressed in human costumes were in the minority. Casanova, Kneissl, and Liz Taylor were exceptions. By far the largest number of guests represented species of the animal kingdom: lions, tigers, cats, every imaginable breed of dogs, donkeys, oxen—wherever one looked. The reason for the predominance of animal costumes was because they were so easy to come by. A cardboard donkey's mask, for instance, could be had for the asking in every toyshop: this on one's head, and one's finery was complete.

There were two costumes that stood apart from the general menagerie. One was a walking tree trunk, which, however, did not actually represent a tree trunk itself but, as a pasted-on sign indicated, a "Termite in Tree Trunk." The other original costume was the inspiration of a young package inspector. He was wrapped from head to foot in a yellow sheet, with holes only for his eyes and mouth, and represented a "Yellow Fever Germ, 98,000,001 times Magnified."

A third group, which was also relatively common, lay between these extremes: the inevitable "ghosts." The

reason for their frequency? The same explanation applied to them as to the herds of oxen and asses. For the
mask of a "ghost," all that was necessary was an old
sheet in which holes for the wearer's eyes could be made.

"Which ones can be my meter-readers?" said
Schweik to himself with a sigh, after an hour had passed
without his hearing from either of them. No sooner had
he said this, however, when they suddenly appeared before him. First came the nervous meter-reader, who hurriedly whispered "Usbek" in Schweik's ear and added
that he had already sounded out a leopard and a castle
ghost, but somehow hadn't been able to come to any
useful conclusions. Unfortunately the nature of his questions was political, there was no getting around it—and
as for politics, these two had declared, they didn't give a
damn about it this evening.

Schweik was lost in admiration for the meter-
reader's costume long after he had disappeared again
into the crowd. It represented a medieval torturer, complete with a strikingly impressive black hood which fell
to his chest.

The second meter-reader, the calm one, had also
been inspired by the Middle Ages. He appeared as the
Iron Knight. His arrival was heralded by a sound like
the rattling of chains. Then came a relatively distinct
"Good evening, Texan." Schweik looked up at the figure that stood before him—whose visor was naturally
lowered—and said, "Good evening. Been sniffing around
too?"

The meter-reader thought mistakenly that the word
"too" was in reference to Schweik himself. His answer
showed that he was on the wrong track. "A little," he
said. "Unfortunately without any results . . . But," he

exclaimed quickly as Schweik started to say something, "that doesn't mean you should tell me about your results yet. No, no! At the moment, they don't interest me in the slightest. The night is long, long enough for me to get an objective picture for myself.

"I imagine," he continued quickly, as he saw that Schweik was still trying to say something, "that you'd like to point out certain colleagues I should go to work on—but would that give me an objective impression? Perhaps, perhaps not. I want to be sure. Afterward, I can always compare your results with mine. But for the time being I want to keep my hands free; I don't want you to point out anyone, not a soul!"

Well, thought Schweik, there was only one person I wanted to point out to you, just to tell you not to bother about him: your colleague from the same office. Never mind, I'll do as you say—you can go chase yourself if you'd rather. I hope the two of you run into each other and sound each other out with a vengeance—that'll do you both a world of good!

And sure enough, fate took its usual course. The two meter-readers promptly did run into each other, although there were nearly three hundred people in the room. It would have been abnormal for fate to forego this coincidence; it is only superficial human minds that find this sort of thing inexplicable. Perhaps this observation is best illustrated for the reader by his being reminded of one of the most common human complaints, daily muttered to heaven by millions of husbands: "Of all the women in the world, why did I have to end up with this one?"

Why? Because fate, which is ever malicious, wanted it that way.

This brief lesson for today is intended for readers who may still have some illusions about fate. Not everyone can be a Schweik. Schweik's continual and intimate experience, ever since he had been old enough to think, had long since taught him what was normal for fate and what was abnormal. Consequently, Schweik was not the least bit surprised, when he danced by the bar in the arms (or paws) of a kangaroo and saw the only executioner in the room standing next to the sole Iron Knight. Well, he mused, there we have it. What, I wonder, will they find out from each other about the political convictions at our freight yard?

Whatever it was, kept the two together for well over an hour. The first one to reapproach Schweik was the nervous meter-reader. "Had any luck yet?" Schweik asked him.

"I certainly have. But not so loud, for heaven's sake!"

"Who did you talk to?" asked Schweik softly.

"An out-and-out opponent of the regime."

"What was he dressed as?" said Schweik innocently.

"He's wearing a knight's armor."

Schweik saw no alternative but to call an end to this wild-goose chase. He felt he couldn't wait until the unmasking forced him to put his cards on the table. "In knight's armor?" he repeated in surprise. "So far as I know, there's only one knight here."

"That's right. And . . ."

"Then you've had a raw deal," interrupted Schweik.

"A raw deal? How come? I don't think so. He didn't make a secret of his attitude—and that's the main thing, after all."

"You mean his being against the regime?"

"Yes."

"O dear!" groaned Schweik. "Then I'm afraid he was only trying to provoke you. And you promptly fell for it."

"Impossible! What on earth makes you say that?"

"It's simply that I know the knight. And here's a surprise for you: you know him too."

"*I* know him?"

"That's right. When he takes off his mask you'll be able to see for yourself."

The meter-reader looked at Schweik as if he was out of his mind—a reaction that was invisible, of course, since his face was still concealed by his hood. His silence, however, spoke for itself. It proved that he was too out of touch with the situation to say anything appropriate. Schweik, therefore, was able to continue uninterrupted. "He happens to come from your office," he said.

"From . . . my . . . of . . . fice?" was the almost inaudible stuttering answer which emerged from the hood.

"Yes. From the SSD."

"From the . . ."

The rest died on the meter-reader's lips. At last the scales fell from his eyes: Schweik was a *double agent!* He must try somehow to stay cool and not lose his nerve. "Where's the john?" he asked with considerable presence of mind, summoning up the last remains of his courage. "I'll be right back . . ."

Those were his last words as an active agent, for that very same night he suddenly turned up in West Berlin, where his request for immediate retirement from the West German secret service was granted, following a cursory examination by a neurologist. The gratifying result for Schweik was that, thanks to the nervous meter-reader's fate at the fancy-dress ball, he was never pestered again by Western secret services. Agent "Usbek" disappeared from the books.

Nor was this the only pleasing result of the ball, so far as Schweik was concerned. Shortly after the departure of the nervous meter-reader, the calm one turned up. He informed Schweik that now at last the problem of the missing quota increase in Schweik's freight yard was a good step closer to being solved. "Have you come across a couple of reactionaries already?" asked Schweik.

"Not a couple—but one!! We'll fix him all right. I just want to bide my time until the unmasking, so that I can arrest him in full view of everyone."

"What kind of outfit is he wearing?"

"A pretty good one—a medieval executioner's, actually."

"A medieval executioner's?" exclaimed Schweik. The ensuing exchange was identical to that between Schweik and the nervous meter-reader, and, as before, Schweik produced his bombshell, "He happens to come from your office."

"He what?"

Now, things got more complicated. "He's the one you asked me to point out last week," said Schweik, "and I'd have singled him out for you right away today, but you wouldn't let me tell you a thing—remember?"

"Good Lord!" groaned the meter-reader.

"Of course it was tough luck that, of all people, you should run into him. Normally, you can't anticipate that kind of thing. Where's he been all this time, anyway? He merely said he was going to the john and that he'd be right back."

"Just think what I said to that guy!" groaned the meter-reader.

"But you only wanted to provoke him?"

"That's right. But the question now will be *which* of us was 'only provoking' the other. That's dangerous. Who will the court believe, that's the question now."

"Must it go to court?"

This simple question of Schweik's brought the meter-reader to his senses again, and after brief consideration he exclaimed, "You're right. If I don't stay for the unmasking, he won't have a clue as to who he was talking to."

And Schweik never saw this meter-reader again either. The latter avoided any problems that might have been occasioned by a chance meeting with the other meter-reader and Schweik by having himself transferred to another division of the SSD, which dealt with agents whose names began with F.

Thus perished agent "Texan."

The only thing Schweik bitterly regretted was having to forfeit the meter-readers' fees.

FIAT JUSTITIA

✳ ✳ ✳ State Attorney Zollner had been ordered to give a report. The State Attorney General himself had sent for him.

State Attorney General Zech was apparently fond of house plants. His whole office shimmered with green —from the leaves of potted plants. Between the greenery there were also fresh-cut flowers. On the wall opposite his desk hung a large picture of Walter Ulbricht, so that whoever sat at the desk could look at it whenever he wanted to. The desk was a valuable piece, hand-worked, old, elegant. Herr Zech was none of these— on the contrary.

Zollner had no idea why the "General" had called him on the carpet, and consequently his face had an unhealthy tinge. In their brief greeting Zollner was servile, the "General" arrogant. Then the latter said, "We visited him yesterday."

Who comprised the "we" remained uncertain, but same was not true of the "him." As he pronounced the latter word the State Attorney General raised his eyes demonstratively to Ulbricht's picture.

Silence. A chill ran down Zollner's spine.

"He gave us two hours of his time."

Silence again.

"He considered the matter important enough."

Now the Attorney General's eyes turned again to the file which lay before him on his desk.

"You know what this is about, Comrade Zollner . . . Or don't you know?" he added, as there was still no sound from Zollner.

"No, I don't if you'll excuse me, Comrade Attorney General, I'm sorry to say."

"You don't know?!" he asked with emphasis, shaking his head in amazement. "Why not?"

Zollner provided the solution to this riddle. "Your office ordered me here without giving any reason, if you'll excuse me, Comrade Attorney General," he said.

The office was a pigsty, the Attorney General said in reply; he couldn't do everything himself. Now, of course, Zollner would not be prepared for this consultation.

State Attorney Zollner somehow sensed from the "General's" words that the "consultation" was not directed against him, and his fears began to subside. They vanished altogether, when the State Attorney General suddenly asked, "Or do you have the Schweik case fresh in your memory?"

"The Schweik case?" said Zollner quickly.

"Yes. It was pending in your department."

"Yes, indeed. I have it fresh in my memory, Comrade Attorney General. I can do without the files."

Not quite so dumb as he looks after all, the old duffer, thought the State Attorney General, a man of middle age. State attorneys general of middle age—or even younger—exist only in Socialist countries. In democratic countries one of the indispensible prerequisites for the position of State Attorney General is to have reached a venerable old age. The most important difference between a Socialist and a democratic State attorney general (that is, between a young and an old one) is their entirely diverse attitudes toward the death penalty. The Socialist attorney general lusts after heads; his democratic counterpart, on the contrary, does not do so. This is perhaps due to the fact that the older a man gets the more spunk he loses. And this latter fact explains why in Socialist countries younger and not older attorneys general are in demand. On the other hand, one should not be misled into believing that it is humanitarian tendencies which render Western attorneys general milder than their Eastern counterparts. This is not so. Humanitarian tendencies are nothing but a brake and a hindrance to any State attorney, be he Eastern or Western. Moreover, people with humanitarian tendencies never become State Attorney General, and that includes those in the West too.

So it isn't humanitarian thinking that causes demands for the death penalty to be fainter on the lips of an old attorney general than on those of a younger one. What is it then? The answer is perfectly simple: It is the so-called wisdom that comes with age. In short, experience. And there is scarcely a field in which there are more impressive and more varied experiences to be gathered than in politics. Therefore, while with age attorneys general become sly, this is no substitute for the nettle shown by their zealous young Eastern colleagues.

"Sit down, Comrade Zollner," said Herr Zech.

"Thank you."

"What kind of a person is this fellow Schweik?"

"I don't know myself," replied Zollner cautiously, since he had not yet discovered what kind of a character the Attorney General had conceived Schweik to be.

"But you've had him in your office often enough?"

"He is small . . . rotund," Zollner began hesitantly.

"Comrade! What sort of nonsense is this! Don't you understand my question? This afternoon Walter Ulbricht will be asking me, 'What kind of a person is this fellow Schweik?' Imagine if I start out with 'small . . . rotund.' He'd eat me alive. So come on now, what sort of personality has he got? His character—*that's* what we want to know!"

"He belongs to the people, Comrade Attorney General."

"Very instructive. Is he cunning?"

"Cunning?"

"Yes. After all, you've had frequent dealings with the man. And the result? Always the same. I imagine I don't have to go into details." He tapped on the file with his forefinger and continued, "What I have been forced to read in here is a perfect fairy tale. I sometimes had to ask myself whether you're already too old to fulfill your responsibilities."

"Comrade Attorney General, if you'll excuse me," said Zollner defensively, "may I remind you of the role played by that traitor and Enemy of the People, Olbert. It was impossible to get anywhere with the incomplete material—deliberately incomplete material—he sent us."

Herr Zech looked up, sat some minutes in silence, lit a cigarette, and said that nevertheless he was not quite happy about Schweik. In fact he wished he had "a bit more intelligence."

First came his suspicion that Schweik might be cunning, and now the opposite—that he was dense. You can never please anyone, Schweik would inevitably have sighed, had he been present.

As a partial explanation why he wished Schweik had greater intellectual gifts, the Attorney General said that this was connected with the role Schweik was to play. Zollner said in reply that he was beginning, please excuse him, to suspect, he was sorry to say, what Comrade Attorney General was aiming at.

It's taken you long enough, you old duffer with your idiotic "excuse me, I'm sorry to say," thought the Attorney General. Idiot! You may well be the least suitable candidate for the role of State Attorney in the trial against Schweik as we envision it. "Comrade Ulbricht," he began again, "would like to have this trial held as soon as possible. As you know, it is without precedent, the first case pending which is connected with de-Stalinization, following the 20th Party Congress of the Soviet Communist Party in Moscow. This fellow Schweik happens to be the accused. That is unfortunate, but it cannot be otherwise. Comrade Ulbricht considers this trial highly significant. It is to set an example. That's the reason he has concerned himself with the matter personally. How far have you got with your preparations?"

"They can be completed any time, Comrade Attorney General."

"What about your arraignment?"

"I finished it long ago, if you'll excuse me, Comrade Attorney General."

"What . . ." The Attorney General paused for a moment. "What sentence have you in mind?"

Zollner thought of his friend Schweik, whom he had promised to have acquitted. Acquittal was out of the question, pure wishful thinking. Schweik will understand that. After all, he's a very reasonable man, thought Zollner to himself. What I can do for him is to recommend the lightest possible sentence. Only an idiot would misunderstand him on that score. The crux of the matter "it doesn't seem to me as if the accused really belongs to eral that Schweik deserves the most lenient sentence, and not the heaviest?

"Comrade Attorney General," he began cautiously, "it doesn't seem to me as if the accused really belongs to those elements which are incorrigible and have to be rooted out. I'm sorry to say, I somehow have the feeling that in spite of everything, perhaps if you'll excuse me, there's some good solid stuff in him."

"So? Then how do you explain the sentences you had in mind for him earlier?"

Zollner cleared his throat. "I believe, if you'll excuse me, that for many years I didn't see him in quite the right light. I'm sorry to have to admit this now, but during the last examination particularly, he made a very different impression on me."

"In what respects?"

"He didn't succeed in freeing himself from Stalinism on the first try, that is correct. However, when he did do so, he succeeded, one must give him his due, totally—if you'll excuse me. And today those of his immediate acquaintance report that not a day goes by without his, how shall I say, damning Stalinism. The expressions he uses are extreme, unsophisticated. For example, he never mentions Stalin's name these days without, if you'll excuse me, adding, 'who, that wart hog!' "

It was evident that the State Attorney General wanted to say something, but hadn't yet found the right words to express what he was thinking. So he remained silent, giving State Attorney Zollner the opportunity to continue speaking.

"And I don't believe he's just paying lip-service to the political turnabout," Zollner went on. "No, no one can cover up as well as that! If only you yourself could witness one of his outbursts, Comrade Attorney General! And I'm sure he won't act differently at his trial."

"You don't think so?" asked Herr Zech.

"No, I don't. He won't hesitate to display his new convictions in court, and he'll repent of his old ones. He's not a bit the stubborn type of defendant who won't give an inch, if you'll excuse me. I bet the press will find in him a worthwhile subject, a fine example to others. If you will permit me, Comrade Attorney General," said Zollner in conclusion—and he had now literally talked himself into enthusiasm—" in short, he will swear to disavow Stalinism with a burning passion. That, I can guarantee."

The State Attorney General looked at his desk, then up at Walter Ulbricht, and thought to himself that here was proof enough of the stupidity and incapability of the old duffer who sat before him. And one has to work with such idiots, he mused. It is all very well for Walter Ulbricht. What had he said yesterday? "I hold you responsible, Comrade, for the trial. Make sure there's no big fuss about Stalinism. I have decided that all that must come to an end in the GDR. The 20th Party Congress has nothing to do with us. Why not? It's perfectly simple: because there never was any Stalinism here, never! Understand! The trial must be conducted with this in mind. So make sure, I repeat, that none of that nonsense comes up."

Easier said than done, Comrade Ulbricht, thought the Attorney General pessimistically. You should have heard this ox of a State attorney talk, then you might feel differently.

Zollner was still waiting for an answer from the Attorney General. Finally, the latter said, "You still haven't answered my question as to what sentence you have in mind."

Zollner, averting his head in anticipation of the storm which would doubtless break loose, said softly, "In consideration of all the circumstances I've mentioned, I would like, if you'll excuse me, to limit the sentence, I'm sorry to say, to the minimum punishment of three years, if you'll excuse me."

Come what may, thought Zollner, Schweik can't blame me for a thing now. I've sacrificed myself for him. But where's the thunder and lightning? Why don't I hear anything?

When the lightning finally struck, it was of an entirely different nature from Zollner's expectations. "You will recommend acquittal," said the Attorney General, and Zollner, slowly raising his bowed head, looked at him in disbelief.

"Ac . . . quittal?"

"Acquittal," repeated the Attorney General with vigor, realizing that he'd still be sitting there next year if he didn't let the cat out of the bag. "I see I have to be blunt with you. Listen, you've got things all wrong. Here, there never was any such thing as Stalinism . . ."

"Whaaat?" This cry came from the breast of an old convinced Stalinist.

"No, never." Herr Zech was drumming on the desk with his fingers. "And in case you have any doubts about it, I tell you that this statement comes from Walter Ulbricht himself. Understand! There never was any such thing as Stalinism here. As a result, we have no need of any display of anti-Stalinism now—at any rate, no more than very mild ones. Any excess of zeal in this matter is naturally to be avoided, since our basic attitude has been the same all along. Had we been guilty of Stalinist excesses in the past—I repeat, *had we been guilty*—then we'd have good reason to broadcast our change of heart."

"Quite right," said Zollner, already back on his toes again. The short crisis he had gone through was over. Every well-trained old People's Democrat is a past master at overcoming such crises with agility.

"As a result," began Herr Zech again, "we don't want any defendant at this trial blabbing about something which never existed. About Stalinism, that is. Schweik must adapt himself to the trial as we conceive it. That's the role of which I spoke earlier. I hope he is intelligent enough for it. Brief him properly, Comrade Zollner, train him thoroughly! You are responsible . . ."

He broke off, opened the file, but then closed it again with a snap and continued, "My information tells me that the cause of arrest was Schweik's exclamation, 'Saintly Joseph Stalin.' SSS Official Sand, apparently an idiot by the grace of God, as Comrade Ulbricht put it yesterday, seems to have made this arrest in the first burst of enthusiasm following the 20th Party Congress. Entirely unnecessary, of course. But what's done is done, and we have to follow this thing through. 'Saintly Joseph Stalin' was a blunder, naturally—or let's say, rather, an exaggeration. Schweik will be called to account for this in court. But he is to be pardoned for it, without any anti-Stalinist tirades on his part. There's to be no branding of Stalin as a wart hog, etc. There's no need for that. That was only a momentary transport caused by a wrongly digested 20th Party Congress, as Comrade Ulbricht said yesterday. You and Schweik can both made a note of that, Zollner. Schweik's defense in court, his appearance, his utterances are therefore to be roughly in line with the following: Stalin was no saint, was not infallible—but nonetheless it cannot be denied that he did achieve certain things. By the way, the most sensible thing will be to prevail upon the accused not to open his mouth unless he is asked something. Will you be able to impress this upon him? I must have a definite answer. Or would you prefer to be represented by another colleague?"

State Attorney Zollner, who had slumped forward during the Attorney General's long directive, now sat bolt upright and said, "Not at all."

In that case, said the Attorney General, he would inform Comrade Ulbricht when he called back in the afternoon that they could count on Zollner.

"Absolutely, Comrade Attorney General."

"Any more questions?"

"No, Comrade Attorney General."

That was the end of the official conference. Zech got up and turned for a moment to more personal matters. He asked Zollner—nothing else occurred to him—whether he had any children.

No.

Why not?

Because he wasn't married, replied Zollner.

But every human being needed something he could care for, said Zech. Even if it was only a hobby. Zollner was about to mention his parakeets, but as his eyes followed the Attorney General's, he realized in a flash what in the present circumstances was the best hobby in the world: potted plants.

The remainder of the conversation between the two men was devoted to botany. Zollner learned the species, age, special likes and dislikes of every plant in the room. When they came to a tiny, fragile, actually rather stunted little plant which stood near the radiator, the Attorney General said, "This is my problem child. She seems quite unable to flourish here. I don't know what to do for her. I've already had a special fertilizer sent in from the West. You know the stuff we produce . . . hopeless. Of course we can't do everything at once. But the Western fertilizer doesn't seem to be doing the trick either. That doesn't surprise me, knowing them. So! what is to become of my plant? I assure you, I've already had nightmares about her wilting away completely."

A plant-lover, this State Attorney General. But only a *plant*-lover. He hadn't had any nightmares yet about the executions under his jurisdiction.

Zollner for his part was an *animal*-lover. The loss of a parakeet could rob him of his appetite for a week. Not so a death sentence for which he was responsible. That didn't upset him for as much as an hour . . .

So Stalinism was a product of the Soviet Union, of Poland, Czechoslovakia, Hungary, Rumania, Albania, and China—but not of the GDR. It follows that the GDR had no need of any anti-Stalinism. What was it the great Stalinist Zhdanov said? "Not all simple things are brilliant. But all brilliant things are simple."

SCHWEIK IN COURT

＊＊＊ Schweik's trial began two weeks later, on a Wednesday. On the courtroom benches, among the usual notorious courtroom fans, sat a number of Schweik's acquaintances: the Buchta brothers, as well as several others who had called their various employers to say they were sick. The bond which tied these gentlemen to Schweik had been renewed countless times in the "Traube."

Two rows had been reserved for a school class, a third for soldiers of the national People's Army. But this was customary, and not connected specifically with Schweik's trial. In the courtrooms of authoritarian countries the organized presence of young people—schoolchildren as well as soldiers—is traditional.

The reporters' seats filled up shortly before the trial was to begin.

On the witness bench sat Secret Policeman Sand, who had arrested Schweik as a Stalinist, the conductor of the train in which the arrest had taken place, and Frau Lehmann. The latter had been crying incessantly, since

long before the proceedings had even begun. What the
court wanted from the train conductor was a complete
mystery for the time being. The conductor himself was
the most mystified of all. So far as he was concerned, he
had been checking tickets during the arrest—but in entirely different compartments. The first he had heard of
an arrest was when he was summoned to appear in court.

Schweik's lawyer was a public attorney, one of
those who are called in when an accused cannot afford
to hire a private lawyer. In those instances, the Court
instructs a lawyer of its own choice to defend the individual standing trial—for a minimal fee from the State
Treasury. A public attorney's defense is no worse and
no better than this fact leads one to suspect. As a result,
the defendant with a public attorney has no illusions
about acquittal. And when the public attorney visits his
hapless charge's cell the day before the trial, in order to
introduce himself to his client, the hardboiled defendant
does not hesitate to tell him that he spits on his "defense." These defendants merely express openly something that everyone secretly thinks, most of all the
dignified justices themselves.

Thus, the custom of using public attorneys is entirely superfluous. Nevertheless it is retained, because
it is a means of paying lip-service to those characteristics
which it is fondly believed distinguish a "civilized state."
Normally, therefore, the fact that Schweik was to be
defended by a public attorney would have encouraged
only the gloomiest of speculations as to the Court's decision.

On the wall behind the tribunal hung a flag with
hammer and sickle. Schweik had had his hair cut and

cleaned his fingernails. He wore a white shirt and a
silver-gray necktie. "That's a must," he had explained to
his friends in the "Traube." "As defendant at a trial in
which Comrade Ulbricht himself is taking an interest—
a singular honor—I can't show up looking like a tramp."

That Comrade Ulbricht was interesting himself in
the trial, Schweik had learned from State Attorney Zollner.

"Damn! Only five minutes until it begins!" said
Schweik's attorney softly after checking his watch.
"And I've only just noticed I've got the wrong file
with me. But now there's no time to run home for it.
What'll we do?"

"What we'll do," declared Schweik calmly, "is
nothing at all. The Court must of course be kept in the
dark. I'll take care of the rest. I've already told you that
I'm going to defend myself. I don't need your services—
God knows I've been in Court so often I'd be a half-wit
not to know my way around by now. All you will do is
add a word or two now and then, purely for form's sake.
Objections—that's really all that's necessary. Only
watch out you don't yak at the wrong moment, when
I'm in full swing. That could be a mistake, because the
more one's in one's stride, the more disconcerting that
can be. That's simple psychology. I can explain it easily,
if you'd like."

Schweik's attorney, a man named Danzer, who
couldn't have cared less, almost nodded, but asked instead—just to show he was on the ball—who the woman
was on the witness bench, the one who had never
stopped crying.

"You've talked to her yourself," answered Schweik
with a smile. "My housekeeper. She came to see you at

your office yesterday to ask how she should behave during the proceedings, so they can't use her statement as a rope to hang her with. You told her you hadn't time to brief her then, but that you'd give her a few tips today before the trial."

"It's too late for that now," said Herr Danzer shrugging his shoulders. "Two minutes to go. Perhaps she's smart enough to avoid the pitfalls herself. Doesn't look it though, if you ask me. That stupid bawling is a bad sign."

"She's been crying ever since the summons came in the mail. It's been some week for me, I can tell you! Also my food was oversalted, because of her blubbering into it! If I told her once I told her a hundred times that we could look forward to this trial with greater peace of mind than ever before. All in vain. She just wailed again and again that it's a crime the way I talk. What can one do with a baggage like that? There's no cure for stupidity, so far as I know. But at least I kept her from pestering you again. You'll notice she's left you in peace today. When she came back from your office I asked her whether she was the wiser for consulting you. I'd already told her there's no point in asking too much of a public attorney. It stands to reason they don't give a damn about their clients.

"Now, don't contradict me, Herr Danzer! Nothing you say can change my mind. Poor clods like us who don't have any money have to look after themselves. That stands out a mile. I haven't a penny to my name, but that doesn't stop me seeing things objectively. Just imagine—here's how I explained it to my friends not long ago—just imagine two defendants, both in Court for the same crime. One has dough, buys himself a good lawyer who does his best. The result? Acquittal, or at any rate the minimum sentence. Now take the other guy who has no dough. Supposing the public attorney were to get the same result? That wouldn't be fair at all. The one who paid through the nose for his defense would be kicking himself, and naturally he'd say to himself 'Never again! Next time I'll insist on having a public attorney and be a thousand marks the richer.'

"Now what happens the next time? A public attorney conducts his defense and he gets two years! That's fair, Gentlemen, I said. Justice must be steadfast as a rock, that's what we teach children from the first grade on; not one thing one day and another the next."

Danzer blew his nose and glanced down at his brief for the defense at Schweik's trial: the wrong file.

When the justices appeared, Frau Lehmann's weeping reached a new climax, so that the Judge felt obliged to say right away in his instructions to the witnesses, "You're not on the defendant's bench, Frau Lehmann, eh? So why are you crying? If you don't stop right away, eh, I shall regard it as a sign that for some reason or other you have a bad conscience, eh."

The Judge was a man with a severe speech impediment. Not an organic one, but one which affected his whole manner of expression. This kind of "speech impediment" is much more common than stuttering or lisping. The judge suffered from the compulsion to say "eh." Other people say "understand" a thousand times a day, before every sentence, with every sentence, after every sentence. If a person really listens and doesn't mentally block his ears, they can drive him crazy.

"Well, now, look at that," said the Judge cynically, "your crying spell is all over already, Frau Lehmann, eh. Eh, I have a way with these things! But no relapse, I beg of you, eh."

He signaled to a Court clerk to read the charges, in which there was much talk about "protection of the Republic." The pertinent paragraphs were tossed around. In conclusion, it was declared that there were "sufficient grounds" for suspecting Schweik of violating these paragraphs.

Schweik nodded his agreement from the defendant's bench, not even objecting to the final sentence about "sufficient grounds." The idiot's made a good beginning, thought Danzer, but then what does that have to do with me?

Then the Judge took the floor. "The accused will please rise," he said. "First your vital statistics, then your life history, eh."

These are the first stages of every court proceedings: the witnesses are instructed to tell the truth; the opening statement with its most important part, the charges, is read; the accused is interrogated as to his personal history.

Schweik's vital statistics were quickly read over. But then Schweik, forthright as he was, tried to prepare the Court for his coming "life history." "That'll take a while, Gentlemen," he announced portentously. "My life history is not so easily docketed as my date and place of birth. A life history is always in quotation marks when it's written down on paper, as the judge of another court once informed me sarcastically. But I had to correct him. There are exceptions that don't need any quotation marks. My life is a case in point. It has been an eventful one, as they say, I can't deny that. But through no fault of my own. My life history is a regular textbook example of a life history, Gentlemen. One whose highlights, as it were, have not been of my own making. There are a thousand proofs of this, right down to my momentary situation on this very bench . . ."

"Your Honor," chimed in Public Attorney Danzer, looking back and forth between his file and the Judge, "the life history of my client has led, if I may say so, through heights and depths. It is in this respect very human."

Schweik was pleased with this interjection. "Absolutely," he added enthusiastically. "Man proposes, God disposes. The result is a continuous service of ups and downs, known prosaically as a life history."

"Which one is God?" queried the Judge, seizing this opportunity to give the press quick proof of his hundred-per-cent Communist convictions, for the sake of possible promotion. "I'm not acquainted with the gentleman, eh. Or has the State Attorney perhaps invited a witness by that name, eh, without informing me?"

Loud laughter, above all from the young people on the reserved benches. There was renewed laughter when State Attorney Zollner rose and declared with a grin that he had not called any witness by that name for the prosecution, or even better, for the defense.

When silence had been restored, the Judge attempted to impose some measure of order upon Schweik's testimony. "First," he asked, "did you have a proletarian childhood? Secondly, did you grow up in settled family circumstances? And third, have you ever been convicted before? If the answer is yes, when was the first time and how often thereafter, eh?"

"First," replied Schweik just as tersely, "yes. Secondly, no. And third, yes and no."

"What is that supposed to mean 'yes and no'?"

"That means yes there are entries in my record, so the records would say 'yes' in reply to your question. But *I* say *no*."

Schweik put such emphasis on this "I," that it had a literally majestic ring. The Judge lowered his eyes before Schweik's gaze; no adequate rejoinder occurred to him. The things he normally would have said to an accused who dared speak this way had been forbidden today, lest the trial take on a harshness of tone that would be out of harmony with the verdict with which it had to end.

Since there was nothing to prevent his doing so, Schweik felt emboldened to continue: "For me a conviction is not a conviction unless I am in fact guilty and am justly punished," he went on. "If I am unjustly punished, I cannot recognize my conviction, and indeed I cannot be forced to recognize it. The logic of this was proved long ago by the philosophers of Ancient Greece and China who thought about the rights of innocent men. Therefore such a conviction does not exist for me, it is zero, a blank space in my mind. And that is precisely the kind of conviction, Gentlemen, which is to be found in my records. Nothing but trifles. *'Failure to Report a Found Object.'* I ask you, Gentlemen, who reports a 'found object' nowadays? Maybe a cardinal—and that's because he only goes out in the street for the Corpus Christi procession, and even then he doesn't find anything because his eyes are fastened not on the street, but on the Holy of Holies. And here in this happy land these processions have long since gone out of fashion anyway.

"So this paragraph, with your permission, Gentlemen, is complete nonsense. *'Failure to Report a Found*

Object'—a paragraph like that flies in the teeth of common sense. And a reasonable law must be based on common sense, we all know that. Those who lose things have only themselves to blame. Scatterbrains like that shouldn't be *rewarded*, on top of everything else, by a paragraph which demands that *'found objects'* be reported. This sort of thing relieves them of any responsibility for their belongings. And where will that get us? In the long run no one will have any urge to keep track of his goods and chattels, and our society will be up to its eyes in *'found objects.'* If that's the purpose of this paragraph . . . well, then, I give up, Gentlemen. All I can say is you're welcome to it."

"Schweik," said the Judge with a friendly expression which cost him no small effort, "what we are concerned with in these proceedings is this question: Are there any political convictions in your records? We can skip the rest, eh, it's not so important."

Schweik threw back his head in a noble gesture of pride, and said with a raised voice, "I have as many political convictions as a bald man has hairs on his head. People have tried often enough to pin them on me, you can see that from my records, but as yet no one has succeeded in doing so. In the end, my innocence has always risen like a phoenix from the ashes, as a public attorney once expressed it."

That public attorney had been the only idealist among all the public attorneys in Schweik's life. Only an idealist could indulge in such an exaggerated tirade. Schweik's acquittal on insufficient evidence had inspired the gentleman with such enthusiasm, it was as if all mankind had come a step further along the path of righteousness. But the normal public attorney is and remains a stranger to such emotions. Every verdict on his client leaves him cold, be it an acquittal or the death sentence.

"Very well," said the Judge, "that will suffice, eh. You may sit down again for the moment, Schweik. Or does the prosecution have any additional questions?"

"No thank you," said State Attorney Zollner.

"The defense?"

No reply.

"Then we can begin the questioning of the witnesses, eh," continued the Judge, and summoned Comrade Sand as the first witness.

Comrade Sand made a rather pessimistic impression. The reason was not difficult to guess. Certainly Sand no longer doubted that there were problems connected with his appearance in court today. Problems born of the changeableness of the Party line. Problems in the life of a Communist. Here today, there tomorrow!

"Comrade Sand," began the Judge, after Sand's vital statistics had been verified, "you are the policeman who arrested the man Schweik. Take a look at the man on the defendant's bench—is that the man you arrested?"

"Yes it is, Your Honor."

"Where did the arrest take place, eh?"

"In a train compartment."

"Why?"

"Why did it take place in a train compartment?" repeated Comrade Sand doltishly.

Apparently the general line of his testimony was to play dumb. However, the Judge nipped this plan in the bud by demanding abruptly, "Why it took place at all, that's what I want to know, eh? Don't play the fool with me. Otherwise we might have to assume that your position in the police force is more than you can handle, Comrade, eh? Once more then: Why did the arrest take place?"

Herr Sand's remorse was plain to see. "It was this way," he began. "The accused more or less forced me to arrest him. Otherwise I wouldn't have done it. You see, Your Honor, I was sitting in my compartment sleeping. Normally I am not in the habit of sleeping during the day, permit me to emphasize that here. The SSD never sleeps. Surely we can claim that. If, as was the case on that occasion, I happened to be asleep, then it was the result of the relatively short night's sleep I had just had. My wife and I, you see, Your Honor, had been chatting in bed late into the night about the future of the Peace Watch of Soviet submarines in allied Albanian Mediterranean ports. It's not unusual for my wife to discuss such subjects: she's a fine example of Communist equality of the sexes. She was formerly a kindergarten teacher, but is now in the process of switching over to military journalism. I only mention that incidentally. So there I sat in the compartment with my eyes closed. Across from me was an elderly married couple. He wore spectacles, she was knitting . . ."

"Come to the point," interrupted the Judge, no friendlier than before. "This couple doesn't interest us at all. For all I care he was knitting too, and she wore two pairs of spectacles. We are interested in the defendant, eh. What happened when he entered the compartment?"

"I didn't notice him until he began to speak. That's what woke me up. He said—these were his very words —'This morning, Comrades, I burned my fingers.'"

Sand looked at the justices with wide eyes, expressing a mixture of melancholy and agitation. The word-less protest written on his features meant: And I'm not supposed to react to *that*, Gentlemen? That's easy for you to say! Consequently, it must have been extremely painful for Comrade Sand to hear the Judge say, "That this expression could be meant literally probably never occurred to you, eh? Instead of that you decided to lure your prey like an ass onto thin ice."

A cough came from the defendant's bench.

"The word 'ass' is not aimed at you, Schweik," the Judge said quickly. "The metaphor was only intended to illustrate a certain process, eh."

Schweik rose with dignity and replied, "On that particular morning I really and truly had burned my fingers. With hot coffee. And if the sleeping gentleman in the corner of the train compartment who is now in the witness stand had taken me at my word and not kept poking around, I really don't know—you're right about that, Your Honor—how our conversation could ever have gotten around to that gentleman with respect to whom Khrushchev, unknown to me, had opened our eyes the day before.

All eyes in the courtroom were now drawn to Schweik as if by a magnet. It was as silent as a tomb. No one dared to breathe. Everyone secretly admired the defendant Schweik, who in a few elegant sentences had relieved the Judge of an important task: getting to the core of the problem. The main act of the drama could now begin.

"You understand what the defendant is implying?" asked the Judge, turning again to the witness Sand. "Describe the decisive moments for us, eh."

Comrade Sand took his time. He shifted his weight

from one foot to the other, looked down at the floor, then up at the ceiling of the courtroom. This phenomenon is often to be observed in people who have to think hard before giving a difficult answer, and consequently is most often met with in the upper classes of schools, where young people are involved. But it also thrives in courtrooms, where of course adults are in the majority.

"The decisive moment came out of the blue, as it were," said Sand at last. "I had leaned back in my corner to go back to sleep, when the accused made sleep impossible, Your Honor, by suddenly shouting out—I quote: 'Saintly Joseph . . .'" Sand's voice failed him, but he forced himself to continue, "'. . . Stalin! There is no one else to touch you—for me, there never will be anyone else to touch you!'"

"What did you think of that?" asked the Judge quickly, in order to keep the proceedings moving and stifle the courtroom murmurs.

"What did I think of that? I thought I wasn't hearing right, that's what I thought."

"And then?"

"Then I tried to avoid arresting the accused, Your Honor. You can believe me when I say I did everything in my power to make it possible for the accused to extricate himself. First I asked him whether his groundless exclamation was intended, in the name of heaven, to identify him explicitly as a Stalinist. His answer was 'Of course!' Thereupon I asked him again whether in the name of heaven he intended to remain a Stalinist. This time he said, 'Until my dying day.'

"Now I don't know whether the accused has denied giving these answers in the preliminary investigation, or whether he's admitted them. If he's denied them, I can swear on oath to the contrary . . . if necessary."

With this involuntary "if necessary," Comrade Sand hit the nail on the head, namely the spirit of the whole proceedings.

"Schweik," said the Judge, "stand up. In the preliminary investigation you did not deny giving the answers the witness has mentioned. But according to the law, what you say during the main trial is decisive—what you say today. Accordingly I must ask you again: Are the allegations of the witness correct, eh?"

Schweik declared that certain features of Sand's statement were new to him—for example his attempts to save him from arrest. But the most important part about the Stalinist outbursts was correct.

"These exclamations of yours," sighed the Judge, "what did you hope to gain by them, Schweik?"

Schweik, mindful of his drilling by State Attorney Zollner, answered, "I merely wished to make sure, as they say, that the baby wasn't thrown out with the bathwater. It was a form of protest against the way people suddenly refuse to leave a good hair on Stalin's head. So I tried to leave him a couple of good hairs, Your Honor. In my opinion he still deserves that today. The man did wrong, I don't doubt that, Gentlemen—but he also did many good things. One mustn't go too far, I said to myself. I don't know whether or not I would have been above reproach had I been in his shoes. And even you can't be absolutely sure about that, Gentlemen. We all of us are only human—and that is how I saw Comrade Stalin, as a human being. That's how I thought of him that day in the train compartment, as a human being who is not infallible and who deserves just as much sympathy as the rest of us with our few merits and many weaknesses. That's the way human beings are, there's no sense in denying it. That's what I meant with my exclamations, Your Honor."

"What do you say to that, eh?" was all the Judge could say. His question was directed at the witness Sand.

"If I could have guessed the motives of the accused," replied Sand in a small voice, "I would naturally never have made the arrest."

Although Sand's remorse was obvious, it could not save him from the damning words of the Judge, who addressed him in a cutting tone. "It would have been your duty to clarify these motives before making the arrest, not to leave them in the dark, eh," he said sternly. "The task of a Socialist police official does not consist of his exercising terror, but his winning the love of the people, who are happy in the knowledge that they are protected by their police. Where is this principle laid down? In the Socialist Police Regulations, Article One. And what do you do, Sand? Exactly the opposite of what you're not supposed to do, eh. Let me give you a tip, Sand. Why don't you apply for a position as policeman in the West, eh? That's where you belong, eh? There you can exercise terror, that's what they want there. But not in the Socialist police force, eh! Understand! Go! We no longer need you as a witness. We will do without your oath, eh. The testimony of a witness like you is worthless anyway. It's just a waste of time. Instead of worrying about swearing you in, I should have informed you at the start that you have the right to refuse to testify, eh, if answering a question puts you in danger of revealing a crime of your own. For I personally no longer doubt that you have neglected your duty. I scarcely need tell you what that means, eh? Go!"

A bundle of misery slunk out the courtroom door. But when he arrived home, Sand soon found comfort from his wife. "Why not, after all?" she said.

"What?"

"That idea about the West?"

"And your military journalism?" exclaimed Sand.

"Well, all in all, I'd be glad to trade that for the nylon stockings they have over there. Come on, let's just pack the essentials."

The Judge called for a fifteen-minute adjournment. Following this "smoking break," Schweik raised his hand on the defendant's bench. "What is it?" asked the Judge.

Schweik asked to be allowed to make a statement.

"A statement?" asked the Judge in alarm. For sudden statements from defendants usually mean an unexpected change of course. The Judge thought suddenly of Walter Ulbricht. During the pause, he had telephoned Ulbricht's presidium office and reaped praise for the way the trial was running.

"What kind of statement, Schweik?"

"Nothing anyone here need be nervous about. I only wanted to let you in on an analogy that occurred to me as I was smoking a cigarette just now. It has to do with the old saying I mentioned earlier on, when I was trying to clear up that business about my allegedly Stalinist exclamations—namely, that one shouldn't throw the baby out with the bathwater. There's a good one on the wall right behind you, Your Honor. There hangs the beloved flag of the GDR. It is partly red. Now, except for a patch in the middle, with that well-known symbol on it, the Nazi flag was also red. If I were crazy, I'd suggest that that makes our Socialist flag less likable. But this isn't so at all! That indeed would be a classic example of throwing the baby out with the bathwater, if you see what I mean. That's all I wanted to add. A good analogy, you must admit. The gentlemen from the press, I notice, have been taking notes like mad. They seem to share my opinion."

The Judge quickly called the next witness, Helbig.

This was the train conductor, a red-faced, beer-loving, primitive old proletarian who was rather short of breath—in all respects the apparent opposite of the Judge, whose manner aroused suspicions of good breeding, abstinence, and intelligence. Helbig wore the Party badge in his lapel. But it would have been a mistake to conclude that this still meant anything to him. He was one of the many individuals whose period of proletarian enthusiasm for the Party belonged to the distant past.

"Comrade Helbig," the Judge began, "you were on duty in the train in which the accused was arrested, eh?"

"I don't know nothing," said a coarse deep voice. "I haven't the faintest idea why I was summoned here."

"I'm telling you why!"

"Why?"

"Because you were on duty in the train in which the accused was arrested."

After this illuminating exchange, which promised to continue in much the same vein, the Judge looked at his companions, the Court clerks. These were a couple of extraordinarily reserved gentlemen who had decided at the very beginning of these difficult and delicate proceedings not to contribute a single word, to leave everything, but everything, to the Judge. The Judge's look

said: Do something, dammit! But in vain. The Judge
had no choice but to fix his gaze on Helbig and continue
his interrogation. "What can you tell us about the incident?" he asked.

"Nothing."

"Where were you at the time of the arrest, eh?"

"How should I know?"

"Good God, man!" cried the Judge flaring up. "You
must know more about it than we do, eh? We weren't
even on the wretched train."

"But I didn't know until I got the summons," said
the conductor, thinking, you stupid bastard, "that anyone had been nabbed at all. So how am I supposed to be
able to tell you today which compartment I was checking
tickets in?"

He was quite right, of course. Several people burst
out laughing. They were delighted at the good swords-
manship of the conductor, a simple soul with whom they
could not help identifying themselves.

"Silence!" thundered the Judge. And then he said
to the witness, in order to save face, "What you and a
few oxen back there don't grasp is that you must declare
explicitly that at the time in question, eh, you were *not*
at the scene of the arrest. In other words, eh, that during
the arrest you were *not* in the compartment with the
accused. Or were you in the compartment with the
accused, eh?"

"No."

"Very well. Why didn't you say so right away, eh?"

Helbig was silent. He only answered mentally:
stupid bastard!

"But surely you had entered that compartment

earlier to check the tickets, eh?" said the Judge, trying a new line of approach.

"Certainly," answered Helbig, although "Certainly" on this point was somewhat equivocal. Conductors checking tickets at one end of a train are often not seen at all at the other end, especially on short journeys.

"And the accused did not make an unfavorable impression on you, eh?" the Judge went on.

"No. He behaved just like anyone else."

"Did you hear him talking politics?"

"No. He was as cool as a cucumber, you might say," said Comrade Helbig generously coming to Schweik's aid once more, although, so far as he could tell, he had laid eyes on him for the first time only that morning, when he entered the courtroom for the trial. Moments later he was assailed by bitter self-reproach. What a stupid ass I am! he thought.

Why? Because now Schweik said to the Judge, "Just a moment, if you'll permit me. May I interrupt? The witness must be mistaken. The fact is that on that day he never came into our compartment at all. I wouldn't want him to make a false statement here by mistake, and perhaps even perjure himself the way I did once—as you can see from those trifling matters on my records which I have already expressed my opinion about today. But at least I was testifying for a friend, whereas witness Helbig, Gentlemen, doesn't know me at all, so there's absolutely no sense in his perjuring himself for me. I'd like to save him from that. I can only offer this explanation for his error: there must have been someone else on the train that day who didn't compromise himself by political remarks. And that's the one he just happened to think of. The resemblance to me is another coincidence. So no reproaches, Gentlemen, I beg of you. The witness only meant well. When so many coincidences like that come on top of each other, they're liable to confuse anyone."

These were the moments which brought on Helbig's self-reproach.

The situation was so extraordinary that something now happened which no one present could possibly have anticipated. Even Public Attorney Danzer snapped out of his lethargy. "Your Honor," he cried, springing to his feet, "my client's remarks are obviously not to be taken seriously. It goes without saying that the witness Helbig is right—not my client! How do I know that? First of all, one must ask oneself what could influence the witness, obviously against his better judgment, to cover up for the accused, whom he doesn't know from a bar of soap. And that's a ridiculous proposition, in all conscience. Secondly, I have here in my file a note on what the accused himself told me: at times, he suffers from disastrously bad memory; a memory with huge gaps in it, Gentlemen, particularly as regards people he has or hasn't met. I therefore believe it to be beyond any doubt that the witness Helbig did enter my client's compartment on that day and noticed his calm demeanor. So I suggest . . ."

"Good," interrupted the Judge, as if he knew what the other was about to suggest. "Let us not labor this point. This objection by the defense seems wholly justified. It corresponds to everyday experience. So let us continue, eh. Or did you wish to suggest something else, Herr Danzer?"

No, that was exactly the point he wanted to make, said Danzer.

But both of them, Danzer and the Judge, had reckoned without Schweik. Schweik now declared with dignity that his memory was no sieve; that he could not imagine how Herr Danzer came to make such a statement. He therefore insisted that he withdraw his statement, or show the court the alleged note from his file.

Danzer paled, involuntarily hid the file behind his back, and was so beside himself that he demanded, shouting, that the Judge break off the proceedings at once and have the defendant's mental health examined. If this demand was not granted at once, he would resign immediately from the defense. Indeed, he yelled, he had a perfect right to do so, with a client like that.

A suspension of the proceedings seemed inevitable. The Judge thought of Ulbricht's presidium office, which he would have to telephone again in an hour or two. He bombarded State Attorney Zollner with looks which seemed to shout: "Is this your way of preparing the accused for trial?"

Zollner requested a short adjournment. His request was granted.

After the adjournment, during which Zollner disappeared with Schweik and Danzer into a room in the State Attorney's office two floors below, everything seemed fine again. An explanation was put forward by Schweik and Danzer, to the effect they had "misunderstood" each other. Then Public Attorney Danzer fell silent for good. He had had enough.

So far as Schweik was concerned, his situation was no more complicated than before. He had wanted from the very first to defend himself. "Your Honor," he said, when the proceedings had commenced once again, "may I direct a few more questions to the witness Helbig?"

"If it is absolutely necessary," said the Judge, sighing.

"I would like to ask him first of all whether my remarks were overheard in other compartments?"

"I didn't hear nothing, anyway," said Helbig, now expressing himself more cautiously than at first.

"Then other people couldn't have heard anything either," said Schweik. "That's logical. Now, did you observe, Comrade, any agitation on the part of the other passengers? Or rather, whether there were any so-called 'centers of unrest'?"

"No."

Schweik turned back to the tribunal. "Very well then! With that, the incitement paragraph also falls flat, Gentlemen. How have I hit upon that? At the regulars' table yesterday my friend Emil Buchta said to me, 'They may try to hang the incitement paragraph on you too, for the protection of the Republic.' He's sitting back there, Gentlemen, in the fourth row, the one with only one ear lobe. Now he's hiding—look how he's trying to make himself scarce. But why, Emil, I beg of you— having only one ear lobe is nothing to be ashamed of. The other ear lobe, by the way Gentlemen, was bitten off by a St. Bernard. But not as he was climbing over a back fence or anything. It would be quite wrong to assume that. It happened quite differently, in a perfectly legitimate way. You can ask him yourself, if you're interested."

But this did not appear to be the case, for the Judge only asked his colleagues and the State Attorney quickly, "Do we need the witness Helbig any longer, eh?"

"No," came the answer in a chorus.

"Does anyone think it necessary to put him under oath?"

Again the chorus "No."

Following this, the last witness was called. This was Frau Lehmann, who was again swimming in tears, although the Judge asked her threateningly whether she had forgotten what he'd said to her at the very beginning.

What good did that do? None. Frau Lehmann shook with fear, now that the moment of truth was at hand; her nerves simply gave way. The moment could not be far off when she would not be the only one swimming in tears. Schweik knew that. He recognized the state of emergency which threatened the whole unsuspecting assemblage, and, in order to prevent the catastrophe, he was forced to commit a breach of "defendants' etiquette." He arose, and, under the increasingly furious glare of the Judge, crossed over to State Attorney Zollner on the other side of the courtroom.

"What's going on, eh?" shouted the Judge angrily.

Schweik only gave an impatient wave of the hand in the Judge's direction and whispered something in the State Attorney's ear. Zollner listened, gave a start, and then went over to the Judge, to whom he whispered Schweik's message.

And behold, the Judge gave an identical start and said rapidly to the witness Lehmann, "Calm down, I beg of you. Nothing is going to happen to you. There's only one thing we want you to tell us: Is it true that the accused, whom you keep house for, burned his fingers with scalding coffee on the day of his arrest?"

"Yes," sobbed Frau Lehmann, now expecting to be called to account for the mishap. She could scarcely

believe her luck when the Judge actually said that would
be all, good-by.

With her disappearance, a bitter affliction was agree-
ably disposed of. The hearing of witnesses had now
come to an end.

"Herr Zollner," said the Judge, turning to the
State Attorney with a sigh of relief, "your arraignment,
please."

Karl Zollner rose for the shortest arraignment of
his life. "Honored Gentlemen of the Court," he said.
"Even the State Prosecutor's office can make a mistake,
if you'll excuse me. We have wrongfully accused an
innocent citizen of endangering the State. That is the
unequivocal result of today's examination, I'm sorry to
say. I am not a reactionary State Attorney, who wishes
regardless to fight for conviction of the accused, as is
customary in the West, for example. No! I am a Socialist
State attorney, inflamed by the ideals of a Socialist
prosecution, if you'll excuse me. As a Socialist State
attorney, I have no hesitation in dropping the accusation
against Comrade Schweik. I'm afraid I can't help you,
Honored Gentlemen of the Court, I'm sorry to say. I
recommend acquittal with all costs to be borne by the
State, if you'll excuse me."

Now, as usual, it was the turn of the defense. Herr
Danzer contented himself with one sentence: "I declare
myself in complete agreement with the recommendation
of the State Attorney."

We're almost through, thought the Judge joyfully, and allowed Schweik the closing statement which
is granted every accused person before the Court retires
to reach a verdict, and in which he normally declares
that he is full of remorse for everything, will behave

himself better in the future, and hopes for a mild verdict. Schweik, however, had no reason to humble himself in this manner. The way things stood, he could do without such "last words." That is what the Judge counted on. But here he was wrong, for Schweik launched into a real rip-roaring closing statement. It was also evident that Schweik had been quite taken with Zollner's expression "Honored Gentlemen of the Court."

"Honored Gentlemen of the Court" Schweik began. "I know what you expect of me: that I will decline to make a closing statement, because it's no longer necessary, you think. But permit me to say that you are forgetting one small thing. That kind of thinking might be all right in the West—but not here, Honored Gentlemen of the Court, not here in the Socialist camp. The proceedings have gone well for all of us, that can certainly be said. But in the process, one important thing has been entirely overlooked, and that is that I must be allowed to criticize my actions. You know that self-criticism belongs as naturally to Communism as the yolk to the egg, one could say. Or still better: self-criticism is for Communism the dot on the i, as my friend Emil back there said day before yesterday at the regulars' table. 'Don't forget, Schweik,' he said, 'to criticize yourself during the trial. Make the walls shake with it, that way you'll squeak out a year less.' The way things have turned out today, I can even look forward to an acquittal, unless I am deceived, Honored Gentlemen of the Court, and I owe this fact to the generosity of a Socialist court. Can I accept it without some measure of self-criticism? That would be ungrateful of me. So, Honored Gentlemen of the Court, I confess that I have made mistakes. First of all, on that morning I made the decisive mistake, I confess, of not reading the newspaper thoroughly, although as a convinced Socialist I should long since have known what that can lead to, overnight. Because of that the most important facts about the 20th Party Congress in Moscow escaped my attention. And as if that weren't enough, Honored Gentlemen of the Court, in this condition of ignorance I also allowed myself to leave the house. That was the second mistake, which I now confess. The third occurred in the train. I permitted myself to be drawn into conversation with a total stranger, although I was well aware that I had only read part of my newspaper. You all know what transpired, Honored Gentlemen of the Court. But believe me, it will never happen again. I promise you that as a solemn vow, for, after all, even the most astringent self-criticism is useless without a promise to reform. Very well. Anything else? No, I think that's everything for the moment. Or is there something else, Honored Gentlemen of the Court?"

The Court's answer was a speedy retreat into the conference room, where the verdict was officially weighed. That the weighing of the verdict was nothing more than a formality was proved by the result: acquittal of the accused; all costs to be borne by the State treasury.

Ovations broke out among the listeners in the courtroom; ovations meant for Schweik as well as for the Court. Only the young fools on the reserved benches looked at one another with less than complete satisfaction.

The outcome of the trial spelled a red-letter day for the "Traube." Schweik's friends accompanied him in triumphal procession. With but one exception, they declared that whatever Schweik drank today was on them. The abstainer was Emil Buchta, who spoke not of the beers he owed Schweik, but of great clouts on his head.

The "Traube" had been informed in advance of the celebrants' impending arrival, so that preparations had already been made when Schweik and his men appeared in the doorway. The reception was marked by one particular characteristic: hearty, unanimous laughter, laughter which swelled from the bottom of a whole nation's heart. It was that laughter which tyrants abhor and against which they are powerless.